Gold in the Clouds

Hayden Thorne

Published by Hayden Thorne, 2018.

Also by Hayden Thorne

Arcana Europa
Guardian Angel
The Flowers of St. Aloysius
Hell-Knights
Children of Hyacinth
The Amaranth Maze
A Murder of Crows

Curiosities
Dollhouse
Automata
Eidolon

Dolores
Ambrose
Echoes in the Glass
A Dirge for St. Monica

Ghosts and Tea
The Ghosts of St. Grimald Priory
Agnes of Haywood Hall

A Most Unearthly Rival
The Haunted Inkwell
The House of Creeping Dolls

Grotesqueries
A Castle for Rowena
The Rusted Lily
Primavera

Masks
Masks: The Original Trilogy
Curse of Arachnaman
Mimi Attacks!
Dr. Morbid's Castle of Blood
The Porcelain Carnival

Standalone
Renfred's Masquerade
Rose and Spindle
Gold in the Clouds
Helleville
Icarus in Flight
Arabesque
Banshee
Wollstone
The Glass Minstrel
Henning
The Twilight Gods
The Book of Lost Princes
The Winter Garden and Other Stories

Desmond and Garrick
The Cecilian Blue-Collar Chronicles

Table of Contents

Chapter 1

The dreaded moment came at the very moment Blythe dreaded the most, and he only had one weapon in his dreadfully measly arsenal: an insult. Turning away from the voice, he pulled his blankets over his head and groaned, "I don't do girls' work, Molly. Go away."

Unfortunately, Molly was nothing if not tenacious, and to add insult to injury, she was also every bit a morning sort. A very early morning sort, at that.

"Oh, you're always such a grumpy puss," she said—or more like sang. To Blythe's thickly fogged mind, his sister's voice sounded as though it was flinging itself up and down the scales with impunity and with no other purpose than to make Blythe want to disembowel himself twice over.

"I'm trying to sleep like the rest of the world. Go away."

"There's no place for me to go to, you little silly thing," Molly replied, her cheerful singsong adding even more weight to the fact that she took far too much delight in treating her youngest brother like a five-year-old. Or, in this instance, a five-year-old she'd just forced into a lifetime of indentured servitude, his sentence set to begin that very morning.

"Yes, you do—your bed. Now will you please go away? I'm sleeping!"

"No, you're not. You're talking to me and being your usual grumpy, silly little puss thing."

Blythe felt his bed sink under her weight as she took it on herself to sit on one edge. Slithering further under the warm blankets, he retorted, "Good God, Molly, leave me alone! I don't want to go!"

Molly had the audacity to heave a deep sigh. "Blythe, if you want to eat and to have a roof over your head, you'll have to make certain sacrifices. You need to work."

"But I don't want to sell bread! That's a girl's job! It was yours! Why do I have to do it?"

Selling homemade bread door-to-door was—and had always been—girl's work, largely because it was Molly's job. In fact, she'd been doing exactly that for seven years straight since she turned fifteen. Unfortunately she'd recently begun to experiment with cake recipes and had apparently hit on a good one, and after having her creation tested on her hapless brothers and a handful of willing neighbors, she'd decided to retire from bread-selling to devote more time to realizing her dream, which was to make a name for herself as a baker. That, of course, meant passing on the early morning tradition to a boy who despised waking up any time before eight o'clock, preferably nine.

Albert, the oldest son in the Midwinter family, was already up to his ears with woodwork, thanks to his talent with the chisel and whatever other insane tool he used in his trade, and barely had time for leisure activities beyond wooing apple-cheeked girls and drinking ale with friends every other week. Or so he'd say, anyway. So the thankless, humiliating job of selling Molly's daily loaves door-to-door fell on Blythe's thin, narrow shoulders. Threats of running away or somehow being abducted, enslaved, ravished, or killed (sometimes a combination of all four) in the course of his fulfilling his duties fell on deaf ears, with Molly either rolling her eyes, pinching his cheeks, or plain ignoring him despite Blythe's best attempts at looking pathetic. By the time he'd exhausted himself trying, Blythe was convinced that his sister simply wasn't born with a heart because somewhere along the line, their parents did something to displease the gods and were duly punished for it.

That day was supposed to be his first day taking over his sister's work, and he bitterly wished he'd made good his threat of stumbling and falling head first down the town well and its poisonous green water.

"Bertie and I started work at fifteen, and after seven years from me and four for him, look where all this hard work and sacrifice have taken us."

"Pfft. A one-room cottage with a fireplace that peppers our food with soot and no marriage prospects for either of you."

"I haven't gone far enough to feel good about settling down. I want to be secure of my future first before committing myself to having a dozen mouths to feed." Molly paused. "As for Bertie, I'm not in any position to speak for him."

As though in answer, a loud, obnoxious fart broke into the hushed conversation. Blythe, now truly and fully awake, stared wide-eyed at the cocooning darkness offered by his blankets. "What on earth was that?" he stammered.

"That was Bertie. He does that all the time. That's all I hear when I wake up before dawn, and you two are still asleep."

"What—you mean to say that all this time, I've been breathing in his fumes in my sleep?"

"That would be a 'yes', yes."

Blythe finally flung the covers off him, and he sat bolt upright, glaring at Molly, who regarded him with what could only be called sincere surprise. "And you let him poison me in my sleep?" he practically wailed, horrified and nauseated.

She didn't even flinch. "I don't think I have the capacity to do something about his arse without seriously damaging him."

"How long has he been murdering me slowly in my sleep?" Blythe glanced at his brother's sleeping form.

Bertie's bed stood a mere three feet away from his, a fact that only deepened Blythe's horror. The closeness couldn't be helped, what with the Midwinter children's too-limited cottage space, which they'd inherited from their poor, dead parents. The cottage was, literally, just four walls and a ceiling, with no attic space and no rooms. One end of the open area was dedicated to the kitchen and the dining room, and the other end was where the beds were set. What little space was there in the oven and hearth area was always used up by piles of firewood needed for baking and cooking. Even washing themselves was a bit of an adventure, and the Midwinter siblings had nothing but a large oval tin tub that had to be dragged near the fire and filled with water. Ensuring privacy was always a bit of an art form that varied according to the bather's mood.

Molly, being the only girl, was saved by her gender because it ensured that her bed would be situated by the wall opposite from the one against which Bertie's bed was set, segregated from her brothers' by two large, ancient chests, which contained all of their clean clothes. She had lots of breathing room, while Blythe…? He felt bile churn in his belly.

Molly just clucked and rolled her eyes at him before standing up. "I think you can safely guess. Now come along, you cranky imp. Your breakfast is ready, and there's a nice fire going."

"What's the point of going about my day now that my lungs have been blackened by Bertie's rancid blasts?"

As though in answer, another fetid explosion sounded from Bertie's bed, and Bertie even had the audacity to groan, curse in his sleep, and then turn under the covers.

"Oh, shut up, Bertie," Blythe retorted as he rolled out of his bed and fled the scene, planting himself before the bright fire Molly had started. Given the god-awful hour of his rising and its accompanying chill, Blythe found the fire a great deal more comforting than he cared to admit. Hugging himself tightly while doing little hops on each bare foot, he nevertheless felt resentful for being forced into work that he never thought he'd ever do, being—yes—a boy.

Glowering and sulking before the fireplace, he watched his sister move surprisingly quickly as she prepared the loaves of bread Blythe needed to peddle that morning.

Molly had spent the previous afternoon and evening baking till she had a baker's dozen—the number being less a cheeky play on terms and more a necessary loaf count because she'd always sold between ten to thirteen loaves each day. Her task in the evening, once the bread had all cooled down, was to carefully wrap each in cheap paper and secure it with string. The following morning would be spent filling up two enormous baskets with the loaves. It didn't cause her too much trouble to get them all to fit, for she never used loaf pans and simply baked them as round loaves.

And perhaps another—and more logical—reason for her daily bread count was the fact that the wood-fired oven her great-grandfather had built into the cottage was large enough for thirteen bread rounds of ten inches in diameter. The oven had always been regarded as an odd thing for a one-room cottage, but Great-grandfather Midwinter decided that, somewhere down the line, his family would produce a talented baker. Before Molly fell in love with baking, the oven had been used only for food meant for family consumption.

In the past, the process of baking and so on would be repeated on her return home from a morning spent peddling loaves. Now, however, with the promise of increased income from her cake sales, Molly found it necessary to remain home all day in order to bake the bread as well as perfect her cake recipe before taking the next and most crucial step, which meant subjecting the world to her newest work of oven art. What was even more unfortunate to Blythe was the too-real possibility that he might be recruited to go out during the midday to sell those infernal cakes—yes, even after he'd already suffered the tedium and indignity of selling bread in the early morning hours. Was his sister really that cruel? He certainly wouldn't put it past her, considering what he was now forced to do.

Blythe nearly soiled his nightshirt when the thought crossed his mind. The dark looks aimed at his sister now gone, he felt his blood freeze as he continued to watch her fill up the baskets.

"Molly," he said at length once he found his voice. "How are you planning to sell your cakes?"

Molly paused and glanced up, blinking. "Why, a stall, of course—on market day."

"Stall? What stall? When did we start owning a stall in the market?"

"Not yet, of course, but we will once we earn enough from our new recipe to afford a table there." Molly grinned at her brother—a bright, blinding grin that was characteristic of her boundless optimism. It was also the kind of grin that weathered Blythe's defenses despite his best efforts at hardening himself against it. Rather than scowl, he could only manage an eye twitch followed by a resigned sigh.

"And in the meantime..."

"Oh—dear Mrs. Pugsley was kind enough to give us some table space at her stall for a small fee." Molly went back to filling the baskets, humming to herself.

Blythe turned that thought over in his head. "But Mrs. Pugsley sells potions for gout and constipation!" he spluttered.

"I know. Isn't she a darling? She's so accommodating. She said her customers would love the cakes, and she promised to press them into buying."

• • • •

BY THE TIME BLYTHE set out—or, rather, was chased out the door by a broom-wielding sister—it was past six in the morning. The early morning air was, indeed, quite chilly, but he brewed enough resentment in his belly to warm himself up considerably. In fact, he didn't even need to bundle up for the trek around town. An old coat he'd inherited from Bertie was all he required. If Molly's beloved wood-fired oven sprouted legs and talked, it would be him.

Blythe didn't walk to town right away, oh no. There was time enough for that despite Molly's insistence that he needed to be wandering door-to-door in Upchurch by six-thirty at most. She'd claimed that people needed the bread for breakfast, but Blythe had doubts. People who could afford to buy entire loaves of bread were most likely ten times wealthier than they, and rich people meant idle people who wouldn't dream of rising before noon.

Rich people, of course, also had servants whose days were already halfway over by the time their masters dragged their useless backsides out of bed, but that was neither here nor there as far as Blythe was concerned.

With that thought in mind, Blythe didn't feel an ounce of guilt as he stood in the middle of the footpath leading into Upchurch, glaring at the misty scene before him. There was no room anywhere for guilt, anyway, seeing as how crippling humiliation had filled up every inch of space in him. He tried not to imagine the looks on his one and only friend's face when he found that Blythe was now doomed to peddle bread all over town, carrying two large baskets to boot, instead of doing something more fitting for a fifteen-year-old boy.

Blythe wracked his brain. Somehow, he couldn't come up with something he'd like to do as a fifteen-year-old boy, but that could easily be because of his nightmarish waking time and the annoyance that refused to abate. He sighed. The only thing he truly wanted to do was to remain in bed, unmolested by chattering sisters and flatulent brothers.

Shaking his head, he forced his feet to move. Prospects were dreadful for penniless boys like him.

Many a poem had been penned in praise of the dawn, a fact that Blythe couldn't confirm because he'd never read one. Then again, with an education that didn't amount to anything beyond reading, writing, and arithmetic, he wouldn't recognize a poem (what it looked like on a page, perhaps) even if it were to come up to him, clamp its jaws around his nose, and tear it off with a couple of shakes. He'd *heard* someone read a poem out loud a couple of times before, and it was only in passing. What he'd heard made him wonder, though, as to how those things were written because when read out loud, nothing seemed to make sense beyond the fact that the words sounded the same at the end of each sentence.

At any rate, none of the breathtaking beauties of dawn warmed his heart or lifted his spirits. The rising sun's soft glow, the gentle hues of blue breaking up the pinks and golds and chasing away the night's ebbing darkness, the light mist swaddling the quiet town and lending it a serenity that early morning risers would appreciate before the daily bustle began...

"Stupid morning," Blythe grumbled, making a face at the sky as he finally crossed the borders of Upchurch. It was about a quarter of a mile of walking from the Midwinter cottage, and then there were those labyrinthine streets connecting houses in the town proper. Blythe forced the reminder of what lay ahead out of his head lest he were to break down right then and there and collapse in an apoplectic fit.

He approached the first house and knocked. As he waited, he suddenly realized how heavy his enormous baskets were. Setting them down on each side, he cursed softly as he massaged each arm, wrist, and shoulder.

At length the door opened, and a bleary-eyed servant peered out. Blythe was at a loss all of a sudden, now that the reality of his predicament finally impressed itself on him.

"Yes? What do you want?" the servant demanded, blinking and knuckling away sleep. She was an elderly woman who apparently had been up for a while now, given the fact that she'd put on her uniform, which looked to be a fairly elaborate ensemble.

"Good morning, ma'am. Would you be interested in buying a loaf of bread?" Blythe wondered if he sounded persuasive enough.

The servant frowned at him. Then she squinted and looked him up and down. "Why, you're not Molly!"

"No, ma'am. Molly's my sister."

"Where is she?"

"At home. I'm taking her place."

"Why?"

"It's a long story. So are you interested in buying a loaf?" Blythe stifled a heavy sigh and picked up a basket to show her.

The woman continued to frown at him while ignoring the basket. "And how do I know that you're telling the truth?"

Blythe muttered, "Oh, for God's sake." Tamping down his spiraling irritation, he pulled out a loaf and raised it. "Do you see this? No one within fifty miles of this wretched town wraps bread like this. No one except for my sister, though I've no idea why she even bothers if this thing ends up in people's bellies all the same. Now aren't you hungry for one?"

"A fine answer," the woman retorted, squinting even more so that Blythe could see nothing but wrinkled slits for her eyes. "How would I know that you didn't waylay the poor girl, stuff her body down an old well, and steal her baskets of bread?"

"Do I look like someone who'd overpower an adult woman, murder her, and get rid of her body?" Blythe pointed at himself. He was small for his age, thanks to several bouts of illnesses throughout his childhood as well as poor nutrition, and it was a fact that rankled and that he refused to talk about. Now, however, provided that unique opportunity to use it to his advantage.

"A puny little creature like you can do some pretty amazing things when desperate enough."

"Ma'am, I'm not so desperate as to murder someone over bread, but I'm fast reaching that point. Now are you buying or aren't you? I haven't got all day, you know."

The old woman snorted and then shrugged. "Very well, then. I'll take one loaf, and if I were to find out that I bought blood bread, I'll make sure you swing for it, you rascal."

Blythe's eyes had glazed over by now as he handed her a loaf and received a few coins in return. "Fine, fine," he said. "Whatever you say." When the door finally slammed shut, he added, "I'm going to die of old age before I'm even done with this." And his premature and utterly unnecessary death would be on Molly's head.

Chapter 2

Considering what Blythe endured on his first day of work—doing a girl's job, at that—he'd expected Molly to feel, or at the very least express, empathy for his now shattered soul. But she didn't, and it was all Blythe could do to dredge up a good deal of self-pity as he sat on a rickety stool, his bare feet submerged in a pail of water. He didn't know what questions philosophers tended to ask, but he was quite sure that the most unanswered one ran along the lines of "Why was I ever born into this miserable world?"

"Now wasn't that a most eye-opening experience, Blythe?" Molly gurgled as she hurried back and forth between the oven and the hearth, where a large pot sat, the stew in it bubbling and letting out a delicious, though too familiar, aroma. The Midwinter household indulged in stew three times a week, and Molly only knew one recipe for it.

"Yes, it was eye-opening," he replied, glowering at a random point on the opposite wall. "I now know which houses to avoid."

"Avoid? What do you mean? The folks in Upchurch are such lovely people."

"Molly, they're either cantankerous hags or saucy wenches who're threatening to turn me into a grown man. And I'm not even counting masters or mistresses who called me a beggarly lout on his way to the gallows."

Molly burst out laughing, and Blythe cringed. "You're such a storyteller. Gallows? You? What on earth would make them say that? Why, I remember you being chased up a tree by Farmer Maul's geese just last year. I've never ever heard of anyone—even children who're younger than you—getting treed by geese."

That was a low blow. For his part, Blythe was absolutely terrified of Farmer Maul's satanic flock, and he still had no idea why they came after him in a murderous rage the way they did.

"Those so-called nice folks took one look at me, saw how poor I am, and decided I'm well on my way to a life of crime."

Molly's amusement didn't abate. Her bright laughter subsided to wild giggles, and she walked up to Blythe and planted a kiss on top of his head. "You're too funny for your own good," she said before sailing off to tend to the stew.

"But I suppose in that regard, we're somewhat even." She glanced over her shoulder to grin at him.

Blythe regarded her doubtfully. "How so?"

"They took one look at my rags and said that I was on my way to being a cheap prostitute. At the very least they bought some bread from me, and they eventually softened on their opinions once they got to know me better."

"Cold comfort, that."

"Just take their money, Blythe, and console yourself with the thought that you got them to part with their money—money that they could've used for something else." Molly paused. "Of course, when I first started out, I used to think that they were all arrogant, miserable bastards, but even my opinion of them changed in time."

Blythe pressed his mouth into a tight line as he stared narrowly at her. Then he glanced around the cottage in a tired and idle attempt at diverting himself until he felt good and ready to stand up and walk again. His gaze stopped on his shared sleeping space with Bertie, and his right eye twitched. He should do something about his nightly ordeal without inadvertently sending his brother to a surgeon for a very embarrassing procedure.

• • • •

"THAT'S A TRAGEDY IF I've ever heard one. Why'd you agree to it?"

"Because Molly was on her way to nagging me to the grave." Blythe paused. "Like your mama, in fact, though Molly's proving to be a darker influence. And she's younger than your mama, which means that I'm doomed to put up with her much longer than you have to put up with your mama."

Jack snorted, tossing a pebble into the river, and the two boys watched it plop, the little ripples barely marking the smooth current. The trees that loomed behind them afforded them quite a bit of comfortable shade against the surprising warmth of the day.

"I don't envy you that, then," Jack said after a moment of lazy silence. "Your sister's younger and has more energy in her for nagging."

"True, although, now that I think about it, your mama has all those years to her credit. I'm sure she's a lot less forceful in the more obvious sense, but she's likely more effective in that sly, clever way that older people are sly and clever."

Blythe glanced at his friend, feeling a touch smug about his philosophical skills and halfway wishing that he could be as sharp as that when confronting his sister over unfair labor practices. Then again, he was forced to concede, the fact that he couldn't was proof positive that Molly was an agent of the fiery depths and was gifted with unholy powers he could never hope to overcome.

For his part, Jack seemed to struggle with Blythe's reasoning, and he sat in baffled silence for a moment, scrunching his face and picking his nose as he deliberated. Blythe tried not to roll his eyes at the mental struggle. Eventually Jack turned to frown at him, dusty, sunburnt face crinkling again, finger still buried in one nostril.

"What was the question again?"

Blythe sighed and groped around for a small stone, which he tossed into the river. "Never mind," he said.

The sound of rumbling carriage wheels broke through the lovely calm, and Blythe looked up to watch a handsome private coach being pulled by an even handsomer team of horses along the dirt road on the other side of the river. The liveried driver sat straight and proud, his nose high even as he guided the gleaming horses with skill and confidence.

"I'd love to have one of those," Jack said in breathless tones.

"You'll have to work for it."

"I know. It's not fair, I tell you."

Blythe followed the coach's progress till it vanished behind some trees and dense shrubbery. "I suppose you can always gamble for it."

"I don't have any money to gamble with, you oaf."

Blythe tried not to roll his eyes again. "Sell something, then. One of your cows, for one thing."

"Mama and I only have one cow," Jack retorted. "I don't think she'll take to selling it. I mean, where will we get our milk?"

"Then find a job, you lazy dog!"

Jack let out a noise that sounded suspiciously like a fart, and he stumbled to his feet, brushing grass and dirt off his ragged trousers. "Dear God, you sound like Mama. Worse, you sound like a wife. I'm going home."

Blythe shook his head as he watched Jack yawn and stretch his long, bony arms, twisting his torso and cracking his back when he did.

"A wife," Blythe said. "That's what you need, Jack. A wife. Preferably a rich one."

Jack made a face and lightly slapped the top of Blythe's head with an open hand. "Don't be stupid. I'll never marry. I'd rather go off on grand adventures and come back rich."

"If so, then you'll have dozens of girls running after you and your money."

"Ha! They'll never get a penny from me!"

Blythe grinned as he threw another stone in the river. "I doubt if your mama will be too happy about that. I'm sure she'll be demanding grandchildren from you someday."

"Bah! I'll be the one bringing home the gold, not her! If she wants to stay on my good side, she'll keep her nose out of my business and let me have my way!"

A sudden movement just off to the right side of the road across from them caught Blythe's attention, and he cackled as he gave Jack's leg a sharp slap.

"Speaking of staying on one's good side, it looks like you haven't gotten that far with your mama."

A plump, red-faced woman walked into view, her ragged gown and smock as well as her bonnet caked with road dust. On one hand she held a particularly large rolling pin, and from what Jack had told him, it was never used for baking.

"Jack Wicket!" she hollered, turning her head left and right. "Where are you, you no good lout?"

Jack stuck two fingers into his mouth and whistled—a shrill siren that always set Blythe's teeth on edge and send nearby dogs howling. Mrs. Wicket stopped dead and caught sight of the two, and if her face was red then, it turned nearly black upon clapping eyes on her son.

"Jack! What the devil are you doing? Get your lazy, bony arse back home right this instant if you value your worthless hide!" she screeched, waving her rolling pin wildly in the air. "Didn't I tell you to chop wood? Didn't I? You've had all this time, and you never bothered to do one simple thing?"

For his part, Jack looked to be taking it all in stride. He stood silently for a moment, allowing his hysterical mother to unburden herself so passionately and convincingly, before turning and saluting Blythe.

"I'll be dreaming of riches while she thrashes me," he said and then strode off, hands in tattered pockets, and sang a vulgar drinking song. As to where and how he'd learned it, Blythe couldn't even begin to guess.

• • • •

"OH, AND HAVE YOU HEARD about that king who walked about in front of his subjects, all indecent and such?"

Blythe, whose eyes had long faded, shook his head and immediately regretted it when he realized that a negative response encouraged further talk. He didn't mean to do it; it was nothing more than a mindless, automatic response to Mr. Ruffle's incessant jabbering. The old man, apparently the eccentric master of the house whose door Blythe now rued knocking on, turned out to be a gossip. And while he was kind enough to purchase two loaves from Blythe, his generosity came at a high price, and he refused to let Blythe go, making Blythe add "courtesy to kindly old people" to his growing list of what not to do.

"Such a thing will never happen on our shores, you know. England's far too superior for idiotic displays that corrupt the ignorant and the poor—and all decent, God-fearing souls." Mr. Ruffle's talk dissolved into an unintelligible string of muttered somethings, and Blythe perked up. Was he finally done?

"And what about those clever creatures in Bremen, eh? I heard they gave a band of thieves a damned good thrashing! I wouldn't be surprised if those animals boast of bloodlines from England in the distant past."

No. Apparently not. Now he'd fixated on non-human subjects of gossip. Blythe's spirits sank even more at the too-real possibility of Mr. Ruffle taking an idle, meandering path to heroic inanimate objects whose bloodlines could be traced to venerable trees and rocks from England.

A tear escaped Blythe's right eye, and he swiped it away. For the next few agonizing moments, he ran his thoughts down the same lines as Jack's usual daydreams, and he was soon lost in wonderful scenes involving riches that could easily buy him ten kingdoms. By the time Mr. Ruffle decided to let him go—that is, by the time the old man's wife hollered for him from the depths of the house because he was holding up breakfast—Blythe had convinced himself that Jack Wicket's methods of making life more palatable had something to them.

• • • •

"WE SOLD ALL OUR CAKES," Molly declared, barely able to contain her excitement so that her normal singsong manner of speaking had turned operatic. "And Mrs. Pugsley claims that they've cured poor Mr. Pex's constipation. Isn't that terribly exciting?"

Blythe eyed her from where he sat—again on the rickety stool, his feet soaking in water—and pursed his lips as he listened, incredulous. "I'm sure some of Mrs. Pugsley's constipation potions had something to do with it. I hope she didn't taint any of your cakes with drops of the stuff."

"I thought about that at first," Molly replied as she alternately baked and cooked, her energy remarkably high. "But Mrs. Pugsley assured me yesterday that the only potions she sold were for gout and disgusting skin sores, not constipation. Looks like we all made a mistake in thinking she did. At any rate, it's terribly reassuring to hear that."

Blythe shrugged. "Maybe Mr. Pex was already on the mend when he—or whoever—bought your cake."

Molly sighed as she raised the lid of the pot on the fire, peering inside and stirring the bubbling concoction, the smell of which made Blythe think even more of constipation cures. They were having soup that night—one of three nights of soup. At least, unlike the stews, Molly knew three different soup recipes to make, though Blythe often wished that those recipes didn't involve the use of poisonous substances, judging from the nearly inedible quality of the stuff. That Molly's talent in the kitchen seemed to have poured itself completely into her baking skills and not day-to-day cooking had always been a source of bafflement for Blythe.

"You're too negative for a boy your age. Mrs. Pugsley—who, you know, is an insatiable gossip—told me specifically that Mr. Pex had reached that point where he could barely walk, no doubt his overstuffed bowels pulling him down with their weight. Then Mrs. Pex bought my cake to soothe him, and within an hour, she came running back to the market, practically hysterical in her relief and excitement over the results. In fact, she says, now he can't seem to stop!"

Blythe absorbed all this, doubt warring with mild nausea. "I suppose it'd be bad form for me to ask if you used certain magical ingredients to make this—uh—miracle happen."

Molly froze at the question, her face now a study of intense philosophical warring within. It was all Blythe could do to wait patiently and allow his sister to sort it all out on her own. At length she blinked, her eyes resuming life, and she regarded her brother with a cryptic little smile.

"I think you're right. It is bad form to ask. Just satisfy yourself with the fact that certain special ingredients were used, and this is a secret recipe that I'll be taking with me to the grave."

It was no small wonder Molly could persuade people to buy things from her. Blythe knew that she was full of cow manure, and she'd used nothing but the same things that bakers used for cake, but he might as well humor her. "That's good to know. Can't afford to have rival bakers discover your special recipe."

"You know, Blythe, I'm now wondering if I should alter my recipe for my bread to make it as miraculous as my cake. What do you think?"

All right, now she was taking things a bit too far.

"I think it's best to spare the poor, unsuspecting breakfast-eaters, Molly." Now he dreaded to think what she used for her cakes.

His sister fell silent for a moment, thinking, further alarming Blythe, though he took care not to show it. "Oh, I suppose. I think that I might need a special name for my special cakes. What do you think of 'Miraculous Midwinter Mounds'?"

Molly as well have been consulting a pile of horse dung. Blythe, at that point, had already wandered off to magical, mythical lands, where he was the most-loved king in the history of forever. He'd just signed into law the prohibition of selling bread by younger brothers, the penalty being exile or death, depending on the severity of abuse done by heartless and hellbound family members.

Later that day, when the Midwinter siblings were enjoying a simple supper of questionable soup and a loaf of unsold bread, a knock on the door interrupted their easy conversation.

"Why, it's Mrs. Pugsley!" Molly cried from her chair as Blythe pulled the door back some more and invited their guest inside.

"Oh, here's little Blythe," Mrs. Pugsley said as she stepped in, pausing to observe him in both surprise and pleasure. Her little gray eyes, practically vanishing under the ruddy, ample mounds of her cheeks when she grinned, moved up and down and sideways in quick, short spurts that reminded Blythe of skittish mice.

"Good evening, ma'am," he said, a little embarrassed.

"Well, look at you! I haven't seen you in a dog's age, I think. I've only been able to talk to your sister when she's out shopping. It's been a long time, hasn't it?"

"Yes, ma'am."

"What a darling, darling boy you've grown up to be. Why, I could eat you whole right now."

"Lord, I hope not. I just turned fifteen. I'd like to go past twenty-one if I could."

"But you don't understand how terribly eatable you are," Mrs. Pugsley insisted, laughing more heartily now, even taking each of Blythe's cheeks and pinching them, almost making him howl in pain. "But there's time enough for that. I've got some exciting news for dear Molly, and it can't wait."

With that, she gave Blythe's cheeks another pinch before sweeping away, still chattering endlessly, as she seated herself at the table. Blythe noticed, with an outraged and resentful glare, that she'd just commandeered his spot, leaving him no place to sit. And as though to dig the knife in more deeply, the infernal woman, so engrossed in her chatter, had begun to eat Blythe's soup without apparently realizing it, and neither Molly nor Bertie even thought to point that out. Apparently, even his siblings found her incessant talking so engrossing that they remained utterly unaware of the injustice that was taking place under their noses.

And as to what news was so earth-shattering that it needed to be shared at the expense of Blythe's fragile health? Why, it had something to do with whose servant had been dallying with a local squire, of course!

Shaking his head, Blythe shuffled off to find a clean bowl, only to discover that Molly didn't cook enough for five people, for there was only enough soup left for half a person. Oddly enough, Blythe thought this to be a rather fitting statement about his young life, especially since part of that half-person portion included soggy, overcooked things that used to be chicken meat and potatoes, and those stuck to the bottom of the pot. It was testament to Molly's skill as a cook that she'd somehow managed to burn soup.

Chapter 3

The young servant girl, who'd appeared at the door wearing a terrific amount of rouge—something that had never graced her cheeks till that morning—insisted on playing the game. Ignoring the loaf of bread that Blythe left on the ground about three feet away from her, she simpered, twirled a curl that had escaped her mobcap, and turned her body left and right in that maddening flirtatious thing that girls engaged in. False coyness, Blythe thought, now annoyed by the possibility of losing a sale.

"Oh, come now, Master Blythe," she cooed, that false coyness now turning a little emphatic—or was it desperate? All Blythe knew was that her girlish twisting had taken on a kind of urgency so that she looked more like a rouged spinning top. "Why would you let a poor, helpless girl come out in the cold to pick up a loaf of bread?"

"Because it's closer to you than it is to me."

That much was true enough. The loaf of bread sat forlornly on the ground five feet from Blythe. There was clearly a two-foot difference in distance, the advantage being the girl's. Blythe might only be fifteen, but he considered himself cleverer by half, and that difference in distance was done on purpose.

"Why, I've never heard of such a thing—a boy leaving something for a girl to pick up. That's not very polite or gentlemanly."

Blythe scowled. So much for politeness, and she was one to talk! Two days straight, she'd practically molested him where he stood weighed down with his baskets, trying to make a humbler than humble living selling Molly's damned bread. The girl had forced his hand in this, and that morning, Blythe not only did his math, but he also took care to set the loaf down on the ground on his arrival at the house, knock on the door, and then run just to the point he'd calculated was necessary for his virtue's sake. The past few moments had been spent with her cajoling him into giving her the bread correctly and "like a proper young gentleman", not force her to retrieve it like a trained dog.

"I'm not interested in politeness," he retorted, pointing at the loaf. "Just the money. All you need to do is pick that thing up and leave the money on the ground. Then we can both call it a day."

The girl finally stopped her twisting and frowned, this time resting her hands on her hips. "I've never had this much trouble with Miss Molly."

"That's because you never tried to do unspeakable things to my sister, especially offer to marry her."

"And? What's wrong with a bit of flirtation? I'm a girl, you're a boy, we're the same age. What are you so afraid of?"

Blythe stared at her. "The unknown," he said and then pointed at the bread loaf again, this time with greater urgency. "Now are you buying that or not? Other people are waiting for their loaves, and I don't have time to play stupid love games."

The girl paused for a moment, considering. "Oh," she said at length, her frown turning into a broad grin that lit her face up with the intensity of fifty glowing hearths, though that also made the rouge stand out all the more in sickly hues. "I see that you're the type of boy who takes his time with things! How sweet of you!"

Was she being purposefully thick? "If you don't want the bread, go back inside, so I can take it back. I'm sure there are dozens in Upchurch who'll be too happy to claim it," Blythe said, flailing.

"Oh, look, you're blushing!" the girl cried. She even clapped her hands, delighted. "What an adorable boy you are! I can eat you up!"

"For God's sake, not again," Blythe groaned.

As it turned out, there was no need to fret over the danger of his flesh being torn off his bones by insane, infatuated girls. The servant—a Harriet, it turned out—took so long trying to entice Blythe into being hers that a furious cook was forced to step in, drag her away by the ear, and finish the long-delayed transaction with Blythe. Spittle flying all over as she cursed useless servants up and down and left and right, she was nevertheless stiffly polite toward Blythe, thanking him and sending him off without much ceremony.

By the time Blythe limped home, he'd sworn to himself that he'd never sell a single loaf to households containing flighty old men and desperate virgin servants of any age. That, unfortunately, meant losing about half of his current customers, but at that point, he'd already stopped caring. For one mad moment, he actually wondered if his technique was terrible, not having consulted Molly regarding what lines to say to get people to cough up money for food.

That mad moment lasted a good five seconds, and he was back to his old sulky, reasonable self, convinced that the problem lay in others and not him.

• • • •

"TOMORROW BEING SATURDAY, we'll both be at the market with Mrs. Pugsley," Molly said as she nibbled on bread and cheese, while Blythe practically breathed in a small plate of shepherd's pie.

It was a small token from the kindly and generous Mrs. Stringer of Periwinkle Cottage. She'd always been that way, according to Molly, adding a small surprise to her few coins in exchange for the bread. She'd given Molly some pudding in the past; for Blythe, it was a small portion of shepherd's pie from the previous day's lunch. Considering all the grief he had to endure to make it to Periwinkle Cottage with his innocence and his sanity intact, Blythe decided that he'd damned well earned someone's leftovers, and Molly let him have all of it while satisfying herself with something light.

Blythe barely spared her a glance. "What, are we supposed to sell her potions as well?" He really would rather not. Mrs. Pugsley, whose offerings appealed to the old and infirm, was good at putting up with annoying and cantankerous customers. That was something Blythe was plain unwilling to subject himself to on a Saturday, especially after all those early morning ordeals putting up with annoying and cantankerous customers, himself.

"No, silly. We'll be there to sell our cakes." Molly took another bite of her cheese-topped slice of bread, chased that down with a drink, and then leaned forward to regard Blythe with a light of excitement in her eyes. "There's been a huge demand, according to her last night, and she and I decided that it would be best for us to be at the market with her, selling more of our cakes. I've been thinking more about it, and I figured that selling cakes only once a week would make people crave more, and they'd want to buy more than one on market day, which is always good for profits. What do you think? Is that clever?"

Blythe just shrugged, his attention back to his food. The subject of cakes never really interested him.

"Blythe, I thought you heard what Mrs. Pugsley said last night."

He sighed and glanced at his sister again, this time sparing her a black scowl as he swallowed his food. "I'd have bothered to listen had I not been starving to death. Not much, if anything, makes its way in here when my stomach's deprived of a proper meal." He tapped the top of his head. "Besides, when I saw that she was bent on talking about servants and squires, I decided that it was best to ignore the rest of the evening and pretend I was somewhere else."

"Well, at least you're making up for your hunger now. I hope that shepherd's pie was good."

"Heavenly."

Molly grinned. "I know that Mrs. Stringer goes to the market every week with a servant. If she sees you there, she might be driven to even more pity and buy you a hot meal."

"I'd rather she take pity on me and bring me something she cooked. Come to think of it, I hope she'd take pity on me and take me in as a foundling. By the way, if you sell a lot of cakes, does that mean I won't have to sell those stupid loaves of bread anymore?"

"Nice try, Blythe."

"Well—I suppose it doesn't hurt." Blythe finished his meal in sulky silence.

For the next couple of hours, Blythe helped his sister clean and wash before being allowed to spend the afternoon "being an idle pup" with Jack.

"Lord, you're well on your way to turning into a productive member of society," Jack said, disdain dripping from every word.

For that afternoon's entertainment, they'd decided to pass the time lounging about a local suicide's grave, which was conveniently located at the crossroads linking Upchurch to the rest of the world. After standing next to the sad, neglected mound that marked the remains of a long-forgotten farmer's daughter, they eventually decided that not much fun could be had in observing a grassy, oblong mound. From there, considering the tiny amount of time it took them to contemplate a suicide's tragic history (two minutes at most, possibly three), they took to wandering around the nearby heath to see if they could gather wildflowers.

So for the next several moments, buoyed by their cleverness, Blythe and Jack walked back and forth, carrying wildflowers and placing them along the grave's periphery, outlining it with some color. Blythe, for his part, was bored out of his mind, but he really had nothing else to do with his time.

"You know, I'm hoping that we'd sell enough of Molly's cakes to afford stopping that ridiculous morning bread ritual." Blythe shrugged as he stepped back from the grave, eyeing it as an artist would eye a masterpiece in the making. "In fact, I wouldn't mind it if we just kept to the market and sold everything there."

"Then why didn't your sister think about this before?"

"Because she didn't have competition selling bread at such a horrible time of the day. I mean, what sane person would go out before the sun rises just to sell bread?"

Jack cackled as they turned around to while more time on the roadside, heads bent, eyes searching for nothing in particular. Blythe had claimed a slender, broken tree branch and was using it to poke shallow holes into the ground.

"What do you want to do?" Jack asked after a moment's silence.

"I don't know. Never really thought about it. I suppose I'm too old to just hang about like this, but I'm also too young to be tossed into hard work like Bertie's."

Blythe sighed as that fact sank in, and for a moment, he wondered if he was somehow being unfair. Molly, after all, had begun working at fifteen, and annoyingly enough, she'd taken to baking and sales extremely well. Abnormally so, if he were to be really honest about it. She'd even once declared that this was her calling, and she couldn't think of a life doing something else.

As for Bertie, he'd discovered his calling at a later age after his first job—seventeen, in fact—but the end result was the same. He saw that he had both the talent and the passion for woodwork, which showed in his commissions, and his employer was more than thrilled to have Bertie work for him as his top wood carver. As with Molly, Bertie couldn't see himself doing something else.

Blythe couldn't help but feel a touch resentful toward the fact that he remained in the dark as to his purpose in life. Several times, in fact, he wondered if there was something wrong with him because life—his future—should be as plain and clear as it had been with his siblings. But it hadn't been, and he still remained in the dark as to what he wanted and what talent, if any, he had.

Blythe made a face as he jabbed a deep hole into the ground. "Maybe there's something wrong with me," he muttered.

"I don't know about you, but I aim higher," Jack said, following that with a characteristically derisive snort. "I'm not selling anything at that confounded market. I'm not planning on getting rich that way—takes too long."

Blythe laughed, swinging his branch left and right without aiming for any-thing. It gave a particularly interesting "whoosh" that Blythe found to be mildly amusing.

"You idiot. How can you gain riches without working? You're not exactly an heir, are you?"

"No, but I believe in luck."

"Oh? How's luck been treating you so far?"

"Not too well, but I'm patient."

The two stopped several yards away from the crossroads. Blythe, for his part, wasn't aware of the distance, having been absorbed in his thoughts for some time, his conversation with Jack nothing more than a vague, peripheral thing. They stood and gazed around them as the clouds of adolescent day-dreams vanished, leaving them blinking against the harsh glare of familiar and too-real surroundings.

"How much longer do you think you're going to wait?" Blythe pursued, this time allowing himself to stare out at the windswept countryside in fixed, glazed bliss.

"As long as it takes."

"That's stupid. What if luck never comes?"

"It will. I know it will."

Blythe snorted, blinking away the bit of fog. "You're pretty sure of yourself."

"I've always been a gambling man in a sense. Mama hates it, of course."

Blythe shrugged and turned around to redirect his steps back to the cot-tage. "I should go home. There's nothing to do here, and I'm bored."

"Upchurch is a boring town."

"It is. It's like a curse, being born to this godforsaken patch of land. I wish something exciting happens." The thought of the coming days turning out to be as brain-numbingly dull as that one depressed him. That the alternative was dragging his reluctant self through the empty streets of Upchurch before the sun rose only made him wonder what kind of life had been determined for him.

As they sullenly retraced their steps, they continued to heap all kinds of abuse on Upchurch as well as their lot in life—though Jack always took care to qualify the curse of his dull peasant existence with the confident hope that he was bound for greatness without once breaking out in sweat under the heat of the sun. They eventually reached the town square, still complaining, but this time, their shared vitriol was aimed at the gleaming carriages that rumbled all over, expertly negotiating their way through foot and vehicle traffic by smartly dressed drivers.

"Look, it's that carriage again!" Jack breathed. He'd stumbled to a halt, shooting a hand out to restrain Blythe.

The impressive vehicle was stopped before a milliner's shop. With an awed cry, Jack hurried forward, taking care to stop behind the carriage so as not to attract the driver's attention.

"Lord, look at this beauty!" he said, his eyes wide as he slowly walked around the back. "Someday, Blythe, I'll be riding inside one of these."

Blythe scrunched up his face as he stared at the vehicle, mystified by his friend's admiration. As far as he was concerned, a carriage was a carriage was a carriage, all polished wood and pretension for all of Jack's breathless praise, with each rich carriage looking not much different from another. Even the handsome team of horses looked no differently from other handsome teams of horses.

He looked around a little nervously. Rich folks never liked the idea of dusty peasants like them breathing on their precious boxes on wheels. When he saw that Jack had begun to run his fingers over the polished wood, he hissed, "Jack! Stop that, or you'll get into trouble!"

"What about? I'm just touching—didn't take me two seconds to do it!" Jack retorted, though he did pull his hand away as though burnt.

The door of the milliner's shop suddenly swung open, and out sailed a small group of fashionably dressed young people. Three ladies and one man chatted among themselves. A very young man—more like a boy—took the rear as he led an older gentleman toward the waiting vehicle. That last pair conversed with each other independent of the others, but they still exuded the same amount of good spirits, alternately talking and laughing in low tones. The older man surely was the father of the younger, judging from the fondness each displayed toward the other. The gentleman also appeared to be suffering from some form of physical disability or illness because he moved slowly and leaned on his son's arm.

The small group made for a picture of perfect contentment and obvious wealth. The driver jumped off his seat and quickly opened the carriage door with a smart bow.

The three young ladies entered first, laughing and teasing each other. Then the older gentleman was helped inside, followed by the young man and then the boy. Surely they were all related to the gentleman, Blythe thought, if their behavior toward each other was any indication. Brothers and sisters, most likely, though they could also be cousins.

Those were thoughts that were vague and fleeting at best, and Blythe had quite forgotten about them within seconds because his mind had fixed itself firmly and squarely on the boy who entered the carriage last. He appeared to be Blythe and Jack's age at least, though more likely older by a year or so, and Blythe found himself observing that boy more keenly and with some amazement.

The carriage soon jerked into motion and rumbled off, and Blythe watched it vanish around a corner, feeling a touch mystified by his sudden and intense interest. The feeling, like those earlier lazy daydreams, however, was gone in an instant, and Blythe was soon following Jack through the busy square, again lost in conversation with his friend as they picked up where they'd left off in heaping scorn on the awful drab life of an Upchurch resident.

Chapter 4

"Why are you doing this?"

"Because we want to sell all our cakes at the market."

"This is ridiculous. And stupid. I never wear all these fancy things!"

Blythe grumbled, cursed, squirmed, scratched various parts of his body in protest, and even threatened to throw up all over himself. None of those, however, moved his sister. Molly just kept to what she'd been doing, her determination to doll up her brothers taking on a grim edge, even, judging from the odd light in her eyes. It was a gleam that was alarming as far as Blythe was concerned.

"Stop your moaning, Blythe, if you don't want my favorite mixing spoon finding its way up your arse." Molly frowned more deeply as she laced and buttoned, brushed and wiped. Then she broke out into a broad grin as she finally stopped, taking a step back to survey the damage. "See, dear? You look positively adorable!"

At least he wasn't eatable, but that dubious honor must be limited to the views of non-family members. Somehow imagining Molly saying the same thing seemed rather disgusting and wrong.

Blythe dared not move. The suit he was being forced to wear was beyond uncomfortable. A loose shirt contained tightly by a waistcoat that felt it should be worn by a ten-year-old, his Sunday jacket, trousers, and old but shiny leather shoes he'd long avoided wearing because they were too stiff and uncomfortable. All he needed was a silk hat to complete the awful absurdity of his appearance.

Hands pressed stiffly against his sides, he said, "I look like something the cat shat."

"You're complaining?" Bertie retorted from where he stood—where he'd been standing for the last several moments in fact, after Molly had finished with him.

Taller and far bulkier than Blythe, sunburnt and scarred from all those years spent in intricate woodwork, Albert Midwinter had the look of a young man no one would dare trifle with. And he'd been in quite a few messy scrapes in the past and was known to show off his battle scars with pride, though those were all moments in which he was forced to defend his honor, not be the antagonist.

For the present, however, he was utterly helpless against Molly, who'd spent a great deal of time earlier fussing over him while Blythe cowered in the corner, watching in horrified fascination his brother's transformation from amiable, gentle giant to sullen, oversized dandy.

Bertie *was* a dandy right then, no different from Blythe. His bulk and his disposition, however, made the current scene a pathetic one, for the amiable, gentle giant couldn't—or refused to—move. As to whether or not it was because he was plain terrified into a fixed state, Blythe couldn't guess. As it was, poor Bertie stood where Molly had left him, all stiff and straight and freshly washed, the light of fear in his eyes a brilliant, terrible sparkle.

"You both complain too much," Molly said, laughing, and gave Blythe's jacket a final brush before tripping away in a whirlwind of petticoats.

"What's the point of looking like scarecrows if this is all about selling cakes? People will just laugh at us for being the most overdressed vendors at the market," Bertie said, the wild light of fear still in his eyes.

"This is embarrassing," Blythe added. "My friends are going to laugh at me."

"Which friends?" Molly asked without skipping a beat. "Jack Wicket or Jack Wicket?"

"That only goes to show that I can't afford to lose the respect of the one friend I have. Have you no soul?"

Molly snorted as she rummaged around for only God knew what. "Considering how much of a good-for-nothing that boy is, I really doubt if the loss will cost you much."

Blythe narrowed his eyes at her. "You're mocking my pain, Molly. Had I known that sisters were born to make one's life a wasteland of misery, I'd have offered myself to an orphanage the moment I learned to crawl."

"I think roaming bands of gypsies are more interesting," Bertie cut in sullenly. Blythe had to agree there.

That only earned both young men another unsympathetic—not to mention unladylike—snort from Molly. This time, though, she at least had the good grace to suppress her amusement, which the strain in her voice gave away.

"Blythe," she said, walking up to him to give his cheek a light pinch, "you exaggerate as always." Crinkling her nose at him, she swept past, adjusting her bonnet. "Come along, you two. Let's make some good money today."

As she threw the cottage door open and walked grandly out, Bertie and Blythe could only look at each other helplessly.

"I tried to offer myself up to an orphanage when I found out how difficult my life was going to be with Molly giving orders," Bertie said, his voice sounding more like a thin bleat than a healthy young man's. "It didn't work."

• • • •

THE GOOD THING ABOUT being forced to play vendor at the market—more specifically alongside Mrs. Pugsley and her potions—was that the stall was nicely situated under the shade of a large tree. At the very least it offered the Midwinter siblings a welcome protection against the sun, and that allayed some of Blythe's initial fears.

But, yes, only some. As it happened, the more pressing matters were never addressed and were, in fact, not only dismissed by Molly and Mrs. Pugsley, but also worsened. Blythe, it turned out, proved to be an effective draw (though not necessarily sales) among the younger customers and a good number of the old ones. The former thought the world of Blythe's "gentlemanly look and airs", and the latter thought the world of his "ill-fitting gentlemanliness"—or whatever on earth that meant. Blythe, in either case, was not amused. Molly, unfortunately, was, and she took care to keep him front and center despite his protests and threats of throwing himself onto the nearest and sharpest farmer's tool.

Flanked by an energetic, beaming sister and a stuttering, awkward brother, Blythe stood behind the cakes with a dead, frozen look in his eyes as he waited out the time. Even his imagination, so lately fired up, seemed to have stopped functioning, and he couldn't daydream his way out of an excruciating Saturday.

Beside them, manning her own table that she'd placed against Molly's, was Mrs. Pugsley and her bottles of gout and disgusting skin sores potions. Blythe had to admit to being relieved by—and especially grateful for—the fact that Mrs. Pugsley never once showed any competitiveness or jealousy, given Molly's unexpected success. She'd been encouraging and supportive, according to what he'd heard and seen during that brief, gossipy visit, and she didn't even cheat Molly out of her rightful profits from those early experiments at selling without Molly present.

He stole a glance at Mrs. Pugsley's direction and found her busy convincing three folks about the magical, miraculous qualities of her potions.

"I hope she stays just as nice for as long as Molly's here," he muttered, wondering as well how much profit they needed to amass in order to afford their own stall.

A pair of young ladies walked up to their table, nudging each other and whispering. Blythe held his breath, though he knew that it was useless; the girls were not only older than he but also obvious admirers of Bertie, who looked like he was about to shit all over himself.

"All yours, Bertie," Blythe muttered, and he stepped away, shuffling to the side before turning around to see if Molly saw what he was attempting to do, which was to magically vanish from the stall and pretend bewilderment on his return.

Unfortunately, there wasn't much room for him to use; even with two tables of goods to sell, there were still four people crowded behind them. No, it was impossible for Blythe to attempt anything. Molly, who'd been busy either enticing passersby to buy her cakes or sharing stories with Mrs. Pugsley during lulls, saw through him easily enough, rolling her eyes when he glanced at her sheepishly.

Sighing, Blythe decided to try a more direct approach. "There aren't a lot of people buying your cakes right now. May I take a few turns among the stalls?" Sensing his sister hesitating, he pointed at Bertie, who was now obliged to chat up his admirers while looking as though he were on the verge of fainting in shame. Red-faced, damp with sweat, and appearing more and more ill at ease in his fancy clothes, poor Bertie's tongue had also knotted itself, and he couldn't do much better than to communicate in broken and nonsensical phrases.

"See?" Blythe prodded. "Bertie looks like he's enjoying himself. Notice how he's able to charm two women at a time?"

Molly just stared at Blythe dully. "You know very well that those two are fighting over him. He doesn't need to make an effort to convince them to give up money for our cakes."

"But if Bertie can do that with his admirers, who's to say that he can't manage the same thing with strangers?" Blythe paused. "Well—just ignore the fact that strangers don't want to go to bed with him."

"You're nothing if not clever when it comes to getting out of work. I'll give you that."

"I can't help it. I'm fifteen. I'm sure you've tried to do the same—oh, hell, never mind. I forgot whom I'm talking to."

Molly clucked. "Oh, all right. I think it's safe to say that you earned a bit of a break. I do believe you helped me give up half a dozen cakes so far."

"Oh, sure—by being a glorified prostitute."

"Blythe, you need to take a walk now before I do something drastic with my foot and your boy parts. And please note that I was born with excellent aim."

Blythe was wandering through an insane collection of colorful stalls no more than two-and-a-half seconds later.

• • • •

HE NEVER THOUGHT HE'D live to see the day when he'd find the Up-church market a delight to the senses. He'd been there a few times in the past, but because of his age, he found those adventures to be dull and tedious. Molly and Bertie had always been popular because of their work, and somehow being their baby brother earned him an automatic place in everyone's regard. For that reason, Blythe was subjected to either strings of compliments expressed in language meant for five-year-olds that set his teeth on edge or the dreaded cheek-pinching or hair tousling, especially among older people. Blythe had therefore learned to associate the market with a perpetual infantile state.

That said, he was pleasantly surprised at the familiar scenes of color, smells, and sounds. Whether or not it was nothing more than an effect of desperately needing to run away from Molly's stall and the shame of being an overdressed vendor, Blythe couldn't tell, but it was a possibility he couldn't dismiss. Perhaps it was a sign of maturity?

He frowned as he mulled that point over while idly scanning the offerings of a wooden toy maker. At length, not finding any rational basis for maturity, he shrugged off such a ridiculous idea and immediately forgot about it. A number of jugglers and wandering musicians negotiated their way through the crowds, momentarily stopping them in their tracks with their tricks and pretty music and collecting a few coins from their audience in their caps or leather purses.

Upchurch, a quiet town tucked away in a remote corner of a remote region situated in a remote part of England, was so obscure and banal a place that nothing could set it apart from the rest of its neighbors. It wasn't until a group of disaffected magicians from God knew where had decided to say goodbye to a cruel world and find refuge in utter remoteness two centuries ago, when Upchurch's dull obscurity enjoyed a bit of a prick in the arse, pun unintended. In the market, stalls hawking all manner of magical toys and entertainment suddenly appeared, and they'd been thriving since, though at the expense of the magicians' respectable standing in society. Once kowtowed to and even revered for their powers, they'd become nothing more than conjurers for parlor tricks when kings decided that they'd no need of those men's powers.

Blythe decided to see what absurdly brilliant offerings they had and directed himself past stalls crammed with food, crafts, questionable art, and even chapbooks toward the Magicians' Corner of the market. It was one of the more popular areas, and it was also the most colorful and alarming. Bursts of stars and smoke suddenly shooting up above the trees could be seen from other parts of the market, and children would drag their reluctant parents to where the source was.

When Blythe arrived, he found the Magicians' Corner just as busy as before, with hordes of families or even small groups of dirty, ragged children milling about in wonder and pleasure, though most couldn't afford the commissions. From what Blythe understood, magicians benefited greatly from support from the gentry and above, though they continued to sell their current bag of tricks at the market in hopes of further exposure to customers from other towns.

A magic puppet show was being held at one of the stalls. Before it the dusty children in rags eventually congregated, gaping at the remarkable puppets that had come alive and were putting on a brilliant theatre production. With characters both delicate and colorful as well as grotesque and dark, this was by no means a regular Punch and Judy show.

Blythe observed the proprietor sitting off to the side, behind a small table. A large journal lay open on the table, and the stern-looking gentleman was poring over its entries. It was likely that the book contained names of the magician's clients, and Blythe thought it amusing that he'd be in the middle of doing something quite serious while his magic continued to work just beside him, breathing life into puppets and making them act out a fantastical story for everyone.

Blythe decided to take advantage of the shade provided by some trees just across the way from the stall, and there he stood, watching the show with growing delight, now that he'd all but forgotten about his embarrassing situation at Molly's table. In fact, he barely even realized that he was still walking around in his best suit, making him stand out among the crowd in the most mortifying way possible.

Before long, apathy and exhaustion born of too much time spent in shame, and the marvelous cacophony of market noise, color, and magic all turned into a potent mix that sank him into a dreamlike haze. He felt as though he were floating inside a marvelous bubble that engaged and soothed his senses, and he would, if he could, live in it for the rest of his life.

Was he smiling? It sure felt like it, but he didn't care if he looked like an idiot.

Blythe didn't know how long he stayed in a strange, hypnotic state, but his lovely escape from reality was suddenly interrupted by movement just off to his right. He blinked and frowned, looking around him at first with an annoyed sigh.

Then he glanced to his right, a curse of his tongue, and with a start, he had to swallow it back. The boy who'd caught his attention at the town square not too long ago was not only there, but also looking at him, a questioning and curious light in his eyes. When Blythe met his gaze, the boy didn't look away immediately; in fact, his unabashed staring seemed to take on an even more curious light, for the boy—absently, it looked like—actually cocked his head a little as he continued to observe Blythe.

The boy didn't come alone. A man stood beside him, and, judging from the fellow's simple and somber clothes as well as the haughty disdain on his face as he watched the puppet show, it was safe to guess that he was likely the boy's tutor. As to why they'd be spending time in the market, which apparently was an object of contempt for the older man, Blythe couldn't guess.

After a few more seconds of gaze-meeting, the other boy was forced out of his remarkable—not to mention embarrassing—boldness and had to turn away when his companion leaned close enough to say something. They exchanged a few private words and then turned around to walk away, but not before the boy stole another glance in Blythe's direction and did something that was even more remarkable.

He smiled at Blythe over his shoulder—a brief but brilliant smile that seemed to linger even as he and his companion vanished in the market crowd.

Chapter 5

Blythe rejoined his siblings more confused than his most confused ever state. He was so deep in a muddle that he barely noticed the surprisingly small pile of cakes that still needed to be sold.

"Where on earth have you been?" Molly demanded, red-faced and scowling. "We were overwhelmed with customers for an eternity and could've used your help."

Blythe, a bit miffed for being dragged out of his confusion (which had just begun to feel oddly nice), sighed as he took his place. "An eternity? And you accuse me of exaggerating? Don't worry. I'm alive. I'm back. I'm ready to suffer more blows to my pride."

"Good. Look after the cakes. It's my turn to disappear for a bit. By the way, I don't know where you've been or what you've been up to, but you're so red, I'm inclined to call the doctor."

Thank goodness she didn't seem to put much weight on what she'd just said because she claimed her shawl, threw it around her shoulders, and vanished. Blythe, for his part, had let out a startled little gurgle and instantly felt his face with a hand.

"Red?" he spluttered. "What do you mean, red?"

"She probably meant red like my face—like blood plague red," Bertie said morosely.

Blythe looked at him, suddenly realizing that he had a brother. Sure enough, poor Bertie's face had turned a sickly shade of red. His hair, perfectly combed earlier, was also unkempt, a sure sign that he'd spent the greater part of the past hour being fawned over by a gaggle of grandmothers who either adored him or wished to clean their hands but didn't have the proper means to do it. As for his face, Bertie clearly had endured a great deal of pride-battering from younger admirers who saw him in public wearing the most ridiculous ensemble that could be worn at an outdoor market. His posture certainly didn't help; he stood frozen on the same spot where Blythe had left him, his shoulders tightly drawn up, his head bowed, his hands deeply shoved inside his pockets.

"I must admit I feel quite sorry for you," Blythe said. "If it'll help, I can always tell everyone that you're a flatulent old troll at night. That should keep your endless armies of admirers at bay, and I wouldn't even be stretching the truth."

"The frightening thing is that some of them might find a flatulent old troll either a challenge or a charming eccentric." Bertie paused, frowning, clarity suddenly dawning in his eyes. He turned to Blythe, now looking outraged. "Wait a minute—a flatulent old troll, you say?"

A woman with about five hundred children in tow appeared, saving Blythe from a proper answer. Offering his most winning smile, he stepped forward and greeted their customer while keeping an eye on her children, who swarmed the table and looked as though they were ready to run off with what they could manage to carry in their small, bony arms. Immediately after her came Mr. Ruffle, the supreme master of early morning gossip terror. He'd instantly recognized Blythe—inappropriately fashionable clothes notwithstanding—and decided to chat him up. Again. As though Blythe hadn't seen him several hours earlier in his usual hellish bread route.

"It's been some time, hasn't it, my boy?" Mr. Ruffle all but bellowed in Blythe's face.

"Yes," Blythe said, drawing the word out as his brain locked itself in a panic at the thought that he'd nowhere to run and hide. "That would be about six hours ago, I think."

"Yes, yes, an eternity!" Mr. Ruffle paused to survey the cakes and then thought better of it. Looking up at Blythe again, his toothless mouth curving into a grin, he asked, "Have you heard about that prince in the north somewhere and his tallow-stained shirt and that long-nosed princess and a pack of trolls—" Mr. Ruffle had gotten so excited that his words simply flew out of him, and he was forced to stop in order to breathe.

"Are you sure you're not interested in a cake, sir?" Blythe asked, a touch desperate. Or at least a touch more desperate now than before.

The old man, still gasping for air, shook his head and waved his hand impatiently.

"No, no, I'm fine," he said after a moment, his voice tight. "It's just—three ells long, my boy!"

"What?"

"Three ells long! That's how long this princess's nose is! Can you imagine it?"

"No, sir," Blythe said, grimacing, and he followed that with a muttered, "And I really don't want to if I want to keep my appetite."

"Trolls—bah! Always a damned nuisance with royalty!" Mr. Ruffle sniffed when he paused. "Of course, they're not that much better when it comes to their dealings with the peasantry or the gentry. Oh, what am I saying? Trolls are monstrous things that are a plague to society."

"Don't you agree, though, that a nice cake like this would ease the effects of trolls on your blood pressure, sir?" Blythe took up one and held it aloft, hoping it looked so enticing that everyone within a hundred feet would fight each other to the death over it. "My sister's baking's known to cure constipation, so it's not much of a leap to expect it to help your health in other ways."

"Eh? I don't need anything for constipation. I've been regular since my first day on this earth."

Blythe set the cake down and raised a hand, silencing the old man. "Will you excuse me for a moment, sir?" When Mr. Ruffle nodded, he sidled up to Bertie and gave him a nudge with his elbow. "Bertie," he whispered, "can you get rid of him?"

Bertie just gave him a narrowed sidelong glance. "I find this to be sweet justice after you called me a flatulent old troll. Go back to your spot, imp, and sell some cakes."

Apparently such was the reward one got for speaking the truth about one's sibling's gastric condition, but Blythe knew a losing battle when he saw it, and with a sinking heart, he went back to subject himself to more nonsensical tattling from Mr. Ruffle.

By the time Mr. Ruffle left, not a single cake was sold, but Blythe could boast an intricate knowledge about the workings of magical northern kingdoms, not the least of which being a pretty gruesome account of a troll getting his comeuppance through the well-aimed horns of a big billygoat. Did trolls populate much of the north? Blythe didn't know, but all the same, if Mr. Ruffle's wild stories were all true, he certainly wouldn't set foot outside England. No proper Englishman would want to soil his shoes on foreign ground, anyway.

Molly returned from her break, and Bertie was let go for the time being. Judging from the child-like pleasure that lit up his face, it was safe to guess that he was set to spend that time in the company of a delightful pint. Blythe fervently hoped that it wouldn't be more than that; nothing battered wrecked pride more than to be seen half-dragging one's drunk brother home while inappropriately fashionably dressed.

"Since it's quiet at the moment, I'm going to buy some carrots and potatoes from Mrs. Luck's stall. She always has the freshest vegetables—and they last for a remarkably long time," Molly said after she and Blythe stood and watched passersby in bored silence.

"What if I need to go?" Blythe demanded. "I can't just stand here and pretend everything's well in the world while pissing away."

"You'll have to cross your legs, Blythe. Now behave, or I won't buy you your favorite jam."

"Well—can't we have something else besides potatoes and carrots?"

"Those keep well, dear. You know I always buy enough for a week, and heaven knows, green things rot sooner than you'd like them to."

Blythe sighed. Yes, that much was true, judging from those horrific moments in the distant past when he was ordered to get some green vegetables from a container and instead found a bubbling, soggy mass that seemed to speak to him in Satan's voice. He'd no idea how long those vegetables had stayed in their containers, but he suspected that Molly had simply forgotten they existed, allowing them to melt or whatever it was green vegetables did when neglected for too long a time.

The downside to his experience, of course, was to be stuck with potatoes and carrots that made up half of their meals, the second half divided between meat and bread, with bread taking up about two-thirds of that portion. Surely, he thought, there must be a vegetable out there that would last a full week and that would enhance their dining experience even if only by a little bit.

"Can we then get different kinds of potatoes? Or carrots in different shades of orange? Do they come in yellow or violet?"

Molly just laughed and tousled his hair before she sailed out without answering him. Perhaps she was stumped, Blythe thought, sighing. Then he shrugged, rubbing the back of his neck. There wasn't much he could do, anyway, with Molly being the one who knew the intricacies of cooking and recipes and vegetables she needed to cobble a decent meal together with. For his part, Blythe figured that having multi-colored carrots and potatoes would be a step up in his meal experience.

The lull continued for a few more minutes, and Blythe had to kick off his shoes because they were simply destroying his feet. At least there was some thick grass underfoot that helped ease the soreness, and he paced back and forth like a caged but ultimately happy animal, sighing in relief at the feel of a soft cushion under him.

For better or for worse, an old man shuffled up to the table, forcing Blythe to take his place once more. At the very least, though, he felt a great deal more relaxed, and he decided that he could help this customer with more sincere pleasure. The stranger looked as though he'd just emerged from a longish trip through the devil's bowels. He was gray-skinned and haggard, his entire person nothing more than leathery skin hanging loosely off sharp bones. His eyes matched his unfortunate complexion, his eyeballs barely kept in their sockets, and Blythe wondered if he should hold both of his hands up to catch them should they pop out without warning. Then again, he quickly realized, the very notion of holding someone's eyeballs was both surreal and revolting, and he forced it out of his mind.

The stranger eyed him keenly at first, his long, dirty, and unkempt hair making him look more like a startled troll (those damned trolls again!) than an old man down on his luck.

"Those cakes look like a real delight," the stranger said after another moment of uncomfortable silence from Blythe's end. His voice cracked as though he hadn't spoken in ages.

"They are, yes," Blythe said. "If you're constipated, they're miraculous."

"I assure you that I'm not, but I'd like to enjoy one." The old man paused and glanced around him warily. Then he leaned closer and whispered, "Will you sell one to me for five magic beans?"

The most overpowering cloud of rot assailed Blythe's nostrils, nearly making him faint on the spot. If he thought before that nothing on earth could beat Bertie's reeking blasts, he now stood immensely corrected. It took every ounce of strength and willpower for him to keep the contents of his stomach from surging upward as he steadied himself.

"What on earth are magic beans?" he grunted, dreading the next wave, which was inevitable when engaged in conversation with the stranger.

"Exactly what I said. They're beans, and they're magical." The old man blinked, looking puzzled. "I don't see how I can be any clearer than that."

"Speaking of clear, I'd love my air to be just that," Blythe murmured, teetering. He quickly rallied all the same. "I can't accept anything but money, sir, or my sister will slaughter me. Besides, I don't think those are really magic beans."

The stranger didn't appear fazed. "My boy, I guarantee their nature. Aren't you curious to see what awaits you in the clouds?"

Blythe shrugged. "Clouds do nothing but piss on us at the worst times. Why would I want to see what they hide?"

"What about adventures beyond your wildest dreams? Wealth? Gold?"

"That sounds ridiculous. The only adventure up there," Blythe retorted as he pointed at the sky, "is God drinking too many pints and ruining our day as a result."

The old man blinked again. Watching his paper-thin eyelids attempt to move over his eyeballs was unnervingly fascinating. "I don't think that's the case."

"It's all rubbish," Blythe replied with a tired sigh. What on earth was it with old men and wild stories? And why did he draw so many of them to himself like so many flies on a steaming pile of horse droppings? "Besides, I still don't see the connection between magic beans and clouds."

"If you plant these in your garden, my boy, they'll grow overnight and shoot straight into the sky."

It was Blythe's turn to blink in confusion. "That's a damned tall plant."

"A beanstalk, not just any plant, but yes—it's a wonderfully tall one, with great surprises waiting at the top for the enterprising boy who isn't afraid of risks and challenges." The stranger paused and grinned. "What say you, then? Have you the pluck? The courage?"

"I do, but I also have a sister who'll skin me alive if she were to find out I exchanged one of her cakes for magic beans."

The old man was insistent. "Have you the desire to change your path in life?"

Blythe coughed, his eyes watering. Once he calmed, he stammered, "I don't have the air to help me think clearly. I also need a very important body part that's in danger of being cut off by a very sensitive older sister."

"And you'll simply allow your destiny to walk away from you? Aren't you tired of being poor and wishing for something much better than this? Why don't you think about what's contained in that dark and cold cottage you call your home, Master Blythe?"

"How'd you know my name?"

The old man merely grinned, shrugging. "Think of your dissatisfaction right now, young man. Where would you like to be instead? How would you like your life to be—comfortable? Everyone deserves to be comfortable and safe and well-fed, aren't I right? You've always been poor—why would you like to remain so indefinitely?"

Blythe hesitated as he thought of his life and, yes, his growing dissatisfaction toward the day-to-day struggles he and his siblings had to put up with. He couldn't see how selling bread and cake would change the Midwinter fortune for the better beyond food and a rare indulgence in clothing. There had to be something better out there, but luck didn't favor them despite their sacrifices and hard work.

As resentment swirled, something stopped him from doing anything more. From somewhere in the depths of his mind, he heard a quiet voice prod him as well.

Is that all you can see, dearest?

His conscience flared alive at the echoes of his mother's voice, and guilt overwhelmed him. He felt himself gently steered away from temptation and the lure of great adventures and treasure in the clouds. "I'm perfectly fine where I am right now," he said at length, dispirited.

"Is that your final answer, my boy?"

"It is, yes. Thank you for your offer, though."

The stranger stepped back, eyeing Blythe strangely again. But he bowed and said, "Then I thank you for your time, Master Blythe. May good fortune favor you as well as you deserve."

Before Blythe could think of something to say in answer, the old man vanished. Literally.

"Dear little brother, I appreciate your efforts at keeping flies from ruining my cakes. But there's no need to take drastic measures for that. Close your mouth, please. You're drooling all over your best waistcoat and unnerving people," Molly said, her voice cutting through the thick fog that used to be Blythe's brain.

• • • •

THE MIDWINTER COTTAGE shook with Molly's jubilant cries and off-key-singing that evening. Bertie was half-drunk, and Blythe busied himself with a minor architectural adjustment to their humble home. He'd dragged a stool—the sturdiest they had, that is, which really wasn't saying much—over to the space between his bed and Bertie's, and he stood on it, closely inspecting the wall with a thoughtful frown.

"All cakes but one!" Molly kept chanting. "We sold all cakes but one!" She danced around the table, waving a ladle above her head. Food cooked in the hearth, filling the cottage with familiar scents of, yes, stew. For all the profits they'd earned that day, none apparently went to an upgrading of their supper, though Blythe was inclined to suspect that it was because Molly wanted to scrimp and save as much as she could.

"Damned brilliant, Molly," Bertie gurgled from his chair. "Keep the magic going, whatever the devil that means."

Another benefit to selling at the market was the fact that Bertie had easy access to his favorite drink, and he'd proven to be quite good at ingratiating himself to Molly, who'd spared him some money for some celebratory ale. On top of all that, they'd also taken home a good deal of unsold food items—mostly green vegetables in danger of rotting as well as purple-skinned potatoes from a farmer admirer of Molly's, who'd insisted on giving them the extras without paying. Those wilting green vegetables went directly into the stew, and it was going to be the only time when they'd be enjoyed. At least the purple-skinned potatoes could be stretched out some more, and Blythe looked forward to seeing unpeeled purple things in his soup or stew in the coming days.

"We'll continue to share space with Mrs. Pugsley again next Saturday, and I'll bake more cakes—maybe about seven more, now that all of Upchurch knows they exist. In the meantime, Blythe, you'll continue your bread-selling, and you'll remind everyone about the cakes maybe twice a week. Be subtle about it, though, and don't make it look as though we're desperate for a sale."

And so on and so forth. Molly continued to chatter on and on about baking and especially about a new acquaintance she'd made during her break that day—a professional baker, it seemed, who owned her own bakery in town.

"I crossed paths with her while looking at the flower stalls during my break. In fact, she was the one who looked for me, and she was told that she could find me at the market."

"That sounds a bit unnerving, Molly, someone shadowing you like that," Bertie slurred.

"Oh, don't be ridiculous. She's very harmless and quite a brilliant woman. Being a professional, she said that she keeps up with everyone else in the trade, and I'm sure someone had said something about our cakes last Saturday, and that was how she found out about me." Molly gasped for air and giggled, tapping her chest.

The woman had expressed interest in Molly's blossoming career and had even gone so far as to advise her.

"I'd like to think that Mrs. Brainswell will agree to be my mentor. She assured me that she'll be visiting our table on market day to watch our progress and offer more advice on how to be better," Molly said, sounding dreamy and breathless. "I can't believe my luck today. I hope it continues." And so she continued to talk about castles in the sky, while Bertie slurred his congratulations before stumbling outside to relieve himself.

In the meantime, Blythe barely took note of everything, being too busy hammering one corner of an old blanket on the wall and securing the opposite corner to his father's old coat rack. When he was done, he stood back to admire his handiwork: a makeshift wall separating his bed from his brother's, ensuring that Bertie's obnoxious blasts and their murderous effects would be limited to the offender's immediate space and no one else's.

Chapter 6

"That was a pretty fool move. Can't believe you just let him go like that." Jack paused to turn his head and spit.

"What on earth would magic beans give me? He told me that they grow straight into the sky or something stupid like that. What can you do with a plant that goes all the way up there? Pick all the beans you see hanging and sell them for a fortune?"

Blythe never cared for beans unless they were cooked into mush or a form that was completely unrecognizable. Yes, like mush. Then again, he was also forced to concede that his biases would be more a product of years spent being subjected to Molly's cooking.

"The problem with you is that you don't have any imagination."

"What's there to imagine with a giant beanstalk? It shoots up to the sky. Oh, happiness."

Jack just snorted in disgust. "You don't know how to think about possibilities. Sure, the beanstalk can reach the sky, but what goes on beyond that? I mean, what's at the end of it?"

"Clouds and some heavenly being who drinks too much and pisses on us at the worst possible times," Blythe replied, sighing. This conversation was getting quite tedious. "Besides, unlike you, I don't believe in luck and getting rich because I happen to be in the right place at the right time."

"Well, I do, and I think that there's a lot more to those magic beans than what that old man's letting on."

Blythe glanced at his friend. "What if there isn't?" he prodded.

"There *is* no 'isn't.'"

"What makes you so sure? You don't have the beans with you, let alone have them already planted in your backyard. I think you're just trying hard to justify the fact that you don't want to work to earn your riches. You just want it given to you for nothing. You sound like one of those people who inherit their riches and act like they deserve it."

Jack gave Blythe's arm a sharp punch, sending Blythe stumbling off the path a few paces with a yelp. "Rich folks are rich through no hard work," Jack retorted, turning to spit again. Icy bitterness edged his words. "I don't see why it can't happen to people like us."

"Accident of birth, fool," Blythe said, grimacing as he gingerly shook his arm. "Ow. You didn't have to hit me that hard, you know."

"Well, you're irritating me. You don't think that poor folks don't deserve good luck."

"I never said that. I only said that I don't believe in luck." He didn't, did he? Blythe pinched his mouth and scowled as he fought off a few ugly thoughts coursed through his mind.

"What if it happens to you? What would you do then?"

Blythe considered for a moment. "I don't know. If it happens, it happens, I suppose, but—I don't think I'll be feeling too comfortable about it."

"That's the stupidest thing I've ever heard. It's easy money, and you won't feel comfortable? What, you want to suffer at work all your life?"

"I wouldn't be earning it, Jack. That's my problem with it." But the temptation, though—Blythe was forced to admit that being gifted with riches was such an amazing dream. There were so many things he could do with the money, so much independence to revel in. The very thought of living in a house that was more than just four walls and a ceiling...

"Lord, talking to you's like talking to a damned wall. Then again, I suppose some people are plain too cowardly to take chances. I'm certainly not one of those."

Blythe scowled at his feet as he listened and pondered. Was he being a coward? He certainly despised his new work, and his experience at the market was nothing short of hideous despite Molly's success. He'd love to see his family rise above their station, but he'd always been told that only one path was available to reach that end: hard, honest work and a good deal of prudent handling of money.

He felt the weight of the baskets on each hand, and his eyes strayed to the one he carried in his left hand. It contained three unsold loaves, while the right basket was emptied of its contents. He'd been reluctant to return home with three loaves left because he was sure that it'd be a sore blow to Molly, who'd always come home empty-handed.

Blythe had spent much of the later morning hours searching for people who might be interested in the loaves, but everyone had already had breakfast or refused him for whatever reason. It all rankled, considering the fact that since his first day taking over his sister's work, he'd always come home with at least one unsold loaf—a depressing reminder of his shortcomings.

Jack happened to stumble across Blythe sitting forlornly at the fountain in the middle of the town square, watching everyone go about their business while cradling the basket with the loaves against his chest. Jack almost had to peel him off his stone perch and force him to walk around idly. For his part, Jack had escaped his mother's cottage because he still refused to chop wood for the hearth, claiming that he'd already sharpened the ax, and it would be a waste of his time if he were to dull the blade again by hacking away at a tree.

"I'm not a coward," Blythe snapped. "I just have a different view of things."

"Oh, sure—like do the safe thing. How predictable. Nothing will happen to someone who won't take risks." Jack let out an exasperated sigh as he kicked a stone and watched it fly off and disappear under the wheels of passing wagons. "Wish I were at the market. I'd have taken that old man up on his offer."

"Jack, he could've been mad for all we know."

The sudden yelling of a man and the neighing of horses forced their conversations to a halt.

"You two! Out of the way! Damned filthy urchins! Out! Out!"

Blythe and Jack whirled around and saw a pair of horses practically breathing down their necks. The driver glared at them and continued his shouts, and with a little exclamation, both boys jumped out of the carriage's way. Jack went in one direction, and Blythe threw himself into the other.

He hit the ground hard, rolling and coughing at the cloud of dust that rose up. He waved a hand before his face and squinted as he looked around him. Sitting up, he saw his baskets a few feet away, the leftover loaves of bread having tumbled out, with two rolling directly into the path of the carriage's wheels.

"Oh, no," he cried, horrified, as he watched the loaves get squashed. "Stop!" he yelled, stumbling to his feet. "Stop! I have to sell—oh, lord."

"What on earth—whoa! Whoa! Get away from the carriage! What are you trying to do, you idiot? Kill yourself?"

Blythe, without once thinking, had run close to the wheels in hopes of saving the third loaf, which had rolled farther out but was also in danger of being run over. Had it not been for someone's quick intervention, he'd have been crushed under the wheels, himself. A bystander, seeing the catastrophe about to happen, had reached out, grabbed hold of Blythe's jacket, and jerked him back roughly and out of harm's way. With the sound of ripping fabric mingled a gasp and coughs because the sudden pull of his jacket and shirt nearly strangled him.

What sounded like a dozen voices started shouting at the same time. Blythe, frozen in confusion, shock, and terror at the realization of having escaped a pretty horrific annihilation, stood in mute helplessness, kept in place as well by his rescuer, who continued to grip his jacket. Blythe barely recognized Jack's furious voice in the mix of sounds that now engulfed him. He wasn't even clearly aware of a calmer, quieter voice asking something—a voice that was close, much closer to him than the others.

The man who'd yanked him out of the way finally released him. "That was a stupid thing you tried to do," he scolded, frowning darkly at Blythe, his weathered features and thick beard lending him an even greater air of rough authority as he loomed over Blythe. "Don't ever do that again. You hear me?"

Blythe could only nod and offer his weak thanks, but those were enough to satisfy the fellow, who nodded, harrumphed, and then ambled off, his soiled and hulking figure melting against the busy scenery.

When Blythe felt a touch on his arm, the spell broke, and he gave a start.

"I asked if you were all right."

He blinked and looked up. The boy he saw at the market was speaking, and he'd leaned out the carriage window and had reached out to touch Blythe's arm. A look of worry darkened his features. Blythe, still confused but this time for a different reason, gave the carriage another look. No, this was a different one from what he'd seen before; perhaps this boy was a great deal wealthier than he'd thought, and his family owned more than one carriage.

Wonderful. Now Blythe felt a thousand times poorer than he really was.

From inside the carriage, a few voices floated out as well—female voices talking excitedly. None of the ladies looked out to see what was the matter, though, but Blythe hardly cared about that.

The realization of just how much of an idiot he was finally dawned on him, the worst part being the fact that the other boy had seen everything that'd just happened. The clear and sincere anxiety on Blythe's behalf only made things worse. Not only was he a failure, he was also an object of pity.

He pulled his jacket more tightly around his shoulders, inwardly wincing at the pathetic picture he made. He was dusty and disheveled, his frayed and faded clothes now sporting a few new tears from his savior's rough handling. His cap had fallen off, and God knew where it was now. With Blythe's luck, it was probably lying in a shapeless heap under the horses and getting thoroughly shat on.

"I'm fine, thank you," he said, meeting the boy's gaze for a second before looking away, his face burning horribly. "I have to go."

He turned away, grimacing as he rubbed his throat gingerly. The savage pull on his shirt and jacket felt as though his throat had been kicked. He looked around for his baskets, feeling the weight of the other boy's stare on his back. Somewhere in the periphery of his awareness was Jack hurling insults at the driver, who, in turn, tossed back a string of colorful references to the nature of Jack's brain. For better or for worse, Jack had the final say, and he gave the driver a pretty rude gesture with his hand as he made his way around the horses to join Blythe.

"Mr. Hood, if you wish to remain employed, I suggest that you leave the boy alone and drive on!" a woman called out from the carriage's interior. Her voice was clear and firm, making Blythe wonder if she were the oldest lady in the group—and whether or not she was related to the boy whose solicitude now shadowed Blythe's existence.

"Yes, ma'am," the driver stammered. He whistled, made clicking noises with his tongue, and the horses trotted onward.

Blythe fought the urge to look up and watch the carriage go, but as it happened, he was at his most vulnerable, which included a severely weakened will. Swallowing, he glanced up and saw that the boy kept his head out the window and continued to stare at him with a worried little frown. At length, because of the growing distance, he was forced to sit back again, and the carriage soon vanished around a corner.

Around Blythe life went on. The earlier incident seemed to have been forgotten completely, or it seemed as though it never happened. Passersby went about their business—walking or hurrying, chatting with companions or looking preoccupied. Blythe picked up his baskets, momentarily inspecting them for damage and feeling some relief in finding none. The loaves were all beyond help. Even as Blythe turned to see where they lay, birds had already descended to feast on the torn remains that littered the cobbled street.

"Here." Jack appeared and held up Blythe's cap. "The horses nearly trampled it to pieces."

"Thank you." Blythe took his cap and stared at it, grimacing. "Oh, blast it. This was my best cap."

"Fool. That's your only cap."

Blythe sighed as he regarded the remains of his unsold bread, wracking his brain for the best way to break the news to Molly. The pang of guilt lancing through him as his mind conjured up images of his sister sweating and covered in flour made his steps drag.

In the meantime, Jack, wholly unaware of his friend's depressed state, ranted on about idiot coach drivers and insensible rich people.

"They don't care about people like us," he spluttered, turning to spit a few times in the course of his railing. After five minutes of that, Blythe sincerely worried if his friend was in danger of spitting himself dry. "They go about parading their damned money for everyone to see, rubbing our noses into their privilege—as if we needed more reminders of how far behind we are as their inferiors."

After a few more moments of this, Blythe couldn't bear to listen to him go on an endless verbal rampage that was generously peppered with emphatic spitting. His mind, having nowhere else to go, had decided to fix itself on that boy. A multitude of conflicting feelings pressed down on him and left him breathless and confused—yet again. Blythe shared a good many opinions about the rich with Jack, and on normal days, he'd be just as vocal in his disapproval of the shabby treatment poor people were forced to endure in the hands of the well-to-do.

Not now, though. Amid the awful sting of mortification at being seen in such a ridiculous—and dangerous—light, Blythe couldn't help but recall the boy's face and the myriad of expressions that had lit it with so much wonderful life. There was that look of contentment and quiet pleasure as he followed his companions—his family?—out of the milliner's shop. The look of open curiosity at the market, which was followed by a friendly and rather bold smile. And now it was a look of anxiety, the boy's gaze a great deal steadier and more deeply probing.

Blythe had never had many friends; in fact, he'd counted Jack Wicket for steady companionship since their childhood. Never, in his young life, had he ever been on the receiving end of such looks as he'd seen from that new—was he new?—boy. Even among those in the same circle he and his family moved in, Blythe had always been largely ignored, patronized for his age, and scolded or dismissed. He'd nothing important to offer, was the message he'd long grown used to receiving, and he'd learned to believe it about himself. And having accepted that, Blythe had sunk into a form of contented apathy and went about his days being—and acting like—a part of the furniture.

Now someone appeared to be paying attention to him, and he'd absolutely no idea what to do. The fact that this someone was rich only made the waters a great deal muddier than they already were.

"Hey! Wake up!"

Blythe gave a start and turned to find Jack glaring at him. His friend had also stopped, though Blythe hadn't, and Blythe sheepishly turned around and retraced his steps back to his friend's side.

"Sorry," he said in a meek, meek voice. "I've got a lot of things on my mind."

"Obviously." Jack sighed and rolled his eyes. "I was asking you if you wanted to come in for something to eat. Mama's still out, but I'm sure she won't mind."

Blythe's surprise deepened as he gazed around him. He and Jack had walked past the last few houses, and they were now standing before the dirt path leading to the Wickets' cottage. Unlike the Midwinters' simple, rundown abode, the Wicket cottage had reached a more advanced stage of deterioration and neglect. It stood against a lush, green backdrop of trees and wildflowers, glowering at the world with its aging windows and shutters that could barely be closed. If one's home reflected one's character, Jack Wicket was perfectly represented.

"I'll have to join you another time," Blythe said, raising his baskets. "I have to go home and tell Molly what happened."

Jack shrugged. "All right, then. Be careful." He waved and sauntered down the dirt path, while Blythe turned around to continue his walk home.

He tried to anticipate Molly's response and fixed his mind on the most promising. "She'll get angry with me and then sack me," he muttered, hope now turning his dragging, reluctant steps into a light, perky trot. "Oh, God, I hope she sacks me!"

Chapter 7

"**O**f course, I won't sack you! Do you really think I'm that cruel?"

"I was hoping you were," Blythe said. What on earth was wrong with his sister? "Why can't you be a real witch to me and take away my job for good?"

Molly chuckled as she busied herself with hanging freshly washed clothes behind the cottage. Blythe followed her, dragging the large tin tub filled with that week's washing.

"I suppose I'll have to resign myself to the fact that you're going through a phase that no one else in the family had ever experienced," she said. "You need to work, Blythe, even if it's what you're so fond of calling a girl's job."

"But when can I move on to something that fits me more?"

"Like what?"

Blythe paused. He still hadn't figured that one out, and being stymied like this really dampened his chances of emerging victorious during arguments. "I'll have to get back to you on that, but I know there's something out there for me. I'm just—one of those special delayed-maturity sorts. Like one of those flower things that get stuck for a while before they manage to bloom or do what flowers do that make girls faint. Delayed blooming, I suppose. That'd be me. And it means a special kind of handling from loved ones—*especially* loved ones."

Molly had stopped her clothes-hanging to turn and stare at her brother with a look that defied description. It wasn't a frown, and it wasn't a grimace. It was certainly *not* a smile. Blythe noted that the safest interpretation would be the kind of look that promised a swift death in her hands.

"Well, you did ask," he countered, and Molly rolled her eyes and went back to her task.

"Blythe, you'll move on when you develop a deeper appreciation of honest, hard work. You're not stealing, and you're no heir. Fortune gave you a specific path to follow, and it's up to you to do what you can with what you have."

"Can't I deviate a little bit here and there?"

"Dear little brother, I'm not saying that you can't, but life's a good deal more complicated than that. I say stick to what you have, and if chances come up along the way, think first before running after them. Some of them might not do you good, but some will certainly help."

Blythe frowned at his weathered shoes, chewing his lip. That sounded awfully familiar. Oh, yes, it was an echo, almost, of what Jack Wicket had said before. "And how would I know if one chance is a good thing or a bad thing?"

Molly sighed. "I can't help you there. It's always a gamble. Lord, I'm gambling with my cake sales, even with our modest success, but I feel in my gut that I'm on the right track, and I'm keeping to it."

Gut instinct? Blythe mulled that one over some more, and in the end, he hoped his gut wasn't so shrunken from years of illness and near-starvation that it wouldn't be sending him the necessary signals to help him determine what was right or wrong with the choices he'd be facing.

Molly stopped her work and eyed a shirt she'd just hung, her wet hands on her hips. Then she glanced over her shoulder to grin at Blythe. "I'm optimistic about our chances. I think we can impress so many people at the market that we'll receive enough orders to keep us busy between market days."

Blythe cocked a brow. "I don't understand. You mean to say that Upchurch has enough residents living with constipation for us to live comfortably?"

"It looks like it, but I'm not too sure yet about living comfortably. It'll be extra income, to be sure, but it's still too early to tell. As far as I know, we've generated enough interest to make me hopeful." Molly held out a hand, and Blythe pulled up a dripping pair of trousers, which she took and wrung out thoroughly before draping it on the clothesline. "Success never happens instantly, Blythe."

"Unless you're lucky."

"Unless you're lucky, yes, and even then, good luck when it comes to riches rarely ever happens."

"I told Jack that, and he says that makes it even more worthwhile to wait for good luck to come your way." Blythe dragged the tub a couple more feet to follow Molly's progression.

"And if it never happens?"

Blythe fell silent, considering. "I think he doesn't believe that. He always says that good luck's bound to happen, regardless."

Molly chuckled and turned to regard him. "It happens to all people, I suppose—even those who murder and hurt and cheat."

Blythe shrugged. "I never bothered to ask him about that part, but I'm sure he's got answers to everything."

Molly rolled her eyes again and indicated the tub. Blythe pulled out another pair of trousers and was relieved to find that no more wet clothes awaited him. "Your friend, dear, is a good-for-nothing who'll justify his laziness in every possible way. Now, I don't like dictating rules about friendship, but I hope that you at least try to think more critically about his philosophies."

Blythe clamped his mouth shut and carried the empty tub off to the edge of their backyard and threw away residual water before taking it back indoors. Molly hadn't said anything new. As she'd done so many times in the past, the key to one's future lay in honest, hard work. And Blythe's questions regarding life and whether or not there was something more to it grew more insistent.

"Never thought I'd say this, but I think Jack's been right all along."

• • • •

IT HAD BEEN ALMOST a fortnight since Blythe was forced to take up the infamous Midwinter Morning Bread Job. He found, when his eyes reluctantly cracked open under Molly's infernally cheerful early morning call, that he *was* getting used to the dreadful schedule. His mood remained black, of course, but it had lightened by a couple of very subtle shades, so he'd describe it more along the lines of "very dark gray"—almost as void as the tomb but with a bit of air to make it ever-so-slightly more bearable. He'd never been good with languages, let alone English, or, worse, poetry.

It also helped that Molly did take pity on him and took care to set aside a bowl or a plate of the previous evening's meal for Blythe to eat in the morning. It helped in keeping him full and energetic, and he'd received a couple of sleepy compliments from bleary-eyed servants about his "improving looks". The heavier breakfast lifted his mood as well, and he found it a tad—just a tad, he was quick to emphasize—easier to convince non-early morning risers of the benefits of Molly's freshly baked bread. Or more like half-a-day fresh bread, however one more accurately described it.

As it tends to happen in life, however, he saw that he'd no choice but to take the bitter with the sweet. Younger servant girls continued to flirt with him, and he needed to come up with a better method of getting them to buy the bread than leaving the loaf on the ground with a little tin cup sitting next to it, waiting for their confounded money to be tossed inside.

The other issue involved Mr. Ruffle, whose energy and enthusiasm for outlandish gossip never once flagged. Oddly enough, Molly claimed to have never been harassed by the old man when she used to sell bread.

"He just smiled, complimented me on my bread, gave me money, and then said goodbye," she said to an incredulous Blythe one time while he soaked his tired feet.

"Why's he doing this to me? I never encouraged him or even ask about the weather. What've I done wrong?"

"I think you just have to the kind of face that invites wild stories and unnecessary attention," Molly replied, tousling his hair. "Now hurry up with your foot soak. I need extra hands for vegetable duty."

• • • •

"I DON'T UNDERSTAND why we all have to look inappropriately decent," Bertie groused from his usual corner as he glumly watched Molly fuss over Blythe. "Nobody buys something because the vendor's dressed up like he's about to be dragged off to church."

Blythe nodded, and he'd have said something had Molly not forced him to wear that same too-tight waistcoat. It was all he could do to wheeze his support of Bertie's complaint and feel a touch sympathetic toward those fashionable ladies who teetered about in bone-breaking corsets. Perhaps it was high time for him to acquire a castoff that was more his size, but the process, he told himself, was going to be a tedious one considering the competition and the low possibility of finding something that fitted him perfectly. Unless he enjoyed a sudden and extreme growth spurt, he couldn't look to Bertie's old clothes for something he could use without spending countless hours altering them, and heaven knew, Molly could do with less work piled onto her already full plate.

He bit back a curse as he pinched his eyes shut. Molly was now putting all her attention on his hair, which she combed vigorously.

"Unfortunately for you two, I received nothing but compliments from several folks who were, apparently, too embarrassed to tell you themselves. And, yes, they bought some cakes from us," she said in that annoyingly sprightly way of hers. She stopped shredding Blythe's scalp with the comb and stepped back to survey the damage with a pleased sound in her throat. "I happened to stumble across them during my quick walk, and they told me everything I'd hoped to hear."

Blythe regarded her dubiously. "I've a feeling you're just making that up," he said.

Molly grinned. "I am. But you can't deny that we're the best-looking stall in the market, and if I want to rise above the competition—and I've got quite a stiff one out there—I need do everything I can to be noticed, pride be damned."

"Cold comfort, that," Bertie muttered as he shuffled stiffly out the door, looking like a well-dressed prisoner on his way to the gallows.

Molly followed him, still chattering endlessly about how "silly" her "two dashing brothers" were and other such nonsense. As Blythe walked out the door, still wheezing, he grudgingly had to admit that Bertie had drawn a great deal of interest among the female crowds, regardless of age. Blythe was sure that, in addition to the motherly urges roused by Bertie's overgrown schoolboy look, there were likely those tender, romantic feelings stirred in the female breast by his "poor gentleman" appearance. The latter was, Blythe reasoned, nothing more than a more grown up description of his brother's overgrown schoolboy-ishness.

As he followed his siblings to the hired horse and cart, he had to stifle a little smile. He also had to admit that Bertie, in his big, awkward, lumbering way, was very much the kind of fellow whom every woman would love to spoil rotten. As for him—Blythe made a face as he looked down at his too-small, spidery body—he'd quite a ways to go. Being stunted his growth made him appear two or three years younger, but he hoped that, with Molly's steady rise up the baking ranks, Blythe would somehow make up for all those physical deficiencies with better, more solid food.

Bertie and Molly sat at the front, and Blythe hopped onto the back of the cart, his legs hanging down as he faced the road behind. With him were the cakes, all carefully set against and on top of each other. For this market day, Molly had decided to wrap each cake in very much the same way she wrapped her bread loaves. They certainly looked more appealing now, though that also meant losing some profits because Molly refused to raise the price of her cakes.

"It was Mrs. Brainswell's first advice to me," she'd said. "She's a professional baker, and I trust her completely."

The ride to the market was quite pleasant. Recovering—though perhaps only momentarily—from their discomfort at being so well-dressed, Bertie and Blythe were easily coaxed into a light, idle conversation with Molly. With other people on the road heading in the same direction, the siblings were soon drawn to a good deal of brief but high-spirited exchanges with fellow vendors and early shoppers. Much of the attention was focused on Bertie and Molly, with Blythe receiving a few scattered pleasantries and praises. Rather typical, Blythe thought, mentally shrugging, but then again, considering how terribly self-conscious he felt now, the friendly dismissals proved to be quite welcome.

As before, Mrs. Pugsley was there, waiting for them, and brimming with her usual good cheer and motherly attention. She'd already readied their table for them, bless her, and she even brought some of her own home-cooked dishes to share with them while at the market, and Molly nearly burst into tears. Blythe used to think that the woman was overly solicitous and even suffocating in the attention she lavished on the orphaned trio; however, he'd softened toward her once he learned that not only was she widowed, she'd never had children.

"Oh, there, there, dear girl," Mrs. Pugsley cooed, leading a red-eyed and stammering Molly away from all the activity while Bertie and Blythe set up the table and laid out both their cakes and Mrs. Pugsley's potions. "You know very well I consider you three to be family."

And so on and so forth. Molly sat on a rickety stool that had been set against the tree, utterly lost to emotions. When Blythe turned to check up on her, she merely waved him away while blowing her nose.

"Lord, dear Molly's such a soft heart," Mrs. Pugsley said, clucking and blushing as she joined the two brothers in finishing up the table.

An idea struck Blythe. Sidling up to the widow after taking care that Molly wasn't watching, he asked in a low voice, "Since you have such a strong influence on my sister, would you be so kind as to convince her not to dress us up so nice for market day?"

They'd busied themselves to finishing up their cake table, while Bertie led the horse and cart around the tree. A good deal of free space could be had, and they didn't need to send both cart and horse back to the farmer they'd hired from. The cart, once emptied of all the cakes, provided them with a place of rest, away from the bustle at the tables.

"Oh, whatever for?" Mrs. Pugsley asked, grinning, as they took turns arranging the cakes in the most attractive yet practical display they could think of.

"We all look ridiculous. Molly insists that we attract more attention that way, but only Bertie gets all of that. Molly must have drawn people, too, but definitely not me."

"Not you? What makes you say that?"

"Well—because it's true. I'm just a child in most people's eyes, and I'm perfectly fine with that if that means giving me a reason not to look so silly. So there's really no incentive for me to go through all this trouble on market day." Blythe swept his hands up and down his front to indicate his appearance.

Mrs. Pugsley regarded him, amusement lighting up her eyes. "You don't want to be noticed? Is that what you're saying?"

Blythe nodded, relieved. "You understand, then."

"Oh, I quite understand, you dear boy. Unfortunately for you, though, you're rather late."

"Late? I don't understand."

"Oh, you." Mrs. Pugsley laughed heartily, her round, ruddy face turning redder, her plump figure shaking. "You've already attracted attention, whether you like it or not. A boy came around quite early today, asking for you. I told him you haven't arrived yet, and he promised to come back."

Blythe nodded as he carefully arranged the last few cakes in a neat row. "Oh, him. That's Jack Wicket, and I already know him. He must've been sent to the market for something, but I doubt if he was able to carry it through, knowing him. He probably wants me to sneak out sometime and go watch the madness at the Magicians' Corner and maybe stuff ourselves silly with some pudding."

"Jack Wicket? That insufferable, lazy lout? Heavens, no! It was a different boy—well-dressed and well-spoken. Very much a young gentleman in every way."

Blythe froze and stared at her. "Gentleman?"

"And quite handsome, too, I might add—though in an engaging sort of way. He's not like one of those overly attractive dandies who prance around for everyone to see. He's quieter and more soft-spoken but so affable and engaging. It's hard not to think of him as handsome, if you get my meaning, with those qualities. Definitely a far cry from that odious Wicket boy." Mrs. Pugsley sighed as she regarded the tables in their shared space with a pleased grin, her hands on her hips. "Oh, but don't worry, Blythe. He did promise to return, and as a gentleman, he's sure not to break such a promise."

Chapter 8

"**B**lythe Midwinter, you're not going to sell a single thing hiding in the shadows and feeding the horse."

"He's hungry, Molly. I'm amazed you never even considered this poor animal's welfare after all that trouble dragging your cakes to the market."

Molly glared at him, hands on her hips. "He's beyond hungry at this point. He's well on his way to being fed to death. And we hired that horse! Don't hurt him, for God's sake!"

Blythe paused, glancing down at the basket of apples and carrots he held. He grimaced upon realizing that he'd lost count of the number of apples he'd fed the horse, who didn't appear to mind much being spoiled rotten by a boy who was utterly terrified of making a new friend. His hands were also both slimy and sticky, and he clucked, turning to set the basket back on the cart. Walking away a little, he approached a small pail of water and washed his hands in it. Mrs. Pugsley had brought it with her, claiming that in her line of work, she needed to wash her hands as often as possible after handling money given to her by those with disgusting skin sores. Were those things catching? Blythe didn't know, and he pondered as he stared at his wet hands. At length he shrugged. If his hands were to suddenly explode with puss-filled lesions or whatnot, he knew what to attribute those to.

"Blythe!" Molly called out. "That's for Mrs. Pugsley!"

"I know. It's too late now. Just try not to shake my hands or something."

He sighed heavily as he walked back to the cake table, wiping his hands petulantly against his jacket when his sister turned around to greet customers. The great tree whose shelter Mrs. Pugsley had long claimed for her stall was a mercifully big one. From where he'd momentarily stood, Blythe could only see one end of each table and fleeting glimpses of his siblings and Mrs. Pugsley as they moved about. The horse and cart provided even more protection from the general public, and Blythe wished that he were ill enough to be allowed home or, at the very least, take refuge in the cart—all day if he could. Unfortunately he was healthy—or more like healthier than he'd ever been.

Unnecessary attention. Blythe sighed again at the thought. Why did he have to put up with such a thing? What was it about him that would rouse a complete stranger's interest enough to ask for him at the market, of all places? Blythe frowned as he picked his way past the tree's monstrous roots. Come to think of it, he'd found himself drawn to that boy as well, and he'd yet to make sense of his interest.

Being fifteen was proving to be a terrible idea. He stopped dead and blinked, the fog lifting as he gazed around him. He'd taken his assigned place in between Molly on his left and Bertie on his right without even realizing it. The cakes—now all nicely wrapped and drawing admiring attention from customers—sat in neat rows before him, with several spaces indicating sales. There appeared to be more people milling around their table, if not slowing down or pausing in their tracks to examine them first and then the cakes. Some asked Molly and Bertie questions about their now legendary qualities involving gastric distress.

Well, more people than he'd seen the last time they were there, that is.

"Oh, I never saw you last Saturday! What a pity!"

"Better late than never, as they say."

"I've heard about your miraculous cakes, and I simply had to see them for myself. Do you have any that's unwrapped?"

"Are we allowed to sample a piece, my dear?"

"Your cake didn't last two hours in my mistress's household. She now demands two."

"I say—I haven't moved my bowels in four days. I think I'll need one of these. Are your cakes only available on market days? It'd be a blessing if I could ensure a regular week, not just the weekends."

"Have a care, Miss Midwinter. My gouty old master declared that the woman who cures him of his digestive troubles will be his next wife after the current one dies. I suppose that means you."

"My dear boy, does your brother have a sweetheart?"

Overwhelmed (and shocked) by what seemed to be an endless crowd at their table, Blythe momentarily forgot his nervousness and was now flittering about, assisting both his siblings in selling the cakes. He also hurried back and forth from the table to the cart, bringing more cakes to the front to fill in empty spots.

After several minutes of this, Blythe slowly settled into a busy but contented state, in which he discovered and savored the role of the youngest, invisible brother. Being the mute assistant was something he could do all day if he needed. Free from mortifying and patronizing attention from customers, he was able to fulfill his role with a good deal of speed and efficiency, which, in turn, kept the flow of customers to a nice, steady pace.

The energy of the moment fed his mind, and he went about his task with unnatural good humor considering his ridiculous attire. He even bandied jokes with both Molly and Bertie, the latter also showing much improvement in his attitude.

The crowd eventually thinned, and Blythe didn't need to run back and forth. He stood at his usual spot, greeting or thanking people with a smile or an embarrassed shrug whenever someone complimented him for something.

"I do believe we're done with the first wave," Molly said, laughing and flushed and looking positively dazed. "Lord, I never expected this."

"I'm shocked," Bertie said, mirroring her look of stunned amazement. "Molly, I say we celebrate."

"Not until after we're home," Molly replied. "But a nice little feast would be a welcome treat. Something to complement Mrs. Pugsley's fare."

Bertie's shoulders sagged at the injunction against spirits while at work, but his humor remained intact. "I'll see what I can find."

Their table was now free of customers, allowing Bertie to flee. Molly, for her part, moved to join Mrs. Pugsley at her table, which still had a small group of people looking over her potions. Blythe didn't know just how busy Mrs. Pugsley had been in the past hour, but he hoped she enjoyed some good sales as a reward for everything she'd done for them, and he felt a pleasant warmth spread over him at this surge of generosity. While the two women chatted with each other and with customers, Blythe busied himself with bringing out more cakes and rearranging their display. The frenzy's energy waned, and he relaxed, finding the mindless ease of his current task surprisingly helpful in settling him down.

"Are these cakes as miraculous as everyone claims?"

Blythe glanced up and nearly swallowed his tongue. The boy—whoever the devil he was—stood before him, regarding Blythe with keen interest and a mischievous little smile. He was alone—for the moment, perhaps—but he appeared to be quite comfortable being on his own despite his youth. It was a clear indication of his privilege; his amazing confidence and easy openness spoke of an excellent education and breeding.

Up close, the boy appeared to be a great deal more attractive despite what most discerning people would refer to as his regular features. Mrs. Pugsley, Blythe realized, was correct in her summation of this young man's attractions. In truth, there was nothing remarkable about his face. Light brown hair worn short and neat, clear complexion, gray eyes that were neither expressively large nor slyly narrow, a straight nose, and mouth that was neither full nor thin, and an unremarkable chin. He was a head taller than Blythe—then again, the rest of the world was at least a head taller than Blythe.

For all the regularities, however, this boy rose well above everyone Blythe knew by virtue of his manners and the intelligence that seemed to emanate from him. He was dressed tastefully, his privilege quite obvious without being ostentatious and vulgar.

Faced with such a young man, Blythe wanted to shrink into himself and slink away. He didn't answer immediately and moved a couple of cakes around as a desperate means of delaying the inevitable. He eventually managed to pull his tongue back from his throat.

"Um—I really can't tell you," he said, forcing his gaze up to meet the other boy's. "Would you be interested in buying one—uh, sir?" He grimaced when he realized his blunder, which was immediate.

"Sir?" the other boy replied, his smile broadening to a grin. "I'm seventeen. I hope I don't look too old."

"Oh. I'm sorry. But I don't know how to address you."

"By my name. I'm Edrik Vicary. A pleasure to meet you finally." Edrik stuck out a hand, and Blythe couldn't help but stare helplessly at it for one crippling moment. Edrik didn't wear gloves, and his hand looked as immaculate as any gentleman's. The very thought of wrapping that hand with Blythe's coarse and bony one made Blythe's blood run cold.

But politeness couldn't—shouldn't—be ignored. Blythe gingerly took Edrik's hand, inwardly wincing at the touch, and offered him a weak smile in return. "Blythe Midwinter—likewise."

He quickly let go of Edrik's hand and hid his inside his jacket pocket, painful self-consciousness gnawing a hole in his belly. It certainly didn't help that he found himself torn between shame, wonder, and admiration for a boy who was his superior in every way.

"Blythe." Edrik paused, mulling over the name, his gaze not wavering. "It means 'merry.'"

"Yes, well—Mama and Papa were enjoying a bit of a merry time when I was conceived, I suppose." Blythe pinched his mouth into a tight line as he squirmed. How long did meetings like this last, anyway?

"I, uh, wanted to see if you were all right. The near-accident a few days ago, I mean." Edrik's easy smile had faded into a look of mild concern, which would've been flattering if Blythe weren't so mortified.

"Oh, that—yes, I'm all right, thank you. I lost my cap and some bread that I couldn't sell, but my sister was very understanding and refused to sack me."

Mentioning Molly suddenly reminded Blythe of his companions. Bertie was still missing, and when he turned to look for Molly, he found his sister and Mrs. Pugsley still standing behind the other table, though both women were now watching him and Edrik, eyebrows raised high.

"That's my sister and our friend, Mrs. Pugsley," he said, jerking his head in their direction. "They enjoy gossiping."

Edrik turned to them and smiled, touching his hat. Yes, he actually wore a hat, not a cap. "They're not talking right now," he said, coloring a little when he looked back at Blythe.

"No, but they will be soon enough." Blythe gave Molly a last look of warning, which only made her raise her brows even higher. He looked back at Edrik. "So—are you interested in buying one of these cakes, Mr. Vicary?"

A momentary shadow clouded Edrik's face, and, looking a bit deflated, murmured, "I suppose Mr. Vicary would suffice." A second later, he was once again smiling and exuding easy confidence. "I don't have control of my money at the moment, but my sister and brother should be wandering here any time soon. I'm sure I can persuade them to part with some coin."

Blythe nodded, still squirming and uncomfortable. "I hope you don't find me rude, but what are you and your brother and sister doing here? Shouldn't your servants be the ones walking around the market and bargaining with vendors? You're getting your clothes dirty just standing there."

Not to mention his hands, Blythe appended silently, now hoping more than ever that he didn't contract any disgusting skin diseases from washing his hands in Mrs. Pugsley's pail and infect poor Edrik unwittingly.

Edrik shrugged. "My family—uh—I come from a family of artists, and everyone has his way of expressing his distaste of the day-to-day strictures of society."

Blythe frowned. "The what?"

"My brother and oldest sister love wandering through markets in different towns, talking to locals and travelers and finding inspiration in being with people outside their social sphere. My two other sisters disguise themselves often and go off randomly to the more remote corners of the countryside. Sometimes they explore ruins or simply sit on a mountainside, absorbing the view and finding their own inspiration that way."

"Why the disguise?"

Edrik paused for a moment, thinking. "How do they put it? Something about going outside themselves as a way of freeing their minds of their unnatural limits and exposing themselves to influences they can't control." He grinned again, the blush creeping back up his face. "I think that was what they said. Whatever it was, they were always very serious about their art and their methods."

"And you?" Blythe asked, his self-consciousness gone as he listened in growing wonder. "Are you artistic as well?"

Edrik laughed. "I'm afraid the artistic magic didn't quite reach me. Oh, I can fully appreciate art and beauty, but I'm not blessed with either the temperament or the talent. I'd rather savor poetry and fiction and watercolors than create them."

Blythe regarded him dubiously. "No? Huh—you seem to be artistic to me, though I really don't quite understand what that means. I mean—" He broke off and made a few vague gestures with his hands. "Lord, I can't think of the right words to say."

Edrik shrugged carelessly, his eyes sparkling. "All right, I'll confess that I'd like to be able to write a book someday, though it's also possible that that's not where my path lies. I've yet to figure out where I want to go, and, bless Papa, he's not pushing me too much on this matter. For the time being, it's all about the schoolroom and endless hours spent with my tutor."

"I saw him last Saturday—your tutor, I mean. I saw both of you at the Magicians' Corner, watching that magic puppet theatre thing. I'm shocked your tutor agreed to go there. He didn't look pleased with it," Blythe said, suppressing his laughter. He stole one more glance in Molly's direction and found his sister and Mrs. Pugsley *still* watching them with their brows *still* raised high. What on earth was wrong with those two? Hadn't they ever seen two boys talk to each other earnestly before?

"I think it's the affliction of all tutors—a low opinion of magical arts."

"At least you enjoyed yourself. When you were watching, that is."

"I saw you there, too." Edrik paused, his grin softening to a fond little smile. He looked at Blythe more intently than ever. "I think I watched you more than the puppet show."

Blythe's squirming turned frantic. "You missed a good deal, then. It was a pretty interesting show—not at all like the more common ones we're so used to."

"Did I? I don't care, anyway."

Blythe coughed. "You should. If you'd like to be an artist type like your family, you ought to pay closer attention to things like that. You know, inspiration and so on."

"I had plenty."

"No, you didn't."

"I saw you smile while watching the show. You looked like you were lost in this wonderful world that no one else could see. Your smile was a little wistful, a little sad, but also hopeful. I can't say much else but that I thought you looked beautiful."

"Ah, Edrik! There you are!"

"Oh, here they come now. Don't be alarmed; it's only my brother and oldest sister."

Blythe gave a start and turned in time to watch a young man and woman sauntering toward the table. They were dressed plainly, their clothes looking faded and well-worn. The woman had even thrown a cloak and hood around her shoulders, and that was just as faded as her gown, with dust and dried mud all over. Both newcomers exuded the same easy confidence and intelligence as Edrik, which also included a careless disregard of social rules. In the latter bit, though, they were a great deal more rebellious than Edrik, seeing as how Edrik still dressed as one from his class would. An old, soiled canvas bag that probably contained artists' materials hung across the young man's body, and for one mad moment, Blythe wondered if he'd someday be allowed to look through their sketches. His conversation with Edrik had stirred his curiosity like nothing ever had insofar as art went, and despite his mortification, he also felt a bit lighter after learning about Edrik's lack of artistic talent or ambition because it mirrored his own. In his case, though, his lack of clear or set goals was of a lesser quality; he couldn't boast anything artistic or even educational. As far as he was concerned, it was all physical labor suited to his station.

"Edith, could you buy one of these cakes? We can have it for tea." Edrik indicated the cakes with a nod. "I heard it's quite delicious—not to mention good for one's health." He gave Blythe an impish little smile.

Edith regarded the cakes in curious silence and then tugged at her brother's arm. "What do you think, Cranston? One cake? Two? Papa should let me have a plate in the workroom when I paint later."

At this moment, Molly appeared, greeting the Vicary siblings and immediately engaging them in conversation. She was certainly on her way to convincing them to leave with three cakes—with Edrik's help, of course.

Blythe could only step aside and watch the proceedings, his brain effectively shut down after his conversation with Edrik. He stole glances in Edrik's direction every so often, but he was now ignored with Edrik being drawn easily into the conversation. Blythe didn't know how long it took before they left with their purchases, but he vaguely remembered Edrik glancing back over his shoulder and bidding him goodbye with a nod of his head.

Chapter 9

Another wave of customers swept over the table, much to Blythe's relief. He saw the look on Molly's face—an all-too-familiar look of curiosity that always preceded a torturous series of questions—after Edrik and his siblings left, three cakes richer and three cakes' worth of money poorer. It certainly didn't help that Mrs. Pugsley was also present all that time, and she'd witnessed everything as well. God only knew what gossipy things now crowded her head. He'd just started to knock his brain about for quick, evasive answers to possible questions when customers started arriving again.

"Oh!" he said, grinning and pointing emphatically at a warty old man who'd just hobbled up to the stall, eyeing the cakes with drool dangling from his sagging lip. "Look, Molly—more people! Isn't that wonderful?"

He only had enough time to see Molly blink in surprise, a question about Edrik obviously hanging in the air, unasked, before he threw himself eagerly—or more like desperately—into the fray. For the next several moments, Blythe had completely turned himself into a remarkable seller—greeting, smiling, exchanging pleasantries, enticing and cajoling. It was all his sister could do to join him in convincing people to part with their money.

They were so busy for the next several moments that Blythe never realized Bertie had finally returned, bringing an armful of sweet things to complete their shared feast with Mrs. Pugsley.

"Lord, what happened?" Bertie asked, wide-eyed and flushed, after the last customer left.

"I think we're well on our way to being rich," Blythe said, dragging a sleeve across his forehead. His face and back felt damp even in the shade, but it was a pretty warm day, and hurrying back and forth to replenish their dwindling stock was now taking its toll.

Molly just fanned herself, laughing incredulously.

"We can't build our hopes up too high," she said. "Today's been wonderful, but we don't know how next Saturday will be." She fixed Blythe with a steady gaze. "See what happens when you apply yourself? You were absolutely wonderful." She paused, her eyes narrowing ever so slightly. "It was as if you were inspired."

Blythe colored. "I'd like to rest a bit and eat some of Mrs. Pugsley's food."

The sly look remained. "Go ahead, love. You earned it."

Blythe gratefully went back to the cart, where Molly had kept the food. There were less than ten cakes left, and it was midday. He was sure that they'd be closing their table much sooner than everyone else. He helped himself to some boiled meat and vegetables and settled himself in the cart, his back against one side, his legs stretched out before him.

Memories of his earlier encounter with Edrik Vicary filled his mind, and he reveled in those moments as he played them again and again. Blythe remained confused and shocked at being singled out by such a boy. The Vicary family was obviously wealthy, well-traveled, well-educated, and blessed with everything the Midwinter family could only dream of. Edrik could have anything he wanted—anything that he surely deserved, given his advantages.

And yet, for some perverse reason, he'd decided to make an acquaintance with a boy who had nothing in comparison. A nobody.

Blythe chewed his food slowly as he puzzled over human nature. In the end, though, he decided that reaching out to underprivileged people was just something that rich and rebellious artists were inclined to do. Edrik had said something about inspiration and the strange and unpredictable methods his siblings often used for their art. Perhaps getting to know Blythe was nothing more than another eccentric attempt at inspiration.

Blythe shrugged. "That makes sense," he muttered as he picked his teeth with his tongue. "He did say that he wanted to write a book someday."

The sound of hurried footsteps and grass crunching put an end to his thoughts. He turned and saw a sweat-drenched and red-faced Jack moving quickly past parked wagons and piles of baskets and other containers toward him.

"Good lord, you're hard to find," Jack said as he stumbled to a halt, panting and leaning a hand against the cart.

"What on earth's wrong now?"

"Mama's driving me mad. I had to get away from her till she calms down."

Blythe sighed. "Is this about that tree-chopping thing that you still won't do? What happened?"

"She's been nagging me to sell the blasted cow—the only cow we have, for God's sake!"

"And what's wrong with that? I thought you told me that you don't get much milk from her—or something. Like she's barren or whatever you call that condition when cows don't give much milk, if at all."

Jack grimaced as he wiped his face with his sleeves—right arm and then the left. "I'm sure Sarah can give us enough milk to live on if either of us knew the proper way of raising a damned cow. I barely know how to milk her, let along understand how best to care for her. Thank God for old Mr. Kettle."

Apparently he and his mother had been depending on the charitable services of an old dairy farmer who was also a longtime family friend. The man would come around twice a day, feed and milk the cow, and take three-quarters of the milk with him as compensation since he received nothing by way of money for his pains. From what Jack had heard, the farmer seemed to be thriving quite well with that extra milk, selling it or making cheese that he'd sell at the market, all in addition to his own modest offerings from his very modest farm.

Blythe blinked as he listened. "And why didn't you ask him to teach you how to milk your own cow?"

"Are you joking? Why would I want to do that? I saw how hard it is. I'm not going to waste my time squeezing an animal's udder twice a day and making my arms and fingers lock up from exhaustion, when I could be doing something else. He knows what he's doing. I'm happy taking a quarter of the milk Sarah gives as long as I don't have to take over the job."

"All right, then. Why do you have a cow in the first place?"

"Mama thought it was a clever idea to own one last year. And we both have a soft spot for livestock. Especially orphaned cows." Jack paused, shrugging. "Well, I didn't agree with her plans, but I've always wanted a pet. Sarah would've been the closest I'll come to owning a dog."

Blythe couldn't help but roll his eyes. "And I suppose you used to depend on your mama to learn how to milk a cow properly."

"She does too much laundry-work for other people. She didn't have time."

"*You* had time, you oaf!"

"I wanted a pet, not a job!"

Blythe set his soiled dishes aside, shaking his head. "You're hopeless," he said, earning himself a grunt. "So what are you going to do now? You can't avoid this forever. I mean—what else can you do besides run away from home?"

Jack scowled, shoving his hands in his pockets and kicking at the ground. "I'd run off with Sarah, but she's a pretty lazy cow."

"She learned from you, obviously."

"Oh, shut up." Jack sighed and looked around him. "I don't want to sell that cow. And I don't want to stay poor forever. I hate my life."

Blythe scooted over to the rear of the cart, letting his legs dangle off the edge as he surveyed the busy and colorful scenes around them.

"Jack, I think it's time for you to admit that waiting for good fortune to happen is the most useless thing you can do." Blythe paused as he carefully chose his next words. "There's no help for it. You have to find a job."

The look of utter horror and disbelief on Jack's face, Blythe had to admit, was priceless.

"And you call yourself my best friend?"

Blythe shrugged in answer, a bit baffled over his lecturing, considering his ambivalence toward his own situation. Perhaps it was nothing more than human nature to hammer someone with a sermon as though he were quite an expert on that subject—firm on his opinion and clear in his mind. Whatever the reason, what came out of his mouth felt natural and easy, though he couldn't help but wonder if all he was doing was echo someone else's—Molly's, for instance—views on the matter.

Jack made a particularly nasty face at him. "I thought you hate selling bread loaves—called it girl's work or something."

"But I'm still doing it because it's important to my family. You know, money and all that."

"See, I don't understand that. Why spend all those hours doing something you hate just to have money?"

"In my case, I'm too young to find work that's better suited to me." Blythe didn't really believe that, but repeating balderdash that someone else came up with was a great deal easier than cudgeling his brain for his own reasoned argument. That said, it also felt rather hollow.

Clearly Jack didn't believe this, given the emphatic eye-rolling he did in answer. Both boys fell silent for a moment, with Blythe stretching and yawning like a contented cat, while Jack sighed and looked bored as he sauntered about and watched the activity around them with restless disdain.

"When can you take a break? I want to see the new magic trees from Mr. Blackdash's stall. I heard they're rather demonic because they can talk, and you can teach them, too. What I'd give to own one and teach it to curse at the rest of the miserable world day in and day out."

Blythe shook his head. "I'll have to ask Molly." He hopped off the cart and then paused, frowning. "Talking trees? That's brilliant! I'd get one, teach it to frighten Bertie into keeping all his bad air inside in the middle of the night. Or maybe train the tree into convincing my brother to get out of bed and go outside to do his business, not poison me indoors."

"I don't know what you're talking about, I'm sure, and I've a feeling I really shouldn't ask," Jack replied, looking both dubious and alarmed.

It was a quiet moment, and Molly allowed Blythe to stretch his legs and enjoy some more free time in Jack's company—though not without regarding an unfazed Jack with narrow-eyed disapproval.

• • • •

THE TALKING TREES WERE beyond amusing, and Blythe desperately wanted one within seconds of laying eyes on those remarkable things. Since he didn't own a pet, a talking tree he could train would work as a good enough alternative. Mr. Blackdash, a very affable old man, was known in that corner of the county as a master of Nature Magic. His spells turned plants, water, earth, stone, and air into the most amazing creatures—all meant to entertain or, in the case of the talking trees and dancing rocks, be owned as novelty keepsakes. And as it was with the other magicians reduced to hawking their wares (and skills) at the market, Mr. Blackdash was also an excellent storyteller.

After marveling at his talking trees—which were, at that moment, saucy potted saplings—Blythe and Jack crept behind the fellow's stall and engaged him in light conversation. It was a spontaneous, idle move on Blythe's part, largely because he needed to forget about all the baffling thoughts he'd been having regarding work and wealth, now made even murkier by Edrik Vicary's sudden presence in his life.

As for Jack Wicket, he agreed to Blythe's unexpected proposal only because Jack was Jack, and he didn't care to go back home to face an irate mother. So in between answering people's questions about his remarkable trees, Mr. Blackdash entertained his young guests with stories of his ancestors' adventures that were alternately successes and failures but ultimately were fuel for wisdom from which magician descendants would learn.

Blythe listened with child-like fascination, vaguely aware of how much he missed his parents, who used to entertain their children with incredible stories like Mr. Blackdash's in a desperate hope of making the little ones forget their hunger. Blythe didn't miss the illness and lack of food, but he missed his parents' determination to better their lives.

"Is that all you see, dearest?" was his mother's favorite line, and she often used it whenever Blythe wept in frustration over his terrible health or lack of toys. It was a gentle reminder of what they had—what little they had, that is—and how much luckier they were than other families out there. It was also her way of making him look beyond the obvious and the physical to something else that transcended his limited scope. Blythe found it easy to do that while his parents were alive and there to ground his perspective, but with them gone, he often felt lost and adrift, even with Molly and Bertie there to guide him. More often than not, he was sure that even his sister and brother were quite lost, themselves, despite their age and their experience.

By the time Blythe needed to rejoin his siblings, his earlier confusion seemed to have deepened. Reminders of his parents' struggles only made him resentful of his family's poverty, particularly during the earlier years. They were doing much better now, though, thanks to Molly's work ethic and Bertie's own modest success in his wood-carving work. That said, Blythe couldn't ignore the fact that they could do much better—indeed, deserved much more than what they now had, considering all the sacrifices and hard work they'd been putting in with very little gains. And the fact that he still didn't know how he could best contribute to their fortune only served to dig the knife further.

With a pang, Blythe thought about Edrik Vicary. The privilege and the resulting ease with which he and his siblings went about their days—surely, Blythe argued, it was easy for them to take on frivolous and idle pursuits like art because they didn't have to slave away for every penny.

He glanced down and regarded his "finery" with growing embarrassment. What "finery" he owned looked more like cheap imitations of the real things. Not only were some of his best clothes ill-fitting, they were also made of poor material and were sewn with not much skill at best. He winced. What on earth kind of picture did he make to Edrik Vicary and his brother and sister?

"Like a pretentious little peasant who's trying desperately to ape his betters," he grumbled, scowling.

Beside him, Jack—apparently inspired by Mr. Blackdash's stories, rambled on and on about all the things he planned to do with his wealth once it fell into his hands. Blythe half-listened to his friend and half indulged in self-pity. He wondered why good, honest people seemed to be doomed to struggle in poverty while the chosen few, either by hard work or accident of birth, enjoyed so much good fortune regardless of their character.

"Well—I suppose I should go home," Jack said when they reached Molly's table. A couple of people were there, talking to Bertie about the health benefits of their cakes. Molly, in the meantime, was sitting on the stool against the tree, enjoying some of Mrs. Pugsley's food.

"So what're you going to do?"

Jack shrugged, looking helpless. "I don't know. I'm running out of reasons to delay things, and Mama's getting more and more impatient with me."

"Lord, anyone with the patience of a saint is sure to lose his mind when living with you," Blythe said, earning himself a sharp jab in the arm.

"Shut up, Midwinter. No one understands where I'm coming from."

"Oh, really? You're pretty easy to read, Wicket. You just don't want to work."

Jack flailed, hissing. "Because my values are different from everyone else's! Good God, how many times do I need to club your thick brain with that? And do I have to remind you of what you did, refusing the magic beans in a fair trade?"

So typical of Jack to aim low when cornered like that, but Blythe knew better than to take the bait. That said, he couldn't help but mimic Jack's facial expressions and wild gestures in a mocking theatrical show, and he was rewarded with a string of curses. "Good luck keeping Sarah," he said at length after his laughter—which Jack didn't share—died down. "Maybe your mama will allow you to buy a talking tree for a pet to compensate for your loss."

Jack made a face. "A talking tree for a pet isn't the same as a live animal, fool. I'd rather have both." With a grunt and a doomed light in his eyes, Jack left for home, his stiff posture and bowed head indicating immense dread of the inevitable.

Blythe took his place at the cake table, feeling relief at the sight of only a few cakes remaining. He was about to celebrate Molly's success when an unwanted reminder clouded the moment.

Molly's new approach to packaging the cakes was likely instrumental in gaining attention. Unfortunately, what opportunities there were for higher profits were ultimately compromised because of Molly's insistence at keeping the price the same.

Blythe sighed, deflated. "I hope that fellow with the magic beans would show up again," he murmured, scanning the crowd eagerly. "I'm willing to make a trade."

Unfortunately for him, the old man never appeared, and Blythe wanted to kick himself for not taking advantage of the strange offer when it was first made. "Fool," he whispered, sighing dejectedly. "You deserve to stay poor."

Chapter 10

The following day found the Midwinter siblings enjoying some much-needed and deserved rest and indulgence. Bertie went off to enjoy time with friends, which also meant an extra trip or two to visit young ladies who fought for his attention. For better or for worse, Bertie had yet to declare a preference for one or the other, and Blythe suspected that his brother was simply enjoying being chased after and not the other way around. In fact, he wouldn't be surprised if Bertie kept everyone hanging until an exasperated father forced him to choose with a sword, an ax, or a pitchfork aimed at his neck.

Molly and Blythe went to the churchyard to visit their parents' graves. It had been a couple of months since they last came by, and Blythe tried not to wither and tear up at the sight of his parents' names on their grave markers. He stood by while Molly knelt between the graves, whispering.

Blythe guessed that she either said prayers or indulged in a one-sided conversation. He never bothered to ask as he'd always considered those moments to be private and sacred to his sister. For his part, he'd already talked to his parents in his head, reassuring them that everyone was doing quite well and wondering if, somehow, Mr. and Mrs. Midwinter could see or, better, hear him. He largely considered that to be too whimsical a notion, but he still couldn't help but wonder as well as take some comfort in the possibility, however miniscule, of his being seen or heard.

Before long Molly stood up with his help. "Well, love," she said, turning to him and smiling. A sheen of moisture made her eyes sparkle softly, but she quickly blinked it away. "I need to buy you a new jacket. I'm also in dire need of a new shawl." She looped an arm through Blythe's and led him out of the churchyard.

Blythe looked at her, surprised. "That's going to be a bit much, don't you think?"

"I saw how many holes are forming in your jacket. And you inherited that from Bertie, who inherited it from Papa. I think it's safe to spend some money where it's needed. Besides, I don't want you to freeze in the morning, and it looks like those stitches do precious little in holding your jacket together."

She paused for a moment, lost in thought. "Also," she said at length, her tone light and sly, "I want you to look good for, you know, friends—especially new ones. I'm sure Jack Wicket doesn't care a jot about finery unless Fortune gifts it, but it's always good to make a proper first impression—and second and third—because who knows where things go when meeting new people."

Blythe gave a start and glanced at her, but she kept her eyes forward. Was that a badly suppressed smirk? It must be. He grimaced and looked back ahead, blinking. "No, he doesn't," he said, knowing that evasion was a good thing in certain cases, particularly this one. "He'd probably complain about looking fashionable even when rich. By the way, are you sure about this? I can always inherit Bertie's castoffs like I always do, though it also means subjecting you to all those hours spent altering them. If we have money, maybe it's better spent hiring someone who can do the alterations, so you don't have to be burdened with it."

He had to admit that the thought of owning a jacket that was new was a terribly exciting one, though.

"Oh, I'm more than sure about it." Molly grinned at him. "We've earned a modest profit from all our sales. We can afford to loosen the purse strings to-day."

Blythe smiled back, elated. "All right, then, though I'll be needing some help in choosing one that's right for me."

The walk to Upchurch's borders—the churchyard was located about a mile away—and toward the bustling main square was spent in companionable silence. Blythe reveled in the scene of mercantile chaos. Fine carriages and weathered wagons jostled for space. People of high and low birth moved among each other, exchanging pleasantries on occasion or, in the case of acquaintances meeting by chance, conversations.

Molly took Blythe to one part of the square—the southern end, where the humbler establishments were located. They walked down a narrow cobbled street called Taggart Lane. Eventually Molly stopped before a shop and ushered Blythe inside.

It was a small, cramped shop that was also dark, and it smelled of old wood and paper.

"Dear Mr. Barnfield's a wonderful tailor," Molly said, her voice hushed. "He's an old friend of Papa, and he's also very quick with his work. I guarantee you that you'll look absolutely splendid in your new jacket."

Blythe gazed around him, full of wonder. Wooden racks filled the little shop. Shirts, waistcoats, trousers, and jackets or every imaginable color crammed the racks, all neatly categorized and organized according to type of clothing, size, and color. While Molly walked toward the back part of the shop, where the counter stood—along with the proprietor's wife, it appeared—Blythe pulled out a jacket whose colors caught his attention and inspected it.

He saw, with a great deal of surprise, that the jacket looked new and was definitely clean, though a touch faded. Blythe realized that Mr. Barnfield specialized in alterations of existing clothes in excellent condition, perhaps worn only once or twice or even not at all for whatever reason. His business was certainly unique at least in Blythe's mind, and it was also quite clever; he grinned at the realization that this was similar to what he'd earlier told Molly about castoffs and alterations, though much, much grander.

For a moment, he mulled over the process, imagining how things went from acquisition of clothing to final alteration and a happy customer marching home with his treasure. He brought the jacket closer to inspect the stitching, his brain turning rapidly at methods that he'd use if he were the tailor in order to improve on the jacket's cut to his taste. Curiosity stoked, he left Molly alone to her devices and entertained himself mentally, delight now surging continued to toy with possibilities as he pretended to be an assistant tailor.

"Blythe, dear?"

He glanced up and saw Molly beckoning him over. He raised the jacket to show her, and she nodded, looking both surprised and pleased at the fact that he'd taken the incentive to find something for himself. Behind the counter, Mrs. Barnfield offered him a warm, maternal smile, and Blythe walked over to join them, lost in utter bliss. This would have to be the first time ever when he'd be treated to something as special and unique as a new piece of clothing, with Molly encouraging him to let his imagination run wild in his choice, adding to the glory of the moment.

With a ridiculous grin that he couldn't squelch, he stood still when Mr. Barnfield measured him, and Mrs. Barnfield took down the numbers. His gaze strayed to Molly, who watched nearby in respectful silence, but the smile she wore rivaled his in brightness. She even let him talk about what he wanted from the jacket without much prodding from the tailor.

• • • •

A SURPRISE AWAITED Blythe on his morning bread route a couple of days later. Jack Wicket's tall, skinny, slouching figure paced in a dejected circle on the road entering Upchurch. Blythe was so taken aback that he'd stopped and gaped for only God knew how long, moving only when the weight of the filled baskets he carried strained his arms and hands.

For his part, Jack remained oblivious to his friend's stupefied presence. Bundled against the early morning chill, he walked round and round with his head hanging down, his shoulders drooping lower than Blythe had ever seen them droop, and his hands shoved deep inside his coat pockets. Even his steps showed a great deal of grief because Jack dragged his feet over the ground, and the early morning calm was rattled by pebbles and loose earth being forcibly rearranged under Jack's worn out shoes.

"Jack?" Blythe stammered, walking forward and grimacing a little from the burden of the two large, filled baskets. "What on earth are you doing here?"

Jack, startled, stumbled to a halt with a gasp, which was followed by a string of expletives that further ruined the poetic serenity of the morning scene.

"Lord, you almost made me wet myself!"

"I did?" Blythe retorted, incredulous. "What about you? I thought you never wake up before ten!"

He set the baskets down once he reached his friend. Gingerly massaging his wrists, he frowned as he looked Jack over despite the still-dim light. Jack, in addition to being immensely put out, also appeared pale and haggard, no doubt the result of being harangued within an inch of his life by a perpetually exasperated mother. For his part, Blythe couldn't help but feel some sympathy for Mrs. Wicket. He sometimes tried to imagine having Jack for a son, and the bleak pictures conjured by those thoughts made him give up with a shudder while silently thanking the heavens that he wasn't a close relative of his friend.

"I'm selling my soul to the confounded devil, Midwinter." Jack sighed heavily as his gaze dropped to the baskets flanking Blythe. "I agreed—all right, Mama made me agree—to follow you on your morning route and watch how you work."

Blythe stared at him. "Whatever for?"

"So I'll know what's required of me—work, I mean. She made me agree to observe you and learn what I can to prepare myself for a lifetime of work." He paused, snorting. "Bah—work? Slavery, more like."

"What—work? *Work?* You let yourself get talked into working? You?" Blythe spluttered, wide-eyed and drop-jawed.

Jack glared at him. "Oh, shut up, Midwinter. I'm more than capable of working, you know, when I'm forced to do it."

"Well, of course, you are—everyone up and down England can see that. It's just—it's a terrible shock to actually *see* you working, if you get my meaning."

"I can see your meaning well enough, you little turd, and if you want to help me, you'd better bite your tongue and carry on. I want to get this wretched thing over with."

Blythe was still in shock, but he pointed at the baskets. "All right, then, take one of these and help me carry them around."

His shoulders drooping even more, Jack sighed gloomily and bent down to pick up a basket. "Dear God!" he cried as he lifted it off the ground. "This damned thing weighs a ton!"

"I'm used to it." Blythe walked forward, his shock finally easing into amazed delight. At last, he thought, he had someone to talk to in the course of going about such a tedious job. With Jack's mood being the way it was, he expected the conversation to be quite a bit fun.

"What the devil does your sister use to make these loaves? Rocks?" Jack grunted. "I swear, I've never carried a basket that weighed this much. I hope you don't have to walk too far to get rid of all these blasted loaves."

Then again, maybe not.

"How can your mama be sure that you'd be doing what she told you to do, anyway? I'm your best friend. I can always lie for you."

"You won't because you're an infernal little do-gooder, and you can't lie, no matter what."

Blythe clucked. Jack had a point, damn him. "Then what guarantee would she have besides your word? And we all know what that's worth."

"Mama's friends with practically every housekeeper, cook, maid, or butler in Upchurch, considering her laundry-work, though I'm no friends with any of them. She'll believe them when she asks if I showed up at their doorsteps this morning, not me."

"Well, then." Blythe grinned, feeling impish. "We'd better make sure they give her glowing reports of your productivity."

"I'd bury you alive if you weren't the only friend I have, Blythe Midwinter."

"Oh, come now—I'm sure you'll find this an eye-opening experience."

Jack muttered another string of curses.

• • • •

"I STILL DON'T KNOW whether to laugh or cry."

"Neither do I. No, that's wrong. I think I'm inclined to cry."

"You poor dear. I must say, though, I'm heartily glad it wasn't me."

Blythe felt a reassuring pat on his arm, and he sighed. He lay in bed with a dreadful headache, his usual foot soak ignored despite his throbbing feet. Molly had given him something from Mrs. Pugsley's potion collection, and he hoped it wasn't a cure for disgusting skin sores. Unless, of course, the human brain was susceptible to its own form of disgusting skin sores, one brought on by the incessant complaining of grumpy friends.

He'd somehow managed to complete his daily route given the burden of dragging Jack Wicket around in a vain effort at opening his eyes to work. And Jack's eyes had been opened, all right.

From start to finish, the irritable boy questioned everything Blythe did—from his method of following a set route that started and ended at the same point to the way Blythe knocked on every door. That, of course, included criticisms of how Blythe sold the bread. Then he had to say something about the price. It was too low, he'd complained, given the amount of trouble Blythe had to put up with to sell the damned things. Every house and every person they came across was a confounded eyesore and a hopeless nuisance, respectively.

Even the early morning mist looked like "the devil's fart". By the time Blythe finished his route, he felt like leaping off the nearest cliff because life simply wasn't worth living anymore, given Jack's endless litany of criticisms leveled against it.

"What a stupid joke work is," he'd snarled, shaking his fist at a harmless bird that sailed past them. Blythe half-wished that the little creature shat on Jack as a way of punctuating the irate boy's views on life.

In fact, rather than help Blythe sell all the loaves, Jack's black mood ruined his dogged efforts at enticing people to buy, actually falling into a heated argument with three servants and almost coming to blows with an ancient housekeeper. Blythe returned home with five unsold loaves in his baskets. It was all he could do to complain about the absurdity of life in general and then wish a plague of dead, rotting frogs on Jack Wicket before staggering off to bed.

Molly was sympathetic toward her brother, though she still couldn't suppress her amusement, and expressions of comfort were broken on occasion by stifled giggles and snorts.

"I'll have to think about how else to serve these loaves," she said. Blythe's eyes remained closed against the horrors of his world as he waited for Mrs. Pugsley's potion to work. As time went, his hopes began to fade, and he almost wished Bertie were there, asleep and filling the cottage with enough fumes to render Blythe insensible for twenty-four hours straight.

"I suppose I can give dear Mrs. Pugsley a couple, considering what she's done for us."

"Yes, you do that."

"I also think I should see if your new jacket's ready. Mr. Barnfield assured me that he'll have it done no longer than two days."

"All right. Good luck."

Molly continued to talk about everything she should do till nothing made sense to Blythe, whose aching brain now refused to take any more information in. Within moments his sister's voice had become nothing more than a cheerful but incomprehensible hum in the background, and much to Blythe's surprise, he found himself lulled to sleep.

At length Molly's voice faced, to be replaced by another one—a young boy's this time. Articulate and affable, the voice talked on and on about magic puppet shows and art, and it was all Blythe could do to listen eagerly.

"Why would someone like you be interested in someone like me?" Blythe asked in his dream. He saw nothing but darkness around him, but he wasn't nervous or frightened. The voice comforted him a good deal, and he would, if he could, make it talk for as long as possible.

Unfortunately the question he asked must have been a bad one because he heard nothing but silence for his answer. It stretched on for a moment or so before it was shattered by Jack's disembodied whining.

"Lord, this stupid road's too rough for my ankles! What the devil are we doing up at this godforsaken time of the day? Where do you go if you want to take a piss in the middle of your route? Oh, go shag the dog, you foul-breathed harpy!"

Dream-Blythe sighed as the voice went on and on and on. "I can't get away from him," he said. And as it tended to happen with dream-logic, he spotted a large club lying on the ground by his feet, and he knew what to do. He picked it up, took a wild swing at the darkness, and Jack howled in pain.

"What the devil's arse are you doing?"

"Getting you out of my head!"

"Do you have to use that thing?"

"Apparently that's the only thing that works unless I drag your mama here."

"All right! All right! I'll stop! Crikey!"

Blythe stood still, club in hand, eyes narrowed warily as he listened. Jack wasn't complaining anymore, but he could be heard muttering in the darkness, and Blythe realized that he'd just exchanged one evil for another when he saw that *that* wasn't about to end anytime soon.

"Damn me, I give up," he said, sighing, as he threw the club away. And sure enough, he awoke from his dream at that moment, sitting upright and looking around him, startled. Molly was gone, and all was nice and quiet in the cottage. Normally Blythe loved having some private time, but at that moment, he wished that either of his siblings were there to ground him and reassure him that he wasn't being haunted by the awful specter of Jack Wicket. He found comfort in a plate of unsold bread and several slices of cheese, ignoring Molly's comment on her return home about his hollow, sunken-eyed stare and how it made her think of freshly risen corpses that'd given up on life within moments of their resurrection.

Chapter 11

The new jacket turned out exceedingly well—beyond Blythe's expectations, in fact. The fit was perfect, the cut comfortable and quite flattering, and the material of a richer stuff than what he'd long been used to.

"You look like a young gentleman," Molly said with sincere pleasure as she made him turn around, his arms held up and out, while she critically inspected every inch of the jacket.

"Are you going to treat Bertie to the same thing?"

"Bertie earns his keep, and he's free to do what he wants with his share as long as it isn't drink, gambling, and whoring. Well—not too much drink, anyway. As long as he sticks to what we agreed on with regard to his earnings' portions, he can do what he wants with his percentage. Someday, Blythe, you'll be doing the same thing." Molly paused, frowning as she cocked her head thoughtfully. She reached out to brush dirt off while tugging at the jacket's hem. "Besides, I'm making good one of the promises I made to Papa."

Blythe looked at her, surprised. "Promise? To keep me clothed, you mean?"

"Lord, don't be silly!" Molly laughed, lightly slapping his backside when he turned around again. "This is all about looking after my baby brother after what he'd gone through in his childhood. A new jacket here, good pudding there, and lots of time spent grounding some good work values into you."

"I've yet to see the good pudding."

"I'm working on it. I never managed to wrap my head around the process of making one, no matter how many times Mama showed me. I suppose it's not a natural talent of mine."

Blythe clucked. "Shepherd's pie, then? Is that hard?"

"Oh. That sounds terrifying."

"What about easing the strain of cooking and just paying someone else for her cooking? Like, well, Mrs. Stringer, for instance. I'm sure we can pay her for an entire day's meal. I can even pick up the food during my daily route since Periwinkle Cottage is one of my loyal customers." Blythe regarded his sister hopefully. "You must admit, that's a pretty clever scheme. Just think—you won't have to fret over cooking, and you'll have all the time to bake. Oh, and do the laundry once a week."

Molly chuckled, blushing. "Oh, I don't know, Blythe. That's an awful imposition, even with money involved. I can't bring myself to do it."

"I've got no shame when it comes to good food. I can negotiate with her if you won't."

"Tut, tut—no more talk about proper cooking, or you'll make me think that you can't stand my cooking. All right, go on and take that jacket off."

Blythe bit back a too-blunt response to the first part of her statement. "Am I expected to wear this on market day? Come to think of it, am I expected to dress up again on market day?"

Molly stood up from where she sat, brushing her smock vigorously. "It's your jacket, so it's your decision to make. That said, seeing as how looking good seems to be working, I insist that we all keep at it on market day."

"And the reputation of your cakes has nothing to do with good sales?" Blythe scowled at his sister as he shrugged off his jacket.

"Of course it does, but seeing as how I hear nothing but compliments about Bertie's looks and yours as well—it'd be madness not to pursue it, don't you think?"

Blythe blew air out of the side of his mouth as he carefully set his jacket down on his bed, giving it one last, admiring look before rejoining Molly in the kitchen area. "If that's so, shouldn't you at least raise the price of your cakes? You've done that extra step of wrapping them individually, and now you're insisting on making us look good. I think you deserve to make more money from those."

"Oh, I don't want to charge people more than what those cakes are worth," Molly replied as she busied herself with gathering potatoes from the old vegetable bin. Blythe noticed, with a disappointed little sigh, that the potatoes weren't colored blue or purple, and he readied himself for yet another evening of indifferent stew. Or soup. He couldn't even tell at this point what was slated for that evening's enjoyment from their two-item menu.

"But shouldn't they be worth more now that you've made those additions?"

"The wrappers are only wrappers in the same way our dressing up is nothing more than a method of catching people's attention. The real prize is the cake inside. Besides, Mrs. Brainswell told me that's the best way to approach things as a vendor."

Blythe sat down and picked up a carrot and started peeling it. "That doesn't make any sense."

"Mrs. Brainswell said she uses that method to sell her own cakes and pastries, and she's doing incredibly well. She owns a bakery in the good part of town, selling her cakes to wealthy patrons. It only stands to reason that she knows what she's talking about, aren't I correct?"

Blythe shrugged and took a bite of the carrot that was so far halfway peeled. "I don't know. I suppose. It depends on how long it took her to go that far."

"Of course she's right! Good lord, child! Anyway, think about it. If our luck holds, I'll be able to open my own bakery like hers, and you won't need to get up and sell those loaves anymore," Molly said, carrying an armload of potatoes to the table. "Imagine that—our own bakery!"

Blythe picked up another carrot and worked on it. As Molly went on and on about this new dream of hers, he couldn't help but wonder how long it would take them to reach that point. He might be undereducated, but even with what little mathematics he knew, common sense insisted that a corresponding increase in price to offset Molly's new expense would be the key to achieving that goal.

"When did you start thinking about owning a bakery, anyway?" he asked at length. "I thought you were happy with market day."

"Don't be silly, you silly thing. Yes, I used to be content with nothing more than a stall, but Mrs. Brainswell changed my perspective completely. 'Don't settle for what's clearly below your abilities,' she said in that firm, superior tone of hers, and I understood—no, I realized—that I've been cheating myself by setting modest goals." Molly gave Blythe a sheepish little smile. "I'm so pleased to have met her. Honored, even. If anything, the way our first meeting went, it was as if she sought me out on purpose, saying that she's heard quite a bit of good things about my cakes and bread."

Blythe set down the carrot he'd just finished peeling and took up another. "You're lucky to have found someone who sincerely cares about you and your success."

"I am. And to think—there are others at the market who're like me, and yet Mrs. Brainswell chose me to take under her wing. It's because I'm the most successful of the novice bakers, she said, and she'd hate to see talent spoiled by inadequate goals." Molly blushed and shrugged, practically glowing as she recounted her new mentor's praise.

Blythe grinned as well. He always found Molly's good humor infectious as long as it wasn't at his expense. "She's blessed with good instincts, then. I'm glad she advises you now."

"Yes. She's even invited me to see her bakery and have lunch with her, in fact."

"Oh? When?"

"I don't know, but I can't wait."

· · · ·

AFTERNOON HOURS WERE designated idle hours, and Blythe always spent those in Jack's company. Given his earlier hellish time with his friend, Blythe wondered if he valued his sanity enough to spend more hours with Jack. For better or for worse, he realized that he was also bored out of his mind and so relented, though he dreaded his friend's mood.

"I never thought I'd ever hear it, but Mama said that she was proud of me for what I did this morning," Jack said, his mood no less sour than it was earlier. He walked around looking the way he did as well—hunched shoulders, bowed head, hands in pockets, feet dragging and scoring two deep tracks in the dirt.

"Shouldn't you be glad?"

"Glad? What on earth for? It means she expects me to be productive and find work! What's to be glad for?"

Blythe sighed. "Well, it was worth a try, I suppose."

The two walked toward the river, intent on whiling away their time in the shade, lost in conversation, while sharing commentaries on the traffic that moved along the dirt road across the river. It had been a while since they last spent time there; Blythe calculated around two days, but he could never be so sure, given his busy schedule.

"Mama's forcing my hand in this."

Blythe glanced at Jack. "What do you mean?"

"I mean she's trapping me in a situation where I'll be forced to agree to her original demand. She knows very well how much I despise work." Jack paused and looked at Blythe, who continued to regard him in confusion. "She's forcing me to sell our cow, fool! And I don't have a choice but to do it."

"That's an odd choice," Blythe said. "How would a cow equal work? I hardly think Sarah will be worth much, command enough money to sustain you and your mama for a month, let alone a year or so."

"Selling her would get Mama to stop her daily nagging, and that's good enough for me. Damn, I'll miss that cow."

Blythe eyed his friend warily. "You sound like you're in love. I never thought you had it in you, Jack."

Jack grimaced before cuffing Blythe roughly on the head. "Oh, lord, I must've died and gone straight to hell," he spluttered, stopping dead in his tracks and grimacing again.

"What now?" Blythe waited for the stars to fade as he rubbed the back of his head. He stopped at Jack's fresh round of mutterings.

"It's those damned Vicary people—they're ahead of us. Let's turn around and go somewhere else."

Blythe's head shot up, and he blinked. "Vicary? Where? Oh."

Several yards ahead of them stood four people—two men and two women. They appeared to be talking, probably about the scenery, because they gesticulated emphatically before them, often indicating the river. Someone suddenly laughed, and his voice carried beautifully in the silence of the general area. Blythe recognized the voice as Edrik's, though he was surprised by the other boy's energy and lack of restraint in the company of others. Blythe squinted and didn't recognize Edrik's companions. They must be friends, then.

"Come on, let's go." Jack gave Blythe's arm an insistent tug. "I don't want to cross paths with anyone from that family anytime or anywhere."

"What—why? Because of the carriage incident?"

"Carriage incident? Oh, that was theirs? Good lord, no wonder they almost killed you!"

Blythe rolled his eyes as he allowed himself to be led away. As much as he'd like to talk to Edrik again, he continued to feel painfully self-conscious about his inferiority to the other boy. Being seen by people who were obviously close, personal acquaintances of Edrik deepened his mortification. No, he could afford to wait another time, when Edrik was alone.

"Don't be stupid," he retorted, panting a little as he tried to keep up with Jack's relentless pace. "What got you running away from them? They're not ghouls pretending to be human, are they?"

"Oh, shut up. No, Mama washes for them, and I've been in their house once because Mama's become great friends with the housekeeper, and we've been invited to have supper with the maids and all. It was all very irregular. I've never heard of such a thing being done in proper households." Jack paused and cast a resentful glower at the still chatting group they were leaving behind.

Blythe sighed. "And?"

To his surprise, Jack pulled him closer, stealing cautious glances back at Edrik's group as though he were in danger of being caught gossiping about them at what seemed like a million feet away. Blythe was forced to admit that there was something morbidly enthralling about the moment for all its absurdity.

"We saw Mr. Vicary walking outside in the dark," Jack whispered, "on our way home. He was having a conversation with himself—or someone who's invisible, possibly a ghost. He didn't stop until someone came out for him."

"Idiot. I heard they're a family of artists, and that's what artists do—be eccentric and halfway terrifying to people who aren't like them."

"The servants keep odd hours like the family, Mama said, and everyone's treated like friends, not hired help." Jack's eyes blazed, and Blythe couldn't tell if it was outrage or shocked respect.

"They're also wealthy, and I'm guessing that rich artists keep the strangest hours—worse than regular gentry or titled folks with no talent to speak of." Blythe pinched his lips in a tight line. "And here I thought you'd be admiring the Vicarys for being strange, moneyed types."

Jack snorted. "I don't trust rich people, artists or no. They always hold themselves up above everybody, and they never let you forget who your betters are."

Blythe fell silent, glancing back at the group. He felt a bit torn because he'd grown up sharing Jack's views on the privileged class, but since Edrik sauntered so carelessly and charmingly into his life, criticisms of the wealthy and powerful were turning into a knife stab in his side. To be sure, ever since he started his morning bread route, a good many things that used to be so clearly defined in black and white had now turned into baffling shades of gray, and he was beginning to yearn for the good old days despite his fifteen years.

"How did you know they're from the family?" he prodded, indicating the group with a jerk of his head. Jack paused, thankfully, for it gave Blythe time to recover from their earlier frenetic pace.

"That braying dandy over there was the fellow who came for old Mr. Vicary, and unless 'papa' has changed meaning recently, I'm quite sure that Mr. Vicary's his father. Now let's get a move on."

Blythe scowled at him even as he obeyed. He didn't quite appreciate the humor, if any, in Jack's use of "braying dandy" in reference to Edrik.

"I think you're letting your prejudices cloud your judgment," he said, fighting the urge not to glance back one more time. "Old Mr. Vicary and his family haven't done anything to you."

"They're rich, and they almost ran you over."

"It was an accident, and I was partly to blame for it."

"Their driver's an arse head. I've met him. He is."

Blythe laughed now, shaking his head. "I can't talk to you when you're being an oppressed peasant. You're both sensible and stupid at the same time, and your arguments and criticisms make my head hurt."

"Shut up. Since when did you turn into a defender of rich people, anyway? You used to agree with me every time, and you added your own brand of spite when you tore them down," Jack retorted, giving him an incredulous look.

"Because I've met them," Blythe said without skipping a beat. "At the market—they bought some cakes from us and were very nice and polite the whole time."

"That's what they've been taught to do, you blockhead. They're supposed to be kind and generous and downright patronizing to their inferiors. Lord, I wouldn't be surprised if they fed your sister's cakes to the dogs and laughed about it."

Blythe blinked, now put out at what he was hearing. "That's utterly ridiculous," he snapped.

"I don't think so. In fact, if they really are a family of artists, they might have used the cakes for their so-called art. Carved them into small sculptures or colored them with paint. Maybe set them on a table and talked to them the way old Mr. Vicary talked to no one."

They'd reached the town's borders by then and paused there. Blythe's earlier excitement at seeing Edrik Vicary—even for a mere moment and at a distance—had evaporated under Jack's ongoing verbal assaults, and Blythe couldn't decide if he was irritated or depressed. In the end he settled for feeling the urge to kick Jack Wicket so hard that his shoe would get lost inside his friend's bowels.

"Well, I believe it's good to think the best of people, especially if you haven't met them like I have," he said after a moment's thought. "I don't care if they have enough money to buy all of Upchurch. I still think Edrik and his family are nice people."

Jack was silent for a moment. "Edrik? You know his name?"

"Yes, I do—he introduced himself to me."

Jack simply nodded and looked around them, his attention divided again. "There's no hope for it, I suppose," he said. "I should go home. There's still this abominable matter regarding my poor cow."

Blythe shrugged. "All right, then. Good luck with Sarah."

Jack scowled, turning to regard him as though he'd just remembered something. The scrutiny was a little unnerving, but Blythe met his gaze without blinking. "You should've seen the look on your face when you talked about Edrik Vicary."

"What? What do you mean?"

"I recognize that look. Have a care, Midwinter. People like him are trouble." Jack saluted Blythe smartly before turning around and walking away, the black cloud of bitterness and envy still swaddling him. It was so palpable, in fact, that Blythe could swear it materialized for a few seconds and then vanished.

Chapter 12

Jack didn't walk with Blythe for the following morning's bread route, thank God, though Blythe felt a little guilty for being relieved. A little. That said, he also couldn't help but brood over his friend's acerbic observations.

In fact, he'd gotten so unsettled by the doubts and restlessness that had begun to fester in his belly like a heavy, rotting weight that he did what he never thought he'd ever do: seek out Mr. Ruffle for some inter-kingdom gossip. He'd encouraged the old gentleman with so much earnestness—more like sullen desperation—that the pair of them eventually settled on a couple of chairs a servant obligingly brought out. Those were set a few yards from the front door and faced east because Mr. Ruffle wanted to watch the sun rise.

"I don't know how many more of these scenes I'll have the pleasure of watching, my boy," he said with a contented grin brightening his face.

"I'm sure you've got plenty more chances. You seem quite hale."

"It usually depends on company. I haven't watched the sun rise with a young person in a long, long time," Mr. Ruffle said, his grin softening to a wistful smile. "That was with my youngest son, who'd long grown up and moved away to raise a family of his own. He'll be a grandfather himself soon enough."

Blythe regarded him. "I'm a poor substitute, I think," he said with a sheepish chuckle.

"Pah! Nonsense! Every person's worth a good deal more than he believes."

"Even criminals?"

Mr. Ruffle nodded firmly. "Even criminals. I believe they were never told or shown their worth, and they learned to believe the worst about themselves and the rest of the world." He paused, shrugging. "Or at the very least that's how they begin, which makes them vulnerable to the darker influences of their fortune. Like poverty, for instance."

"And that's all there is to it?"

"Well, the matter's a great deal more complicated than that, Master Blythe, but I do think that self-worth figures largely in the equation. Remember as well that a person's worth can never be measured in gold."

Blythe decided to simply nod despite the fact that he still needed time to turn Mr. Ruffle's philosophy over and over in his head. Considering the godforsaken hour, he felt the need to avoid anything requiring deep thought till the next convenient time—which could be the weekend or sometime the following month or so.

"And what about our friendly neighbors, sir?" he asked. "Anything new and interesting in the continent?"

Mr. Ruffle let out a grunt of approval and slapped his knees. "Why, yes! Funny you should ask. Word's gone out about some bad contracts made between a queen and some demon-dwarf over straw and gold."

As the old man recounted the story, Blythe scowled upon realizing that it had something to do with riches and the shortcuts and bad decisions made in order to secure them—though, to the queen's credit, she also needed to do what was necessary when faced with the king's threat of death.

"It's all luck and nothing else," he grumbled, taking care not to let Mr. Ruffle hear him. It wouldn't have mattered, anyway. Once encouraged to chatter, the old gentleman kept on with his gossip, completely unaware of Blythe's presence for the time being.

"Ah, and there's this ghastly account about a false bride who was really a princess's waiting-woman, and she'd turned the tables on her mistress, etc." Mr. Ruffle carried on about a sordid tale involving a long-suffering goosegirl and her dead horse's talking head.

Again, Blythe noted, the story involved wealth, luck, and in the case of that cretinous bitch of a waiting-woman, deceit. What on earth was he supposed to take away from these accounts other than the fact that they were outlandish rumors spread by dubious travelers and perhaps embellished by the wild imaginings of lonely old men?

"Begging your pardon, Mr. Ruffle, but have you anything about humble families and not kings and queens?" he asked, waiting for his companion to pause in his storytelling in order to take a few gulps of air.

"Well, there *is* one about a brother and sister and a witch who lured them with a pastry cottage and tried to fatten them up for her food."

Blythe grimaced. "Lord, sounds like something Molly would do if I were to test her patience about my work."

"I'd keep an eye on her if I were you, my boy. When she starts making plans for a pastry cottage and a large oven that can house a youngster like you, I'd run away to France unless you've no objections to retreating in a monastery some-where."

Blythe sighed, resting his chin on one hand as he watched the sun creep its way up the horizon. "Are all these horrible stories from the continent?"

"Yes. A pair of mad brothers with a flair for the romantic, I understand, are the ones either starting or spreading these rumors in their kingdom. Some folks say they come from Hesse, but who knows? They could very well be a figment of people's imagination, given how surreal and fantastical their accounts are, and God knows where these rumors really come from. For my part, I'll have to stick to that pair of mad brothers. It sounds much more interesting than other possibilities." Mr. Ruffle took a deep breath of fresh, morning air, exhaled loud-ly with a satisfied sigh, and slapped his knees again.

Blythe turned to look at the sun again. "Makes you proud to be English, doesn't it?"

"Indeed. We don't have dark, sordid stories about mayhem and ghouls. We don't need them, anyway. We have our hands full with France."

· · · ·

BECAUSE OF THAT IMPROMPTU detour spent in Mr. Ruffle's company, Blythe was late in selling the rest of his loaves, earning himself a good deal of scolding from irritated and hungry customers. Some even threatened to stop buying from him, but he knew better. Nobody else in town offered early morn-ing bread sold on people's doorsteps. It was easy and convenient, and no one would want to set off for the main square in search of bread. There was, also, the issue of taste, with Molly's bread being a touch sweeter than what was normally sold in bakeries. People simply loved the stuff, and Blythe was sure that, for all their grumping and threats of abandonment, his customers wouldn't dream of going through with them. If they knew what was good for them, they'd forgive him that one morning's delay.

Yes, Molly was a genius as a baker and an amateur businesswoman, and giv-en the opportunity, she could rise above everyone and be just as successful as Mrs. Brainswell. It was just unfortunate that Molly's road to success was long, meandering, and unpaved.

On his way home, Blythe decided to spend a bit more idle time lounging about town, mostly to pay his respects to Mr. Barnfield and ask a few meek questions about tailoring. The kindly old man was busy attending a couple of customers, however, so Blythe was obliged to retreat after thanking him for a lovely jacket. When he stepped outside, a touch disappointed, he told himself to come back another day and engage Mr. Barnfield in an illuminating conversation about his trade. Perhaps, Blythe thought, that was where his future lay. It only made sense, seeing as how his interest had been stoked from the first moment he'd set foot inside the little dark shop, and he found that questions about particulars kept coming whenever he inspected his new jacket.

"That's a start," he said, his spirits rising.

Still feeling the need for some lazy time, he wandered about the main square, even venturing down side streets and narrow lanes to explore what those areas offered by way of shopping experiences. As he made his way down one of the larger streets in which shops catering to wealthy customers were situated, he spotted Mrs. Brainswell's bakery, which was conveniently located just a couple of doors from the junction of the main square and the side street.

Even with other bakeries scattered everywhere, it was easy to find this one, for a great big sign hung above the door, the ornate letters painted in vivid colors: *Brainswell's Baked Beauties.*

Blythe stood at the window for a moment, eyeing the baked goods on display. "Molly can do these, I'm sure," he muttered, impressed.

So far his sister had only shown her skills in baking excellent bread and equally excellent but basic cakes. Perhaps it was high time for her to expand her offerings. Blythe entered the shop, flinching a little at the sudden jingling of the bell above the door and the attention he drew from customers who turned to see who'd just come in. He found it a touch difficult not only opening the door while carrying two large baskets, but also maneuvering around, deftly avoiding accidents. It didn't take him long to realize that he needed to move slowly and look around a lot, ensuring that he didn't touch any of the displays and risk catastrophe.

The bakery's interior was gorgeous, to say the least. Every inch of dark wood was polished to perfection. There was nothing overdone or ostentatious in the decorative details of the interior. If anything, the bakery seemed to be devoid of those things, with Mrs. Brainswell smartly opting to let her own creations be the decorative elements. Mouth-watering and colorful confections, pastries, and cakes all seemed to clamor for his attention, and Blythe was only too happy to admire them as close as he possibly could without causing any damage.

"Pardon me, young man, but you must be in the wrong shop. Old Mr. Hodge's bakery's in Taggart Lane. I'm sure you'll find what you're looking for there," a voice said, clear and sharp.

Blythe turned around, startled. He didn't know if he was looking at Mrs. Brainswell as he'd never seen her before, but a thin woman stood behind the counter, eyeing him with undisguised disdain.

"Oh—I was only looking, ma'am," he stammered.

A few customers were in the shop when he entered, and while most opted to ignore him, there were a few who stared, looking him over from head to foot before leaning close to each other and whispering. They were three young ladies about his age, all fashionably dressed.

"Yes, I know, and while I appreciate your interest, I'm afraid I can't help you. Like I said, though, Mr. Hodge will most certainly have what you need."

Nothing quite sank in with Blythe at the moment, and all he felt was some confusion at being told that Mrs. Brainswell's bakery had nothing to offer him. He saw several pastries and cakes, in fact, that he found delectable and that he wished he could afford to buy.

The small group of people had stopped their whispers and sniggering and had moved on to deciding what to buy.

"Thank you," he said, his confusion slowly wavering as something more un-savory began to tickle the edges of his mind. "You have some excellent selec-tions."

"Of course I do," the woman retorted, her words clipped. "I only make the best for my customers."

So this was the legendary Mrs. Brainswell, then? Was now a good time to mention Molly? Something told him not to.

"I quite like the sugar dolls. They almost look good enough to play with, and I'd probably do it if I were much, much younger." Blythe had never been one for eloquence, and he stumbled a good deal finding the right words as he gave his effusive praise for the remarkable treats he'd seen.

The woman only listened, the hard look on her face turning stone-like, while the small group of young customers erupted in wild giggling, glancing over their shoulders to regard him with amazement. Blythe watched them titter and snort, his confusion returning, and with it, that awful feeling that swelled with every look shot in his direction.

"Like I said, young man, I'm afraid I don't have anything here to suit you. Good day," the woman finally said, her face turning red and her jaw tightening.

Blythe made his way to the door, once again taking care to keep his baskets—his old, soiled, and weathered baskets—from hitting a table or a neatly arranged delicacy. He said nothing and looked at no one when he left the bakery, and he barely even noticed the brightness of the outside when he stood in the sun. His mind seemed to have emptied itself so that nothing but a hollow darkness remained, though the past several moments continued to play themselves out in a never ending cycle of amusement, contempt, and rejection. A weight now pressed down on his chest, and he moved aimlessly forward, eventually pausing before a shoemaker's shop.

Blythe looked at his reflection in the window's glass. He appeared a little disheveled, his hair slightly unkempt and his old clothes rumpled and dusty. The baskets provided an absurd touch to the image, and he couldn't quite come up with the right words for it. He glanced up and saw his eyes—large and a touch haunted, definitely edged with pain and that same confusion he first felt inside the bakery.

"Well, well, Blythe Midwinter! What a surprise!"

He gave a start and whirled around. Edrik stood before him, grinning with unabashed pleasure. Dressed as always like a young gentleman, Edrik looked in every way Blythe's counter image. Every article of clothing fitted him perfectly, not drape over his body like a too-roomy sack. Not a speck of dirt seemed to touch his skin and neatly combed hair. Blythe gave up at the idea of observing Edrik's shoes because he didn't think he had the stomach for it.

The more Edrik drew himself up, squaring his shoulders, and lifted his chin, the more Blythe sagged and slouched, his head drooping and his feet shuffling lightly or toeing the ground.

"I'm on my way home," he said, meeting Edrik's gaze once before looking away.

"With empty baskets? Shouldn't you be filling them up first before you go home?"

Blythe hesitated for a moment, wincing inwardly and fixing his gaze on a carriage that slowly drove past. He looked at Edrik again and then at something else, shrugging. "I sell bread loaves for a living. I'm done now and want to go home."

"Oh—well, if you'll give me a moment, I can escort you."

Blythe nearly choked on his tongue. "No," he said, almost grimacing as his gaze darted back to meet Edrik's, this time for good. "No, I'll be perfectly fine. Besides, I can't stay long. I've got things to do, and my sister's waiting for me."

"But I won't be a moment," Edrik said. He appeared to remain oblivious to Blythe's discomfort. Then again, Blythe silently berated himself, he must be too subtle in conveying his distress. "I only need to take my leave of someone, and I'll be all yours."

There was something in the way Edrik said "all yours" that made Blythe's heart skip a beat, leaving him confused—yet again—and for entirely different reasons now. It certainly didn't help that Edrik not only stepped closer, but also softened his grin into something else. A fond little smile or something like.

Blythe gulped, hoping Edrik didn't hear it. "I swear I'll be perfectly all right. You really don't need to trouble yourself."

The smile wavered, and a faint shadow of regret dimmed Edrik's features. "Pity. I was looking forward to spending some time in your company."

Blythe sighed, drooping again, turning his gaze back to the busy square as he shuffled and toed the ground, utterly torn. The very idea of Edrik Vicary clapping eyes on his family's cottage was enough to send him into a near-apoplectic fit. Being seen walking around with those confounded baskets, disheveled and dusty, didn't improve matters for him, given what had just transpired in Mrs. Brainswell's bakery.

All the same, he couldn't help but feel ashamed of his response, with Edrik being so solicitous and all...

"Oh, all right, then," he said after another moment of going back and forth with his conscience. He looked back at Edrik and was a little aghast at seeing the other boy smile so brightly. *Damn*, he thought. *I can't take that back now.*

"Brilliant! Wait here, while I look for my sisters and cousins. They've all split up, pillaging different shops and threatening me with countless hours spent in indecision. I'll look for Edith, and she can tell the others."

Edrik bounded off, quick and energetic as a young buck, and Blythe watched him in helpless admiration. Blythe moved off to the side to allow passersby more room while reassuring himself that it shouldn't hurt having his life, in a manner of speaking, laid bare to a boy he barely knew but he now realized he liked a great deal.

A swarm of people momentarily blocked his view, but Blythe waited until the scene cleared to search for Edrik again.

He found him, all right—talking to Edith, whom Blythe recognized even from a distance. She was once again dressed oddly, and it was very likely that she'd been out searching for inspiration for her art. Brother and sister stood before a book shop, lost in conversation, but they weren't alone for long.

From around a corner a small group of girls appeared, and Blythe recognized them to be the same ones in Mrs. Brainswell's bakery. To his horror, he watched them approach Blythe and Edith, interrupting their conversation as they chattered and showed off their purchases. Edrik cut them off, laughing and talking, and turned to point in Blythe's direction. When the girls followed his finger and saw Blythe, their eyes widened, and they all dissolved into another fit of hysterical giggling. One of them tugged at Edrik's arm, pulling Edrik close to whisper something to him while the others continued to laugh and look at Blythe with contemptuous amusement. Edith appeared baffled by everything, her look of surprise turning to a slight frown as she listened to them.

Thank God for the midday bustle. Another wave of people blocked Blythe's view, and he took full advantage of the protective cover they offered. Turning on his heels, he ran off, taking a longer, more roundabout route back home through the narrower and dingier alleys that he figured Edrik wasn't familiar with. Surely there was no way Edrik would be able to follow him.

Chapter 13

"**B**lythe, do stop being so difficult. Get up. It's late."

From behind the blanket divider that, miraculously, remained up, a prolonged, languid, wheezing fart sounded. Like a mournful trumpet blast from a Herald of Hell, Blythe thought, his mood dipping all the more. He still didn't know what Bertie consumed that would turn him into his brother's murderer. As far as he saw, they all ate the same thing throughout the day, with Molly making sure that Bertie packed some food to take to work in order to avoid unnecessary expense.

Perhaps Blythe could somehow convince Mrs. Pugsley to part with one of her potions if she had a formula meant to cure Bertie's flatulent ills. If not, surely she could be persuaded by the tearful pleas of an innocent fifteen-year-old whose lungs were well on their way to shriveling up into blackened lumps.

What did lungs look like again? Like slimy sacks or something like that.

Blythe wondered if he accurately remembered what he'd learned from an impromptu anatomy lesson given by a traveling surgeon who loathed children and terrorized them with horror stories about cut-up cadavers and what he found inside. Blythe was only around seven when he met the ghoulish fellow, but he could still remember the moment vividly and the gruesome details that made his mouth hang open but failed to make him run away. In fact, he'd actually shadowed the snarling grump for about half a mile outside Upchurch before his mother realized he'd wandered off and had sounded the alarm. Had it been raised too late, Blythe was now sure that he'd have ended up being one more lifeless body on the surgeon's slab, his entrails and severed appendages scattered all over a remote countryside.

"Blythe Midwinter, I'm not joking." Molly did sound a bit peevish. "Get yourself up and out of bed this instant, or I'll throw you out into the cold without breakfast."

Blythe snorted. Of course his sister would never do that. While it was true she'd threatened him with it countless times in the past, she was too soft-hearted to follow through on her threats. That said, her nagging skills were another matter altogether, and it was to Blythe's advantage that he'd get up now before being driven mad.

"Yes, yes, I'm coming," he snarled, throwing the blankets off him and sitting up.

Molly stood at the foot of his bed, scowling. "What on earth's gotten into you?" she demanded. "You've been moody and withdrawn the past few days, and it's getting almost impossible putting up with your sulking. Now I know how life can be a festering boil on your bottom when you're fifteen, but this is ridiculous. What happened? Did someone bully you or something?"

Blythe winced. Molly was treading dangerous waters, and he didn't know how to respond.

"It's nothing," he said. His motivation had taken a severe hit, as if they needed any more trouncing. He barely had the mental strength to do more than make himself crawl off the bed and land face first on the cold, stone floor while Molly watched with a look of morbid fascination. "I haven't been feeling as energetic as I used to," he added, now using his bed for a prop to drag himself to his feet. "I think I'm dangerously close to being sick."

Did that sound convincing? Blythe hated lying to anyone, especially his family, but he didn't want to admit to feeling shame for his poverty. For being terrified of having Edrik Vicary see how much his family struggled day to day, while he and his cousins could sail into shops meant for wealthy, discerning clients. For realizing that Jack Wicket's hopes for good luck were now his own because he was simply too embarrassed by that accident of birth that had stuck him in such a hopeless situation.

Molly worked terribly hard to ensure that her two younger brothers were properly fed and clothed. While food remained meager and clothing was more of a luxury they could rarely afford, she'd still managed to ensure that they never went without a meal or decent castoffs on their backs.

As for Bertie—the genial giant did his part in helping them pay their bills and maintain the cottage's integrity, inside and out. He'd never complained, though there'd always been that possibility of his marrying and settling down that had shadowed future prospects for Blythe and Molly, who'd have to find another home—or more likely rent a room somewhere. If that were to happen, Molly's beloved oven and all her dreams of succeeding in the baking business would surely go up in smoke. Blythe hated thinking about that possibility, but there it was.

He'd been thinking about Jack's rants. Where was the fairness in all this? How would Edrik's cousins compare to Molly and Bertie by way of character? From what Blythe had seen, the disparity was quite glaring with the disadvantage—also glaringly unfair—being on the side of his sister and brother.

Blythe was ashamed of their poverty, but he was also more ashamed of feeling that way. He refused to talk to anyone about it, and for the last two days, he'd been tiptoeing through town, alert and on guard, ready to shrink and vanish into the shadows should he catch sight of Edrik anywhere. And perhaps the worst part of all this was the fact that what self-consciousness he felt before had tripled, and he went about his morning bread route painfully aware of doing work that yielded little results.

He followed Molly to the dining table, where his breakfast awaited him. Even the welcome, cheerful light and warmth of the hearth failed to invigorate him. In fact, catching sight of the blazing fire only reminded him of yet another sad fact: that the only reason why they could easily splurge on firewood was because of the fact that the man who provided them with ample stock was madly in love with Molly even if she continued to refuse offers of marriage from her admirers.

"How long have you been feeling like this?" she asked as Blythe sat at the table and poured himself some coffee.

He shrugged. "I don't know. It just crept up on me all gradual-like. I can't really say." That much was true enough, at least with regard to the progression of his mental state.

"Tsk. Why didn't you say something before?"

"I didn't think it was going to get this bad. Besides, I didn't want to worry you." So many lies kept pouring out of him that Blythe was amazed he hadn't swallowed his tongue yet.

Molly walked up to him and pressed a hand against his forehead. "I don't feel anything, but that doesn't mean you're well." She paused, narrowing her eyes as she looked at him more closely. "You do look tired and haggard."

"I don't feel well," he muttered, but it was in reference to his conscience and the thrashing it was going through every time he opened his mouth to talk.

"Well, then, it's best to prevent a catastrophe from happening."

"It's a little too late now," Blythe murmured, sagging at the table.

"While you're out, I'll go to Mrs. Pugsley and have her mix a potion for you." Molly kissed the top of Blythe's rumpled head and walked off to continue packing the baskets.

Blythe sighed, making a face at his coffee. With any luck, Mrs. Pugsley would put together a potion that induced forgetfulness. God only knew, there was much to be said about ignorance and bliss, and if Blythe could go about his days as thoughtless and as ignorant of the world as a newborn babe, he'd be deliriously happy.

Molly went on and on about variations of potions that she believed would benefit her brother. From the farthest corner of the cottage, another languid trumpet call ripped through the air. Blythe couldn't help but eye Molly's flour-dusted rolling pin sitting on the table. Surely, he thought, that thing would work wonders as something to shove up Bertie's offending arse.

• • • •

THE DREARY WEEK FINALLY ended, those days spent in bleak self-aware-ness climaxing with what threatened to be an equally dreary Saturday. Blythe had spent Friday helping Molly bake and wrap the cakes, flabbergasted by the fact that she'd decided to "improve" on her decorative wrapping with some-thing a bit more costly.

She'd moved from simple "cake paper" as it was called to one that was pat-terned, the ribbon holding everything together also enjoying a bit of an up-grade to one that looked and felt like silk.

"Are you sure you don't want to bring the price up?" he asked Molly as he stared in disbelief at the growing collection of prettily wrapped cakes.

"Blythe, this is an investment. Yes, our profit will go down compared to last time, but that's only natural." Molly, covered with flour and sugar from head to toe, went about her work diligently and with careful, methodical precision. Blythe sat across the table from her, doing his utmost to wrap cakes as well as she did. "If you'd like to know, Mrs. Brainswell said that was how things were with her when she first started her business. In fact, she was in a great deal of debt for three or four years before her profits finally caught up and surpassed her expenses."

He stared at her, jaw hanging. "Three or four years?" he echoed. "How on earth can we afford to do the same for even a year?"

"Oh, stop being such a pessimist. Business requires a great deal of tactical skill and risk, Mrs. Brainswell said, and judging from the looks of things where her business is concerned, I say I'm quite up to the task. If you want to get ahead in this world, you need to take chances and not be afraid of failure." Molly paused to get up and check on that evening's meal (soup!), which was boiling in the hearth. "As for what we can do to offset lean times, we've got our bread sales and Bertie's woodwork."

Blythe tied a ribbon around a cake he'd just wrapped. "I suppose you're very lucky to have a guide like Mrs. Brainswell."

"Oh, absolutely. I'm still quite shocked that she's taking the time to advise me like this. She could easily have ignored me as an amateur competitor of hers but she didn't. I'm so humbled and honored."

"I never see her at the market. What does she look like?" Blythe cautiously glanced up, but Molly's back still faced him as she fussed over the soup.

"Mrs. Brainswell? She's quite tall and thin—very stately, in fact, the way she carries herself, and I think that's nicely reflective of her strength and determination to succeed. She told me that she started with nothing, you know—quite poor, no better than us—and look where she is now. If I only had half her virtues..."

Molly's words faded into an embarrassed chuckle. Blythe had never told her his adventures in Mrs. Brainswell's bakery, and he was convinced that he shouldn't compromise Molly's good standing in the woman's eyes by making his sister turn against her mentor. Blythe might have been treated badly, but he understood how valuable Mrs. Brainswell's success was to Molly, and he resigned himself to holding his tongue while the two women's professional friendship flourished.

"Did you go have lunch with her like you said? Have you been inside her bakery yet?"

"No, I haven't. I'm still waiting for her to make good her promise. But you know, love, she's a very busy woman. I really shouldn't impose."

· · · ·

MARKET DAY TURNED OUT to be as busy as the last one, but there was a palpable difference. Blythe saw that, while customers found the new wrapping to be quite pretty, not everyone who'd purchased from them in the past didn't question what was inside. A few returning customers frowned and demanded a confirmation from Molly that the cakes inside were the same as what she'd sold before.

"How do we know that you're not cheating us by hiding it behind colorful wrapping?"

"I need to open one up and make sure."

"It was far easier for me to determine the quality of your cakes when you didn't have them wrapped."

"Is all this really necessary? Wait—is the cake smaller this time around? It looks to be that way."

New customers were also intrigued by the packaging but in the end asked for the same guarantee, and Molly was obliged to sacrifice a couple of cakes. She unwrapped one first and cut it up into slices for people to sample since they couldn't see the cakes' quality now that they were safely hidden away. A second cake had to be unwrapped and used as a sample when the first one was completely eaten up by customers. Blythe noticed that only half of those who needed convincing bought something from their table, the newest customers looking disappointed on their sampling of cake slices.

He wasn't sure if he'd heard correctly, given the noise around them, but he thought a couple who'd sampled a slice walked away without purchasing a cake, saying, "The cake doesn't do justice to the wrapping. What a pity."

Molly, however, remained unfazed as if she didn't hear anyone's complaints. She continued to smile and cajole and praise her creations to the heavens, and she also had their winning appearances to fall back to—on a subtler level, that is. Blythe was obliged to wear his new jacket, and Molly had taken care to cut his and Bertie's hair the day before despite their protests. While Blythe was previously admired as a "young gentleman," he now withered under praise of him looking like a "gentleboy" (or was it "gentlechild"?). And he did look like a child with his previously shaggy mop trimmed short and neat, though Molly had insisted his haircut now highlighted his eyes.

His only consolation was the fact that at least he wasn't as big and broad as Bertie, which made looking like a gentlechild a little less awkward. Poor Bertie, for his part, couldn't be described with much precision beyond looking like a "hulking, robust, and sunburnt ten-year-old." For better or for worse, that only seemed to stoke girls' protective instincts, and they fawned all over the flustered young man.

Edrik hadn't appeared—yet. Blythe was anxious about the possibility of the other boy showing up because he was at a loss as to how to converse with him, now that Edrik's cousins had recounted Blythe's humiliating experience in Mrs. Brainswell's bakery. He wondered if they stretched the truth for titillation's sake; he wouldn't put it past them, judging from their behavior in and out of the bakery.

At the same time, though, a quieter and calmer voice argued, "He's already seen you working at the market, and your position didn't change the fact that he enjoys your company and is keen on developing your friendship. What kind of a scurvy rat are you, thinking the worst of him when he's shown you nothing but good?"

Blythe sighed as he brought more cakes to the able to fill in the gaps, which weren't many. The self-consciousness was still there, and he wasn't sure if it was going to go away anytime soon. His experiences at the bakery affected him in a way that nothing else beside his parents' deaths had. And he didn't know what it would take for him to get over the shame that now bore down on him.

"Midwinter! Hey!"

Blythe gave a start and looked up, blinking away the haze of self-indulgent brooding. There were no customers at their table for the moment, and Molly was resting and chatting with Mrs. Pugsley, while Bertie had sauntered off to the cart to get something to eat.

Not too far away stood Jack—with a cow. Jack waved at him and then beckoned him over.

"Blimey," Blythe muttered as he waved back. He went up to Molly to beg some rest time, and Molly allowed it but not without giving Jack and his cow a puzzled but dubious look.

"I hope to God your friend didn't steal that poor animal," she said.

"No, he means to sell her."

Molly fell silent and stared at Blythe, looking at a loss. "Jack Wicket's doing something productive?"

"I know. I'm just as much in shock as you are."

He walked around the table and picked his way past other folks to reach Jack's side. "So this is the day, eh?" Blythe stroked Sarah's neck.

"Yes. As to how Mama expects me to do this without a damned stall or pen with other livestock, I don't know." Jack stooped down to pick up a sizable rectangular board and gave it to Blythe. "All I could think of was to make a sign and find a spot somewhere."

Blythe looked down at the sign he held. In bright red paint—symbolic of Jack's spiritual agony, he was sure—the words "cow fur sell" were scrawled in forceful, tragic strokes.

"Jack, I don't know if they'll let you stand around with poor Sarah."

"Then they'll have to take it up with Mama," Jack retorted, rolling his eyes as Blythe gave him back his sign. Giving the rope he held a gentle tug, he said, "Come along, my darling. Let's get this over with."

Sarah obligingly followed, tail swishing, leaving a trail of great, steaming piles behind her. And judging from the sudden cries of disgust and dismay that rose around him, Blythe guessed that Sarah had slyly shat along the main foot path leading up to Molly's table.

Chapter 14

Blythe sat on the ground, munching an apple he'd taken with him (and which he'd stolen from the sack of apples meant for the horse). Three feet away stood a sullen Jack, holding on to Sarah and soothing her whenever she started to shift restlessly. She'd been milked earlier, which was a good—no, merciful—thing, considering what she now had to be subjected to. Jack had secured the sign around Sarah's neck with rope he'd brought for that purpose, and Blythe could swear that his friend was on the verge of bursting into tears when he did so.

Blythe sighed, shaking his head. He hated to admit it, but he felt quite sorry for Jack. The other boy appeared to truly love his cow—his pet?—judging from the way Jack petted and talked to her in low tones. Other than Blythe, after all, Jack never did have any friends, and he and his mother never really got along. Or at the very least, something was, indeed, there, but neither seemed to know what to do to bridge the gap and make some sort of connection with the other. That Jack never knew his father must have something to do with his behavior, and it was an issue that had always terrified Blythe.

His own parents might have passed away when he was younger, but he at least was lucky enough to be raised by them and to have enduring memories, however fuzzy, of his mother and father. Blythe simply couldn't fathom growing up without knowing one or the other.

"You're in the way!" someone hollered. A man pushing a small wheelbarrow loaded with sacks of something walked past them, glaring at Jack. "Find a space somewhere off the main path!"

Jack ignored him and turned to pet Sarah again. "Ignore him, Miss. He's just frustrated because he can't get it up for the wife." He paused to look back over his shoulder at Blythe. "That's what Mama said about him, anyway. She's as bad a gossip as the worst of the lot hereabouts."

"Should I take over for a bit? You should rest."

"No. I don't think Sarah's going to like being looked after by a stranger."

Blythe tossed away the remains of his apple and scrambled to his feet. "The least I can do is get you something to eat. Wait here."

Jack, bless the little bastard, gave him a grateful smile after a moment of wide-eyed shock. Blythe had some money on him, and he decided to go to one of the food stalls for something freshly made. Those were located in the middle of the market, a ring of stalls offering hot dishes to fellow vendors and regular customers alike.

With the time being close to midday, the food court—as vendors often referred to it—swarmed with activity. Blythe walked around, taking in each offering, before deciding on jellied eels and what he called "rock sized bland pudding". The latter item he suspected was nothing more than steamed dough made of white flour and water. The cook, it seemed, wasn't too keen on spices, but at least these small dumplings provided a bland complement to jellied eels.

Carrying the hot bundle, Blythe pushed his way through the crowds. Somewhere along the way, he felt something press against his arm, and he glanced back and nearly tripped over his own feet.

"I was hoping to find you here," Edrik said, looking worried and doubtful. "I tried to catch you at your sister's table, but your brother told me you've wandered off." Edrik paused, frowning a little as he considered his next words. "And he asked me to tell you—if I were lucky enough to find you—to 'get his bony arse back to the cake table'. That's word for word, not a paraphrase."

"Are your cousins here?" Blythe spat out, not caring whether or not Edrik noticed the vitriol.

"No. Just my tutor." Edrik jerked his head to the side, and Blythe caught sight of the same gentleman he'd seen in Edrik's company several days ago. He stood at a polite distance, though he did nothing to curb his disdain toward the market and especially the people who frequented it. In fact, not only did he stare down his nose at everything and everyone, he also covered said nose with a bright white handkerchief.

"I don't think your tutor thinks much about my world."

Edrik sighed and blushed. "I'm very sorry. That's also with regard to my cousins, who aren't very open-minded about a good deal of things." He observed Blythe for a moment, chewing his lip as he struggled with the awkward moment. "They're here visiting, and truth be told, none of my sisters particularly care for any of them."

"And you?"

"I'm not exactly happy with the way they behaved toward you."

Blythe smiled faintly. "The master of understatement—that's you."

Edrik blushed again, shrugging. "I'm fumbling my way through my first courtship. I feel a bit lost half the time."

He certainly never showed it as far as Blythe was concerned, and Edrik's easy use of "courtship" made him soar in exhilaration as well as shrink in embarrassment. The reminders of what had happened in the bakery put an end to that, though, and within seconds, Blythe was again swimming in resentment.

"They all laughed at me in that bakery because I was a dirty stray who accidentally wandered inside a place I shouldn't have."

"I know. They told me. I'm sure you saw everything since you ran away from me."

"I might be poor, but I still have some pride."

"You do. And I'm sorry. I wish I could make up for what you had to put up with." There was no doubt as to Edrik's sincerity given the pain that shadowed his face, his quieter manner and tone, and the loss of his confidence, which left him coloring and stammering. It looked as though all the worldly trappings had been shed, and an ordinary seventeen-year-old boy now stood before Blythe, doing his damnedest to mend things without knowing for sure if what he was doing was right.

Blythe nodded, the tension easing from him. "Your cousins are utter snobs." When Edrik chuckled, he stifled a grin. "They are, and I'm not sorry I said it. There."

Edrik was still chuckling, but his gaze seemed to have softened with a contrite light as he regarded Blythe. "You've every right to be critical, and I promise to keep them away from you whenever they come around to visit, which happens once a year. It can't be more than that, or my sisters will murder them."

"Wait." Blythe shifted his weight from foot to foot as he mulled things over. "Are you saying that you still want to be my friend after all that?"

"I don't see why not." Edrik paused and stole a glance in his tutor's direction. The man was now distracting himself with a juggler in tattered, colorful rags. The fellow was weaving his way through the astonished crowd without looking where he was going and without dropping any of the faded balls he was skillfully juggling. Edrik then leaned forward, holding Blythe's gaze. "I'd dearly love to spend more time with you, Blythe Midwinter, if you'd only let me."

Blythe's face burned, and he was again soaring and shrinking, the insane tug-of-war going on in his head and heart threatening a thorough emptying of his stomach's contents all over Edrik's fine shoes. "I still don't understand why you'd be interested in me, of all people."

"What, are you criticizing my judgment?" Edrik smiled as he dropped his voice to a volume that made Blythe's skin prickle in a good way.

"I'm not exactly your equal," he stammered. "I don't know why you should be reminded of that."

"I've been told countless times in the past that I've got excellent taste in art. And I daresay I know beauty when I see it." Edrik kissed him on the cheek. "I'll stop by your cake table at closing time."

Edrik's words barely got through the fog in Blythe's rapidly melting brain. "Oh—um—Molly usually sells her cakes quickly, and we leave before the market closes. But I can meet you at the stone bridge west of Upchurch. It takes you to the other side of the river."

"All right, then. In two hours, maybe?"

"Make it an hour. I'll see if I can be excused for the rest of the day."

Edrik beamed, his relief palpable. "An hour it is, then." He moved away, still smiling brilliantly and making Blythe's breath hitch again. Then he turned and walked toward his tutor, who continued to gape after the juggler. Within moments, they were both gone.

· · · ·

AFTER FEEDING JACK, Blythe had to go back to Molly's table, feeling oddly light. He remembered nothing of his friend's complaints about heartless people who couldn't appreciate Sarah's value as a personal milk source. He also wasn't sure if he really heard Jack wish the plague on those who offered him a ridiculously small amount for such a peerless cow.

Blythe, moreover, barely recalled urging Jack to move Sarah to another place in case the other boy had chosen badly the first time around. Perhaps the best prospects for cow-selling could be had elsewhere, and it was only a matter of trial-and-error in finding that out.

No, nothing filled Blythe's dreary world other than Edrik Vicary and his fine clothes and his brilliant smile and his earnest solicitousness and his confidence bordering on arrogance and...yes, and that kiss.

"Oh, lord," Blythe murmured.

"Blythe Midwinter, while we appreciate your oddly happy mood, you really need to stop grinning overly much and unsettling people. You're making them regret their generosity."

Blythe's golden haze lifted—a bit—and he glanced at Molly, who was regarding him with a mystified frown as she handed change to a customer. He was going to pooh-pooh that bit about unnerved customers, but he found them eyeing him with varying looks of uncertainty.

"I had jellied eels," he said, shrugging. "And I think they're horribly underestimated as a dish."

"Jellied eels? Someone's selling jellied eels? Here?" Molly asked, shocked.

Blythe nodded. "Mr. Drubbing only sells the stuff once a month, he said. It's too much trouble bringing fresh eels to Upchurch from London. He sells black pudding for the most part."

"Bob Nobley told me jellied eels give him gas," Bertie piped up. "I hope you're not going to stink up the cottage later."

"*You* should talk," Blythe said, rolling his eyes. Then he fell back into that lovely, warm, golden fog, once again oblivious to anything other than Edrik Vicary and that sauciest of saucy words, courtship.

"I must say, though, that however unsettling your mood might be, you're able to draw quite a few people to our table," Molly said. "Can't say I understand it, myself, but we'll take what we can get." She frowned thoughtfully for a moment. "It's been difficult selling cakes today even with the wrapping. Then again, I'm sure Mrs. Brainswell would say that it's part of the struggle of establishing myself."

Bertie regarded a glassy-eyed Blythe for a moment. "I say it's morbid fascination on people's part."

"I think you're right."

"How much time do I have left being a subject of verbal abuse, Molly?" Blythe piped up as he arranged the number of remaining cakes on the table. There seemed to be more than he expected. He'd normally regard a successful market day—or in this case, successful enough—with either indulgent pleasure or plain indifference, and for today, it was plain indifference.

Molly didn't answer right away as she surveyed the scene with a tired and somewhat baffled smile. Then she turned to Blythe and waved him off. "Oh, go ahead and go, dear. We've not much left to sell, and I reckon we'll be out of here within two hours."

It was Blythe's turn to beam. He gave Molly a quick kiss. "Brilliant—I need to check on Jack and see if he's all right."

"I must admit I'm still shocked at the thought that he's out there, being productive. Yes, go see him and make sure he's still sane."

"I will. And I promise to stay up late to help you with the cleaning and all that." Blythe hurried out, waving at Molly and Bertie. "Thanks, Molly!"

"He's going to be farting tonight," Bertie noted in a loud enough voice.

"I wouldn't be so critical if I were you, love. Now come along and look sharp. I think I spot a gaggle of your admirers drawing near."

"What, another one?"

The noise of the market soon swallowed up the conversation as Blythe hurried away in search of Jack. He reached the spot where he'd left his friend and found it empty.

No, not really empty because it was yet another main footpath, and it was, of course, swarming with activity. Blythe made a face as he considered his friend's next move.

"He probably moved to another spot," he said, looking around him and craning his neck as he tried to follow the flow of traffic.

The market, unfortunately, had a particularly intricate maze of pathways that intersected or ran parallel to each other, connecting vendors from all corners. Jack could easily have moved to any random path, and no matter how hard Blythe searched, it was next to impossible for him to stumble across his friend.

It was all Blythe could do to ask people if they'd seen Jack and Sarah.

"What, that sulky brat with the cow? He went down that way."

"Tell him he's in everyone's way! He cursed me and my descendants for telling him to get out of the path. Can you believe the cheek?"

"If you want to find him, just follow the obnoxious trail his cow left!"

Oh, yes, that. How could Blythe have forgotten? He quickly ducked his head and stared at the ground. He hurried one way, turned down a side path, and so on.

"I can't believe I'm using cow dung to locate Jack Wicket," he grumbled after turning what felt like the billionth corner. He paused momentarily as he thought that over. "Oh. Come to think of it, it's rather appropriate."

Blythe's efforts paid off at length, and not a moment too soon. He spotted fresh dung along one path, with some of them squashed, which could only mean unsuspecting people stepping on them. Gingerly picking his way past the steaming piles, Blythe finally spotted Sarah's backside up ahead, her tail swinging left and right in an idle rhythm. She appeared to be moving, being led forward maybe to another spot. Or, Blythe appended silently, she might be going home, Jack failing to sell her at the price he wanted.

Blythe trotted forward, wracking his brain for what to say to his friend in the event of a disappointment. As he drew near, he realized that he didn't have anything to offer other than a sympathetic ear.

He opened his mouth to call out, but the words died in his throat when he realized that it wasn't Jack who was leading Sarah away. The man who strolled along, occasionally reaching out to stroke Sarah's neck, was old and dressed in rags. Blythe frowned as he stared hard at the man's back, trying to remember if he'd ever met him before because the old man sure looked awfully familiar.

A voice calling his name halted him in his tracks, and with an irritated sigh, he turned and found Mrs. Stringer of Periwinkle Cottage hurrying through the crowd, waving at him. She looked a bit harried and a touch distressed.

"My dear," she panted once she reached him, "is your sister at her cake table today?"

"She is, yes. Is there anything wrong?"

Mrs. Stringer only patted her chest as she gulped air. "Nothing for you to worry yourself over," she replied once she found her voice. "But—oh, some people are just no good! I must speak to your sister at once. Thank you."

She hurried away, leaving Blythe blinking and wondering, but it didn't take him long to reset his mind on his purpose. Reminding himself of Sarah and her new owner, he ran down the path where he'd last seen them, eventually spotting them in the endlessly moving crowd.

Blythe increased his pace, and with his eyes glued to the figure several feet ahead of him, it was nothing short of a miracle that he never tripped or stumbled on the uneven dirt path.

When the old man slowed down, his shoulders visibly tensing as though he felt Blythe's gaze burning a hole through his back, Blythe felt like he'd swallowed a boulder, and it was trying to negotiate its way through his bowels. The old man glanced over his shoulder to look at Blythe, and he grinned.

"Oh, for God's sake," Blythe breathed, stunned. "The idiot sold the cow for magic beans?"

As though he'd just heard Blythe, the old man cackled, the light in his eyes cold and almost mocking—at least to Blythe, who remained shocked. That he could actually hear that little sound of amusement despite the noise around him only confirmed his suspicions that this stranger was very likely a magician or even a dark-magic-practicing sort. He hoped not, anyway, as concern for poor Sarah's welfare loomed quite large in his mind, and he didn't have the means to buy her back and keep her safe.

Then the ragged stranger turned around again and continued to lead Sarah through the market crowd without breaking his stride, reaching out to stroke the cow's neck every so often. Blythe, for his part, stopped in his tracks, gaping and feeling the urge to tear his hair out over Jack's idiocy.

He would've done it, too, had it not been for the fact that he was off to spend time with Edrik Vicary, and he needed to look his best for the other boy. Sporting a head peppered with bald patches all over simply wouldn't do.

Chapter 15

Edrik was already there when Blythe arrived at the bridge, making him wonder how long the other boy had been waiting. Since Molly had dismissed Blythe earlier than planned, he expected to be the one waiting.

"I wasn't waiting too long—maybe ten minutes," Edrik said. "I didn't want to go home and then go out again, so I told Mr. Woodham to go on without me, which took a bit of doing, I'm afraid."

"Your tutor, you mean?" When Edrik nodded, Blythe suppressed a grin. "I'm guessing he suspected that you were planning to undermine all that hard work he's put into your gentlemanly development."

"I wouldn't doubt it. Papa meant well when he hired Mr. Woodham, but at that point, the damage has already been done, and I was on my way to turning out just like my brother and sisters." Edrik was about to lead Blythe away when he stopped all of a sudden. "No, wait. I forgot."

He moved off to the side of the bridge and stooped to pick up a small canvas bag. Blythe didn't even notice its presence, considering where his mind lay, and he mentally laughed at himself for being such a dolt in the realm of boys' romance. When Edrik returned, he was smiling sheepishly.

"I went to Mrs. Brainswell's bakery and bought you something sweet. I hope it's not too much of an imposition."

Blythe took the bag and saw that it contained a small pastry box. He looked up at Edrik, unable to come up with something to say. "You did, didn't you?" He paused, hesitating, and then let out a soft breath. "Consider us even with this, then." He raised himself up on his toes to kiss Edrik on the cheek. "There. And thank you."

Edrik's grin looked comical, and Blythe guessed that the other boy was simply caught off-guard, just as Blythe was earlier.

"I was afraid that I made a terrible choice, going to that bakery for something to give you, but I prefer to look at it as a way of subverting her will." Edrik sniggered.

"What would she do if she were to discover that one of her exclusive offerings was being enjoyed by the person she'd practically chased out of her business?"

"A wicked part of me wishes that you stole whatever it is you have now if you really want to subvert her, but I wouldn't want anyone to do that, especially for me."

"I'm not as big a rebel as I think I am."

Blythe laughed. "I'm happy with what you are now, really."

He took Edrik's hand and led him away in the direction of the shady and quiet footpath that ran parallel to the river.

The two walked along the path, taking a random direction. Blythe didn't care a jot, having been given the rest of the afternoon to himself. They could wander off to the next county and beyond, and he'd be perfectly fine with it. He was too enthralled and in quite a bit of shock still, and he kept stealing glances at Edrik as a way of reassuring himself that the moment was truly real.

"What's the matter?" Edrik piped up after another moment's silence. He looked at Blythe, amused. "Looking for awful flaws? I'm afraid I'm born plain. I can't even boast anything unique or odd anywhere."

Blythe laughed, blushing. "I never cared about that. I was just wondering—uh—"

Edrik nodded and gave his hand a gentle squeeze. "Wondering why I like you, you mean?"

"I know, I know. I shouldn't worry about that, and I keep bothering you with it, but I can't help it."

"Do you like me?"

Blythe's embarrassment spiraled as he nodded, meeting Edrik's steady and earnest gaze. "I do, yes."

"Can you explain why? Like you said, we're not equals in situation. I'm nowhere near the handsomest boy in Upchurch."

Blythe had to laugh, and he shrugged. "I suppose you got me there," he said, dropping his gaze to his shoes and feeling the warmth and gentle pressure of Edrik's hand in his more keenly. "I can't explain attraction. It's such a strange thing, and I've never experienced anything like this before."

"You've never liked anyone until now? Really?" When Blythe shook his head, Edrik heaved a sigh of relief. "I must be the luckiest person alive, then."

What a flatterer, Blythe thought, grinning. "What about you?" Blythe paused, making a face at himself. "Oh, lord, what am I saying? Of course I'm not your first. I'm sure there've been others before."

"Others!" Edrik echoed before dissolving into light, bubbly laughter. "I'm only seventeen, Blythe. I'm really not as well-traveled as you think. I never even went to school. Mr. Woodham is it for me. I've been to assemblies and ballrooms and picnics, but I've no experience in steady, close quarters with the same group of boys year in and year out."

Blythe stared at him. "No? Really? But—"

"My upbringing's what most would call unconventional or even scandalous. Papa raised everyone himself, with Mama dying in childbirth with me." Edrik gave Blythe's hand another gentle squeeze. "Mama was just as much an artist as Papa, though, and she'd made him swear to bring everyone up as he—as someone with keener sensibilities than most others—saw fit, not constrained by petty rules. My brother and sisters had governesses through the years, but by and large, we were all taught quite radical views, which we've all embraced."

"What, their governesses agreed to that?"

"Not all the time. A couple resigned from their posts because my sisters were too 'godless' in their opinion, but Papa eventually found one who had a streak of the rebel in her." Edrik smiled wistfully as he stared ahead. "I think I only spent a year being taught by Miss Spratt before she passed on. Lord, I miss her."

Blythe shrugged. "You still enjoy the services of a tutor. Mr. Woodham might be just as much a snot as your cousins, but he seems to be a good fellow."

Edrik chuckled. "Bless you for the reminder. I hope he doesn't get wind of this conversation."

"Ha! I doubt if he'd want to readily converse with me. Anyway, I interrupted you."

"Well, Papa expected us to grow up and determine our own paths, and he'd even said that if we chose to reject his world of liberal philosophies, he'd welcome it. I suppose you should know that Papa was groomed to enter the church, but he was obviously the radical in his family. We're still amazed that he wasn't cut off for pursuing art, of all things. I mean, you know—sensuality and excess and everything the church preaches against." Edrik glanced at the sky and squinted at the brilliance above them. "Grandpapa wasn't pleased with his choice of wives since Mama was just as bad as Papa was, but he couldn't do anything about it. In the end, he'd said that it wasn't his place to dictate a grown man's life, and we knew deep down he loved Papa and couldn't bring himself to make him unhappy."

"That's nice," Blythe said, smiling. "My grandparents were both gone even before I was born, so I never knew them."

"I'm sure they'd be proud of you."

They fell silent for a moment, with Blythe absorbing what he'd heard so far. Thank God no one else was strolling along the same footpath and interrupting their private time, or he'd surely be seen looking rather stupid and slack-jawed as his brain worked furiously.

"I'm rather surprised to see Mr. Woodham staying put," he said at length.

"I'll admit I am, too," Edrik replied with a quiet laugh. "Lord, he's made it quite plain, though, that my—uh—lack of discipline or direction galls him since he can't seem to 'cure' me of those."

"Do your sisters shock him, too?" Blythe sure hoped so.

"You've no idea! The way he looks at Edith, Corliss, and Guendolen—one would think that he'd been sentenced to an eternity in the company of witches. My sisters know, of course, and they take too much delight in shocking him even more."

Blythe laughed along, falling silent for a moment and enjoying the slow, idle walk. "I'd like to get to know your family," he said, the self-consciousness returning, though not in that awful, crippling way.

"You will. Cranston and Edith have been asking about you, in fact. 'So when will you be inviting your new friend to dine with us?'" Edrik changed his voice to mimic his sister's. "I told them to wait, seeing as how everything depends on whether or not you accept me."

"That's quite a bit of pressure to put on me," Blythe said, coloring again. "Considering how little we know about each other and all..."

"There's no pressure as far as time goes. I like you enough to want to spend as many hours as I can in your company, getting to know you better."

Blythe stopped and looked at him, thrilled and yet mystified. "That's what we're doing right now. I know, I'm telling you what's obvious, but I feel a bit compelled to say it. It's my way of getting used to this sort of thing, I suppose."

"I'm sorry if I shocked you."

"No, no—I think—I really should stop fretting too much over this."

Edrik grinned. "You've no idea how relieved I am." He nodded at the bag in Blythe's hand. "Now are you going to share that or keep it to yourself? I've never talked this much in anyone's company other than my family—no, not even my cousins. And I'm hungry now for some sponge pudding."

Blythe had to ponder that for a moment, much to Edrik's delight. At length he agreed to share, though he demanded the right to dictate portions, which Edrik readily accepted—with much theatrical head-shaking and sighing.

They claimed a spot on the riverbank, and there they spent the rest of their time together watching the quiet flow of the water and the occasional white swans that took advantage of the currents. Blythe could barely remember much else about Mrs. Brainswell's sponge pudding (with treacle!) other than it was good. He thought about giving Molly a portion of it to sample, so she could determine its ingredients, but he enjoyed Edrik's company so much that he decided against it in the end, having fed the other boy half of the small cake. The sacrifice was well worth it. Edrik demonstrated his gratitude with a long, deep kiss, from which Blythe emerged later sporting blades of grass in his hair and clothes.

· · · ·

BERTIE HAD GONE OFF to enjoy the rest of his day with friends and some excellent ale, which meant that Molly was the only around to hear about Jack Wicket's remarkable sale.

"He's such an idiot! I can't believe he'd actually make good his threat of exchanging his cow for magic beans!"

Blythe rambled on and on as he swept the floor after helping Molly wash the dishes. Molly, in the meantime, didn't seem to have much to say about that. All Blythe got out of her was a quiet "Mm-hmm" or "Indeed" before falling silent as she prepared vegetables for that evening's supper. Blythe just shrugged it off. Molly was understandably tired, and besides, she'd always thought of Jack as a lazy good-for-nothing. What Blythe was telling her added nothing to what she already knew about Jack's character.

"I'll have to go find him tomorrow and kick him. I only hope he's still alive." Blythe grimaced. "I can't imagine what his mama would do to him after finding out what happened today." He wouldn't be surprised if she damned well flayed her son alive and buried him in salt.

After he'd done sweeping, he went to the pail of water next to the table and washed his hands. "What would you like me to do next?" he asked, wiping himself dry.

"Hmm? Oh—here. Help me cut up vegetables. You know, the usual thing," Molly replied, her manner distracted. She pointed at a bowl of carrots she'd just peeled. "Cut them into large pieces."

Blythe returned to the table with a knife and a cutting board and was soon lost in his work, his mind wandering back to his time spent in Edrik's company. When his imagination began to move toward the kiss, he squirmed a little as his face flared up. Stealing a few glances in Molly's direction, he saw that his sister wasn't paying him any attention, her mind obviously bent on her own thoughts as she peeled vegetables with a frown. Blythe also noticed that she looked rather pale.

"Is there something wrong?" he asked.

"Wrong? No, why?"

"Well—you're very distracted. And you look a bit ill."

Molly smiled wanly. "I'm just tired, dear. It's been a very busy few weeks for me what with your bread sales and market day. And all the usual chores I have to do on top of those—I'm afraid I'm starting to feel the strain."

Blythe nodded. "In that case, perhaps we can skip one day—like Sunday, for instance. I'm sure everyone can make do with one less day of dealing with me on their doorstep."

Molly seemed to pale even more. "Absolutely not," she replied a little too sharply. "No, I don't care how tired I am. We'll continue what we've been doing."

"Are you sure? Since we've been doing quite well on market day, I thought—"

"You thought wrong, Blythe. Fatigue's never an excuse. I refuse to use it as such." Molly nodded at the bowl of freshly peeled vegetables. "Now go on and finish up, so I can start cooking. We've got a lot of baking still ahead of us."

With a start, Blythe realized that she hadn't even started on the following day's bread loaves. "Huh," he muttered as he cut up vegetables. Molly must really be exhausted to have lagged on that.

• • • •

SUNDAY MORNING BREAD sales were good—surprisingly so. Blythe's baskets were emptied of their contents, and his little leather pouch hanging from his belt felt heavy. He couldn't wait to tell Molly about his good luck because she needed it. She'd retired the previous evening looking drawn but grim, and Blythe worried about whether or not she was coming down with a fever.

He took a detour on his way home, redirecting his steps toward Jack's home. Since it was close to midday, he knew it was safe to visit, with Mrs. Wicket already out and doing laundry work.

The cottage seemed to look back at him with the same baleful, sullen gaze that Jack always had. Blythe regarded the structure with a shake of his head, wondering if a house's owners could somehow transfer their personalities and moods to their domiciles. By some form of domestic magic, perhaps? Maybe what had been said about fairies dwelling in houses was true. Invisible supernatural creatures or forces could very well work in such a way as to infuse a structure with its owners' essences, whatever they might be.

Bythe walked up the weed-choked path to the door and knocked. The door looked as though it had been fashioned from long dead and decaying wood that Blythe forced himself to soften his knocking for fear of breaking the decrepit thing to pieces.

The door was eventually opened, and a stupidly grinning Jack stood there, blinking and swaying on his feet. "Well met, stranger!" he gurgled, waving a hand.

Blythe regarded him blankly. "You're drunk, aren't you?"

"Me? Nooooooo. Why should I be?"

"What happened?"

Jack shrugged, made a face, and gestured vaguely with his free hand since he still clung to the door. "Don't know," he said, belching. "I sold Sarah, you know."

"Yes, Jack, I know."

Jack blinked again, and he frowned. "You do? Who told you that?"

"I saw the man walk away with your cow when I went looking for you."

Jack sagged against the door, now looking distraught, his face flushed. "Sarah—my poor cow! She's never done anything to deserve being sold like that." He raised a finger. "I made him swear, though, to treat my poor cow right. And he said he will. Where he comes from, he told me, cows are protected and cared for. Apparently milk gives magicians strength—or brain power—or something. Maybe good cheese."

Blythe scowled at him. "For what price did you sell her?"

"Oh, come on, Mama, you've already asked me that! How many times do I have to tell you?"

"I'm not your mama, but that's neither here nor there," Blythe retorted. "I can't believe you sold her for magic beans. What were you thinking?"

Jack pinched his eyes shut, grimacing, as he waved Blythe off like a pesky fly. "Oh, go away, Midwinter! I've had enough of that rubbish from my mother!"

Blythe snorted. "I don't even know why she bothers nagging your ears off when you obviously lack any common sense to understand anything."

Jack just mimicked Blythe, contorting his face while mouthing Blythe's words.

"So what're you going to do now that you've wasted an entire cow for so-called magic beans?"

"I threw the damned beans in the back, you boy-harpy! Mama practically tore my head off yesterday and ordered me to throw the beans out before she left for work this morning! Now go away! I don't need you here, pretending to be my conscience!"

Jack stepped back and slammed the door in Blythe's face before Blythe could get another word out.

"You made your own bed, Jack Wicket," he said, shrugging, as he turned away to head home. Fortunately for him, the empty baskets and heavy leather coin pouch reminded him of better things, and he hurried back to his cottage, eager to share his account of excellent sales with his sister.

Chapter 16

Molly appeared to be in a better mood, though she still seemed a bit distracted, often lapsing into a thoughtful silence with a frown. Moreover, she'd become quite doting as well—overly fussy, as a matter of fact. She fed Blythe almost immediately on his return, and she shooed him off and ordered him to soothe his feet in his usual foot soak of plain clean water. For this final bit, she even had hot water waiting for him, when before, Blythe had to go about heating the water himself.

"I don't know what's going to happen to Jack," he said after a comfortable pause in his endless chattering. He leaned forward and rested his chin on one hand, his elbow digging into his thigh, and he watched his bare feet in the water. He wriggled his toes a little and diverted himself with the way the ripples distorted his feet.

"Sound like he got punished well enough," Molly said as she came back inside the cottage, the baskets newly shaken outdoors. It was another task that usually fell on Blythe's shoulders. He'd take the baskets outside and shake them upside-down in order to rid them of bread debris and other things that might've ended up inside them in the course of his bread route.

"He can be a bit of an arse head, but I do feel sorry for him. I hope his mama didn't thrash him too much."

"You say he was drunk when you saw him?" Molly set the baskets aside and turned her attention to the wash.

"Very. I'm surprised that he still managed to stay upright. He was also coherent, which only makes me wonder if he's so used to getting his brain soaked that he can manage anything when he's like this."

"Then he was thrashed quite thoroughly, but it's more like a tongue-lashing than anything else. Mrs. Wicket might be driven mad by that boy's laziness, but I know she'd rather die than hit her son." Molly flittered around the cottage, gathering soiled clothes and throwing them into the large tin washtub.

"I wonder how he'd have turned out if his papa were around. He'd probably be a great deal more practical than he is now, I'm sure."

Molly straightened up after collecting the last article of clothing for washing. She rested her hands on her hips and twisted her torso left and right, grimacing when she did. "Day-to-day work for people like us isn't exactly a mag-ical experience," she said. Did she just curse under her breath? Blythe thought she did, and he stifled a grin. "I might call your friend a lazy good-for-nothing, but even I can't say that I blame him for looking for gold in the clouds."

Blythe picked up the ragged towel that sat folded on the floor next to his stool. He spread it open to use as a drying mat for his feet. "I'll help you with the wash," he said.

"Oh, thank you, dear."

"Someday we'll be able to afford hiring our own washing-woman, won't we?" he asked as he briskly dried his feet. "Seeing as how we've been doing so well with our sales lately."

Molly didn't answer right away. "Yes, of course," she replied, smiling faintly at her brother.

• • • •

BLYTHE DIDN'T SLEEP very well. Nightmares wracked him through the night, and he didn't know what they meant. He remembered seeing that old man again, the grinning face appearing in the heavy fog Blythe was lost in.

"You should've taken the magic beans for your cakes, boy," he kept saying before cackling like a witch—only male. "You work so hard, sacrifice so much, and what do you get in return? An altered jacket."

Blythe would shrink away from the leering, foul-smelling face, turning around to run in another direction—only to have the infernal creature appear again, stopping him in his tracks while mocking him for his bad choices. He was startled awake several times, and he stared in dismay at the darkness for a few moments before drifting off again.

By the time Molly roused him for his bread route, Blythe felt quite ill and tired. And as he set out with his filled baskets, he could still hear the old man's voice taunting him, laughing at him with every attempt at selling a loaf of bread.

"Lord, leave me alone," Blythe hissed, scowling and shaking his head the way a wet dog would shake itself.

He didn't know if something more sinister was at work because he'd had nightmares before, and none of them continued to haunt him the way this demon-man now haunted him. Blythe felt the urge to take a different route from what he normally followed. It was almost random, taking him around Up-church, following the town's periphery.

The mist that morning was also heavier than normal—no, it was a fog, Blythe corrected himself as he hurried along. He looked around him, feeling a little unnerved by the sense of isolation the darkness and the fog stirred up in him. His fatigue certainly didn't help. It made him vulnerable to suggestion, and Blythe thought he was being watched a few times.

"If that old man suddenly appears in the fog—if that old man's *face* sudden-ly appears in the fog like it did in my dream, I'm going to scream worse than a girl," he muttered, more irritated than frightened.

The fog gradually lifted as the sun rose, and Blythe was still on that lonely road, not once redirecting his steps to a nearby house. He'd only sold four loaves before his unplanned detour, and he knew he had to get a move on if he wished to sell all loaves before mid-morning.

Once he could see more clearly, he checked the cottages to his right, and he realized that he was close to Jack's home.

"As long as I'm not lost," he said.

The road meandered a bit before taking him to the intersection of the nar-row dirt path that led to the Wicket cottage. Blythe stopped at the junction and gazed at the fuzzy silhouette of the small, run-down structure.

"Maybe I can lure him out this morning," he said. "I'm sure he'll need some company after yesterday."

He was about to debate himself over the virtues of having Jack shadowing him during his bread sales when a woman's scream tore through the early morn-ing silence. Blythe froze, stunned, vaguely wondering if he'd just wet himself.

"Jack! Jack!" the voice cried. In the stillness of the morning, Mrs. Wicket's screams carried extremely well.

Blythe ran down the path in a panic. "Something's happened to Jack," he panted as he flew down the path, his baskets and the annoying weight com-pletely forgotten. He could be leaving a trail of unsold bread loaves behind him for all he cared.

"Mrs. Wicket!" he cried when he reached the door. "Jack!" Blythe still had the presence of mind to set his baskets down carefully, not drop them, and he knocked as hard as he could.

The fog had lifted some more. No one answered the door, and Blythe could hear raised voices toward the rear of the cottage. Picking up his baskets—again barely taking note of his protectiveness of his livelihood—Blythe ran around the corner toward the back. He heard Jack matching his mother's frantic screeching so that their voices sounded like some kind of demonic mating call.

"Jack? Mrs. Wicket?" Blythe panted as he rounded the cottage's rear corner.

Then he skidded to a halt with a horrified yelp. Before him, rising up from the small patch of land that made up the Wickets' backyard, was a gigantic beanstalk. It rose up in a thick collection of green, twisting vines, from which sprouted countless leaves and green beans ready to be plucked and turned into a day's healthy meal. It didn't follow a straight line, either, the mass of tangled and twisting vines curving here and there, sometimes mimicking a short spiral, sometimes moving farther off in one direction, only to turn on itself and return to its center point, where it once again curved and turned. If one were to imagine its growth during the night, the beanstalk probably looked as though it danced and slithered up to toward the sky.

"What on earth..." Blythe's jaw dropped—along with his baskets as his hands lost all strength and let baskets and bread loaves fall at his feet.

He followed the beanstalk's progression up, and he had to tip his head far back in order to keep it in sight. The fog hid parts of it, but he could see where it terminated. A strange cloud, hanging above the Wicket cottage, a heavy, gray cover that seemed to threaten rain, but Blythe could smell nothing in the air. It hung low, too—much, much lower than ordinary clouds, looking very much within reach for anyone mad enough to want to climb up the beanstalk in order to touch it even though the height was still quite formidable from where Blythe stood.

Another thing about the cloud that struck Blythe as unusual was its movement. It stayed put on the whole, but it moved on itself the way storm clouds curled and did all sorts of things to make him wonder if it were the alive and breathing. Blythe could see movements akin to the ebbing and flowing of ocean waves—as he understood the ocean's movements, of course, based on stories and descriptions given by folks who'd actually seen the sea. Then he'd see swirls and spirals, curlicues and floral-like patterns. All the while, the great, gray cloud remained fixed in space, with the beanstalk shooting up and disappearing in the sluggishly heaving mass.

"Oh, my God," Blythe stammered once he found his voice again.

"Blythe? Is that you?"

Blythe started out of his shock and turned to find both Jack and Mrs. Wicket staring at him from an upper window. Jack appeared to be fine—pale and stunned as everyone else, but fine.

"I heard Mrs. Wicket scream," he said. "I knocked on the door but ran back here when I heard voices—what on earth is *that?*" He pointed helplessly at the monstrous plant nearby.

"It's from the fiery depths of Hell is what it is!" Mrs. Wicket said, wringing her hands. "It's the Devil's work, and Jack sold his soul for eternal damnation!"

"I sold the cow, Mama," Jack retorted, though he continued to look just as stunned as before. "And this isn't hellish—it's magic."

"It destroyed my poor backyard! Where am I going to hang our laundry now? Look at what that thing did to yesterday's wash!"

And sure enough, Blythe saw clothes not only strewn on the ground but also hanging off parts of the giant beanstalk where the clothesline had tangled with the leaves after being snapped from the trees where they were secured.

"So, uh, what's going to happen now?" Blythe asked, glancing back at Jack. He noticed his friend had regained his composure and the usual flush in his complexion. In fact, Jack appeared to eye the giant beanstalk with sly but cautious interest.

"We're going to chop that thing down is what we're going to do," Mrs. Wicket spluttered.

"I'll do it, Mama, but not until after I find out what's up there." Jack pointed at the clouds.

"Hell and damnation, that's what! And you'd better not be climbing up that thing!"

Jack snorted. "Hell's underground, for God's sake."

"Well, that sure doesn't look like Heaven to me!"

Blythe scowled at the cloud. "Do you really think that there's something up there?"

"Of course I do! What a stupid question!" Jack said.

"I've never heard of people walking on clouds, blockhead," Blythe retorted.

"That's because no one's ever tried. All right, well, granted, no one's been given the means to do it until now."

"We don't even know if that's a real cloud. I mean, it looks really odd."

"That's because it comes straight from the devil's pit!" Mrs. Wicket exclaimed.

"Oh, lord." Jack vanished from the window, leaving his mother red-faced and distressed, still wailing about the surging armies from the fiery depths and her poor laundry.

At length the rear door burst open, and Jack hurried out. He paused and looked up, his hands on his hips as he mulled over things.

"Do you really think there's something up there?" Blythe asked.

"There's only one way to find out."

He chewed his lower lip as he turned things over in his head. "Jack, it could be a trap."

"Then again, it might not be." Jack glanced at Blythe, cocking a brow. "So are you coming?"

Blythe stared at him, not sure if he heard his friend correctly. "What? You want me to go up there?"

Jack turned to him now and moved closer, dropping his voice to an excited whisper. "Come on! Why not? I could've just kicked you to the side and claimed this thing for myself, but I'm not, see? You were the one who told me about the magic beans, and we're best friends, so why shouldn't I give you a chance to share an adventure with me?"

Blythe narrowed his eyes. "You mean to say you're terrified of climbing that monstrous plant and want company because you need to feel good about the stupid choice you made."

"We can share the spoils! If any, that is. I've got a good feeling about this. We'll go up there together, and we'll see what's waiting in the clouds together—like a poxy married couple, but who cares?" When Blythe continued to eye him narrowly, he sighed and nodded. "Yes, yes, I'm damned terrified of what all of this means."

"Then don't do it! Are you mad? That looks like a ridiculous height we have to climb!"

Jack looked up and grimaced. "I know. I've never climbed anything that high before. Trees are nothing compared to this monster beanstalk."

"It'll take us at least a day to get up that thing," Blythe noted, blanching, as he tried to measure the beanstalk's height and failing when he suddenly got dizzy just staring at something that shot up at such a distance.

"Jack Wicket!" Mrs. Wicket hollered from the window. "I hope you're not trying to corrupt your friend into doing another fool thing! Master Blythe works—and he works hard, unlike you! Leave him alone and chop that giant green monstrosity down before the devil comes to claim us all!"

Jack barely looked at his mother. He pinned Blythe down with a desperate, hopeful look. "Please, Blythe? We can do this. I'm sure of it. Look, I'll give you more than half of the spoils. What do you say to that?"

"I say you're out of your mind. And your mama's right. I've got work to do. What do I tell Molly when I disappear for a day or even half a day, and I come home with baskets filled with bread that I never got to sell because I went off to a grand adventure with you?"

Jack stared at him as though he'd just sprouted an extra eye on his forehead. Or nose, whichever part of his body was the most unnerving with an extra eye. "Show her your treasure, for God's sake. That should stop her nagging."

"This conversation's going nowhere because we're just going around in circles, with me about to say something rude about the possibility of us *not* finding anything up there, and you saying something like, 'But you can't say that until you actually go there and see for yourself!' By the time we're done, I'd have shat all over myself trying to make heads or tails of everything." Blythe sighed, scratching his head. "Can't we try to explore another time, Jack? Don't cut the beanstalk down yet. I need to figure out how to get out of my morning work without making Molly suspicious that I'm up to something."

Jack made a face, his head and shoulders sagging as he kicked at the ground. "When do you think you'll be ready to climb with me?"

"I wish I knew."

"That's not a good enough answer."

Oh, the pressure. Blythe wracked his brain and chewed on a fingernail as he looked at the beanstalk, laying out possible scenes in his mind and doing his damnedest trying to predict outcomes. In the end he found that he was so rattled by the reality of magic beans that he didn't even know where his own arse was.

"I'll come back later and tell you," he said. Then another idea came up. "I can go home first after my bread route, ask Molly to let me go for the afternoon, and come back here, so we can go off on our adventure. What do you think?"

"Are you going to tell her what you're going to do? That's awfully cheeky of you," Jack replied, incredulous.

Blythe rolled his eyes. "No, of course not, you idiot. She'll only lock me away! I'll tell her after we come back and only if we have actual treasure to show."

Jack hesitated. "You promise to come back?"

"Of course! I must admit, I'm a bit excited now, the more I think about it."

"Good! All right, then, I'll see what I can do to pacify Mama. She doesn't want me to go up there, either. I need to wait for her to leave for work before trying anything."

"Jack! *Jack!* Stay away from that poor boy, you hear me?"

It was Jack's turn to roll his eyes as he stepped back and saluted Blythe. "Yes, yes, I'm moving away from my one and only friend in the world, Mama!" he hollered back. "As you can see, Blythe's safe from my dark influence, and he stays just as pure and chaste as he's always been."

Blythe pursed his lips. "Actually, I've been kissed already, and it was the kind of kiss that leads to pregnant servant girls. I'm guessing that I'm not as virtuous as your mama would like me to be, though I'm quite sure I won't be walking around with a swollen belly in a few months."

He must've spoken in too low a voice because Jack merely blinked and then made a face at him while saying in a voice that was purposefully loud for his mother, "I've absolutely no blasted idea what you've just said, Blythe, but I hope you have a very good and very successful day selling bread like the honest, hardworking bread-seller that you are."

"Yes, dear, go on and take care of your duties. You're an inspiration and a role model for other boys your age," Mrs. Wicket called out, leaning over the window ledge and giving Blythe a sweet, encouraging smile. If she could, she'd probably wave a white handkerchief or something to help send Blythe on his way.

Chapter 17

So much for clever plans. By late morning, all of Upchurch knew about the giant beanstalk. Many hurried over to the Wicket cottage to gape at it and at a hysterical Mrs. Wicket, who was reported as "possessed by lesser demons" as she ran around and around the beanstalk, alternately gathering her displaced laundry and screeching for her lazy, insane son to chop the thing down.

In the end, with a few soothing glasses of good ale, she was convinced to go forward with her day doing her usual laundry work. She finally left for work, slurring threats of a thorough thrashing to Jack should she come home and see that the beanstalk—or what she now referred to as "Satan's monstrous pizzle"—was still standing like a vulgar reminder of manly shortcomings.

That, apparently, was one person's account of what he'd seen when he'd gone off to gawk at the magic beanstalk. He'd left the Wicket cottage to spread his bit of news, and Blythe happened to be one of those whom he'd tattled to.

"Damn," Blythe hissed, looking at his baskets. "I want to go there now." The temptation was truly a huge one, but he found that he couldn't, in good conscience, lag on his duties and deprive his family of at least an average day of bread sales. So, fighting off the urge to double back and hurry to the Wicket cottage, Blythe marched forward like the determined soldier he was and continued knocking on people's doors.

Unfortunately for him (again!), he continued to run into folks who'd gone there and were now too eager to spread all sorts of gossip about the strange, dark magic that had taken over a poor widow's back yard and laundry. No one had seen Jack, at least from what Blythe had heard, but it was very likely that Jack had taken cover in the cottage, what with the sudden swarm of people now moving in and out every five minutes or so in his property.

From what Blythe had heard, some men and even young boys had offered to climb up the beanstalk in response to playful, maybe even drunk, dares. Oddly enough, according to wide-eyed gossips, the miraculous beanstalk kept them from going beyond five feet off the ground.

"How can anyone get up this thing? It's too slippery to hold on to!" some had complained.

"It kept moving. Like it was trying to shake me off."

"I swear I saw a face in the middle of the vines and leaves. It was staring at me from the shadows. It gave me a fright, let me tell you! I'm not going anywhere near that thing. No, not for any money."

"It's haunted! I heard a voice coming from the tangle of vines—calling my name and laughing!"

And so on and so forth. Before long, everyone who'd gone to the Wicket cottage were convinced that the beanstalk didn't want them near it, let alone touch it. Then again, Blythe saw, at least a third of those who'd given their accounts were also drunk, and as for the rest, well, life in Upchurch was simply so excruciatingly dull that people would say anything to validate their existence. And the farther into the day they went, the wilder the stories became.

Yes, so much for clever plans.

That morning was Blythe's worst morning for sales, and he was still left with one full basket of unsold loaves. Most of his usual customers had ignored him after hearing about the strange beanstalk. Half of those had run out to see for themselves, and the other half shooed him away while turning to their neighbors, lost in fresh morning gossip. Annoyingly enough, Blythe also had no one to blame but himself, for he'd used the beanstalk as a desperate conversation starter when faced with reluctant customers. Once their interest had been piqued, Blythe couldn't get them to buy a single thing because mysterious gigantic beanstalks were too delicious a subject to ignore.

Yes, life in Upchurch had gotten *that* miserably dull, it seemed.

Once he heard the distant clock tower signal the usual hour for him to return home, Blythe drooped. Would Molly be all right with the unsold loaves? She shouldn't blame him, should she? Blythe did try his best to sell them all, but no thanks to Jack's giant beanstalk, all his hard work had been undermined.

"Molly knows I've been working very hard since my first day doing this," he said as he paced in an agitated circle by the stone bridge, his baskets on the ground and serving as a dark reminder of his situation as an unlucky casualty in Jack Wicket's Remarkable Turn of Fortune. No, not even the bridge's associations of his glorious afternoon spent in Edrik's company eased his mind. He chewed on one fingernail after another. "She can't send me out again to sell the rest of the loaves. I'm sure she's clever enough to come up with a plan to get rid of them without involving me."

After several moments of awful doubt and desperate hope, Blythe made himself stop so much useless thinking in spite of his ongoing doubts. He couldn't afford to waste more time. Jack was waiting for him, and they both needed to go off on their first grand adventure together as the best of best friends before Mrs. Wicket came home. Gathering his baskets, he took a deep breath and jogged back home, his long and detailed excuse ready to spill out of him.

• • • •

MOLLY, AS FEARED, WAS quite upset—a good deal more than Blythe had anticipated, in fact.

"What are we going to do with all these?" she cried, unpacking the basket. "We can't sell these tomorrow morning! They won't be fresh!"

Blythe stood awkwardly by the hearth. Fidgeting with the hem of his jacket, he said, "But can't we give them away somewhere? Or turn them into something else—like pudding?"

"Why would I do that, for heaven's sake? Do you want me to lose out on profits?"

"I thought we could afford to lose a little. Isn't that what you've been telling me when you started wrapping your cakes for market day?"

Molly shook her head, the look of distress on her face quite alarming. She stared at the loaves before her, her complexion a sickly pale shade. "Yes, but we can't afford to lose any more, Blythe. These bread loaves earn us far more than the cakes, and if we're losing on market day, we *have* to make up for it the rest of the week."

Blythe frowned as he watched her closely. "Are we losing more than you expected on market day?"

"I'm afraid so," Molly replied, sighing deeply. "There was some resistance to the wrapper idea, and we didn't sell as many as I wanted. Given that we've also sacrificed a couple of cakes for people to sample, we didn't take home as much as I'd like, even with the expected loss."

"I'd hate to be unsympathetic, Molly, but I wish you never listened to Mrs. Brainswell. Her methods might have worked for her, but it doesn't mean it'll be just as good for someone else."

Molly raised a hand to silence him. "No more talk about her, Blythe. I don't want to hear it."

He narrowed his eyes at her further. There was something else she wasn't saying, and it was obviously weighing her down. Did it have something to do with her much-admired mentor? It must have, or she wouldn't have shut him up so abruptly. What on earth did Mrs. Brainswell tell her this time? That she was useless if she didn't earn such-and-such in profits by such-and-such time? He wouldn't put it past her, given what he'd seen of her character.

"Molly, what did Mrs. Stringer say to you?" he asked, suddenly remembering the kindly old woman and her harried state at the market. "She appeared really upset when I saw her."

Molly blinked in surprise and looked at him. For a moment she remained silent but then surrendered, and she sagged, looking distressed and haggard. "I shouldn't keep this from either you or Bertie, I suppose. Considering what you two have done for me, I owe you this much. The thing is, Blythe, Mrs. Brainswell wasn't intending to help me at all. Mrs. Stringer had heard her talk badly about us and how gullible I am to 'suggestions' she'd made." She sighed and looked at the bread. "Those suggestions weren't made to help me. She wanted to ruin me by making me lose profits."

"Where did Mrs. Stringer hear this?"

"At Mrs. Brainswell's bakery, of course. Mrs. Stringer was there earlier that day, looking for something special for her husband's birthday, and—well—apparently Mrs. Brainswell started gossiping with a friend who'd entered while Mrs. Stringer was deciding, and there it was." Molly shook her head. "I feel incredibly stupid for thinking that someone would want to be so generous toward a complete stranger. I've never done anything to hurt her. She's got her own business, and it's not as if there's no room for one more baker. I might not even be as successful as she is, no matter what I do, but she still..."

"She's a damned predator, Molly. I'm sorry you had to put up with her nonsense like this, but I'm glad you found out about it soon enough."

"I know, dearest. I know. I still can't help but feel so stupid and dirty for being so gullible."

No, it wasn't Molly's fault, but Blythe knew better than to push the subject, so he kept quiet even if his mind continued to whirl, and a new resolution started to form.

Molly sat down by the table and folded her arms on it, resting her chin with an air of dejection that was uncharacteristic for her. Blythe found that he couldn't—dare not—move from where he stood, the intense discomfort keeping him from doing something despite the urge to ease himself with even a simple walk around the cottage. Guilt had also cemented his feet in place, and the fact that he didn't know what to tell his sister to make things better for her only added to his frozen, useless state. He squirmed, glumly regarding the bread loaves, his mind also tearing itself as it wandered back to his promise to Jack.

If he went with his friend and returned with treasure, all this nonsense about being mentored by a despicably snobby baker wouldn't even be a concern. Molly wouldn't need to have thirteen loaves sold every day. She'd buy her own bakery and dazzle everyone with her skills, hopefully putting Mrs. Brainswell to shame with her recipes. Even Bertie wouldn't need to pursue woodwork if he wished; he could settle down—if he'd actually found a girl, but that was unlikely—and live comfortably enough to ensure that his wife and children would never want for anything.

He could still ask her to give him the afternoon off. He wanted to surprise her with the solution to her livelihood problems, and things would be fine with them. He cleared his throat and said, "Molly, if it wouldn't be too much trouble, I'd like to have the afternoon off, please."

Molly sat up and shook her head. "Dearest, I wish I could give you the time off, but we simply can't afford it." She stood up and started gathering the loaves and filling up the basket again, making Blythe's jaw hang low. "No, you can have tomorrow afternoon off, but for today, I need you to go back out there and sell these."

"But—it's too late for anyone to buy these loaves, isn't it? These are meant to be sold in the morning like you've always said."

"I know what I've said, and considering how many are left, I think we should take advantage of every chance we've got to sell bread. Just take the basket and try again, and don't come back until you only have one or two loaves left. We can waste that much if we have to."

Blythe tugged at his jacket again as he furiously tried to come up with a way out of this. "But there's nowhere else for me to go, Molly. I've already been through the main town."

"Not the north side, though. That's never been in our plans, but I'm afraid we'll have to use it as a last resort. Blythe, don't look at me like that. Just do it. No more arguing. I've got so many things to do still."

Numbly, Blythe picked up the basket again and walked toward the door, his steps heavy and dragging, delaying as much as he could. He couldn't find a way out of this mad scheme of his sister; if he were to set the basket aside, ignore her orders, and follow Jack to unknown places, what guarantee did he have that he'd return with enough gold to buy themselves out of their current difficulties? He couldn't even guarantee that to himself! And if he returned home with the basket still full, what story would he give? The truth, he supposed, but that would also mean a great deal of grief, considering the way Molly regarded their loss of profits as more catastrophic than expected.

"Ugh," he whispered, scrunching his face and forcing himself to refrain from hitting the side of his head with the heel of his free hand. "I can't think of anything! This is so stupid!"

If there was one thing Blythe Midwinter was terrible at, it would be clear-headedness during moments of emergency. When he paused at the door, glancing back to find Molly watching him with her brows raised high, her expression both questioning and challenging, he gave up. He sighed, waved goodbye, and slipped through the door.

"So stupid," he grumbled, this time hitting the side of his head with the heel of his free hand.

* * * *

"OH, ISN'T THIS QUAINT? A little ragged boy at our doorstep! And he's selling bread! Doubly quaint!"

Blythe pursed his lips as he suffered through ten million different variations of that startled yet delighted exclamation from servants of households from the north side of Upchurch—the wealthy side of Upchurch. If he wondered why on earth Molly never included this part of town in her daily bread route, he knew why now. Why couldn't these servants say yes or no and be done with it? He wasn't looking for conversation, let alone deep, abiding friendship. All he wanted was to make up for his earlier difficulties in the shortest amount of time as possible and then run off to join his friend, who was quite likely chewing a hole through the cottage walls as his patience wore out, waiting for Blythe.

Staring dully at the servant who'd even let out a girlish squeal upon opening the door and seeing him there in all his dusty glory, he asked, "Would you be interested in buying some homemade bread, Miss? It's fresh, and it's uh—round shaped, which I think is more interesting to look at than the typical rectangular shaped loaf." He paused as he wracked his brain for more nonsense to use. Then he snapped his fingers. "Oh! The oven used for baking this was made during Charles I's reign!"

The girl just listened to him, practically bouncing on the balls of her feet in utter delight. When he'd done, she held up an emphatic hand.

"Wait here while I tell my mistress. I'm sure she'd love to buy one or two from you."

She turned and vanished in the great house's shadows. Blythe sighed as he waited, glancing around him, his impatience growing every time his gaze caught the beanstalk in the distance. No matter where he was in Upchurch, he could see the infernal thing, shooting up and disappearing into the strange low-hanging gray cloud as though mocking him.

After what felt like an eternity, the servant reappeared, money in hand, and the wicker basket gave up two loaves, much to Blythe's delight and relief.

"Oh, do come back," the girl trilled as she held the bread as though they were gold. "We never, ever have poor people come around, which makes it so dull hereabouts." She paused, mulling over something. "Just make sure to be your sweet little self, or you'll be threatened with the dog."

The door slammed shut, and Blythe turned around, now dreading the next doorstep he needed to blacken with his presence. "Oh, lord," he muttered as he forced his feet to move, a grimly determined soldier on his way to the battlefield with no hope of coming back alive.

"Oh, my goodness, what do we have here? A darling little chimney-sweep? No, you don't have a broom, and you look cleaner. Alice, come quick! There a sweet creature at the door, trying to sell us something! Hurry!"

• • • •

ONE OF THE HOUSES HE visited—if one were to call it that—turned out to be a surprise of the unpleasant variety. It was really too bad he only had one loaf left to sell, and this had to be the next house he needed to get to.

"My mistress doesn't need your bread, thank you. She's more than capable of making her own." The servant paused, her eyes moving up and down Blythe's person. "And she earns plenty enough through her bakery. I'm sure you've heard of Brainswell's Baked Beauties."

"I have, yes."

"Then you understand what I mean."

Blythe smirked. "Oh, surely your mistress hasn't forgotten about her past. You know, where she came from and how much she struggled before getting this successful."

The servant looked genuinely shocked. "Mrs. Brainswell? What gave you that idea? She's always had money, for heaven's sake. She married well and was given the bakery because she had so much time on her hands and needed something to do. Poor, you say?" She burst out laughing. "Oh, dear, the things that gossips would say about her."

Blythe carefully catalogued that in his mind. "I'm sure her competition's falling away one by one if she's so good."

"Yes, I'd like to think so. You don't stay on top without being ruthless toward your rivals."

"Like deliberately tell them to do things that'll ensure their failure, I suppose?"

The servant shrugged. Blythe had suspected as much. "It's a hard world, dearie. If you want to be ahead, you'll do everything to make sure that everyone else falls behind. Now go along. I've got plenty of work to do."

The door slammed in his face, and Blythe regarded it icily. "And so do I, Miss."

• • • •

BLYTHE RAN TOWARD THE Wicket cottage, his basket emptied of its contents, finally, and swinging wildly. He had no idea what time it was, but he was mortified at being so late in joining his friend. Mrs. Wicket would still be away, but now, they didn't have much time to do what they wanted to do. Heaven knew how long it'd take them to climb that confounded beanstalk, which meant that they'd probably only have no more than an hour left to explore the clouds. That is, if they were lucky. Things could still happen along the way as they clambered up that monstrous plant, delaying them further.

"Maybe he'll agree to waiting till the next day," Blythe panted as he stumbled up the dirt path, finally, toward the cottage door.

A handful of gawkers stood by the beanstalk, talking among themselves and pointing at the clouds. Blythe ignored them as he walked up to the door, where he suddenly noticed a piece of torn paper nailed to the wood.

Surprised, he stared at it and realized it was a note.

Couldn't wait and had two goe. Will tell you all about it two morrow. Jack.

Blythe tore the note off the nail as he reread it, blood boiling. "Oh, you scum-bastard!"

"You really caused a stir in my side of town yesterday," Edrik said as he walked beside Blythe, carrying one of the empty baskets. "I wish I'd been there, urging you on."

Blythe shrugged, embarrassed. "I survived. It was a little unnerving being looked at like a traveling puppet-show, but I was able to make up for my mistakes earlier."

"You did what you could to get people interested in talking to you. Don't kick yourself for living in a town with nothing better to do than go after gossip before satisfying their hunger."

Blythe had told him everything except for his mad scheme of following Jack up that enormous beanstalk. He suspected that Edrik wouldn't take too kindly to the idea of his new friend (beau?) charging off into unknown territory without a second's thought, ready for some wild adventure that, hopefully, also meant returning home triumphant and drowning in treasure.

"I suppose. Still can't help but feel awful for ruining Molly's profits, though."

"Hmm." Edrik paused and gazed thoughtfully ahead, the sun lighting his features very nicely, and Blythe tried not to stare too much. "I hope, for their sakes, they bought your sister's bread willingly and not to be patronizing to someone who's at a disadvantage."

"Oh, I really didn't care in the end, Edrik. I just wanted to earn money and be done with it."

Edrik glanced at him, frowning slightly. "You don't care about why they did what they did?"

"No. It was mortifying at times, sure, but in the end, I got the better deal, right? I had their money, after all."

"I'm just worried about the price it cost you—the hits your self-respect suffered in the name of profits."

Blythe smiled, now flattered by Edrik's sincere concern, and he took the other boy's free hand in his. "I did it for my family. If you were in my place, you'd do the same, I'm sure." He grinned. "You really do sound like a rebel. Looks like your papa did a splendidly thorough job raising you to be a cynical genius. But, really, you shouldn't worry about me. I know what I'm doing. I'm learning how to work my way through our difficulties day after day, when before I started selling bread, I didn't care a jot—just wanted to enjoy my freedom and do whatever I wanted with my time even if Molly didn't care for my choice of friends."

Edrik laughed. "Yes, blame my breeding. I honestly doubt if things would have changed had my mother lived."

"I'd have loved to have met her. I think we'd have gotten along quite well."

"I think so, too. Fortune just has an odd way of making things work, I'm afraid." Edrik stopped, tugging Blythe close. "And speaking of meeting one's parents, Papa would love to have you over for rebellious, artistic tea."

Blythe swallowed as he stared, wide-eyed, at Edrik. "He does? What do you mean by 'rebellious, artistic tea'? That sounds a bit unnerving."

"You'll have to come to find out, imp." Edrik kissed him lightly once, twice, which sent Blythe's soul soaring despite his own awkwardness in reciprocating. He'd have to get used to physical intimacy like this. Perhaps he needed a little more practice, he thought, which sent a wave of heat coursing through him till he felt a too-familiar warmth stirring his nether regions.

"Oi! Get a room!" someone barked.

The two broke apart, red-faced and sheepish. Edrik pulled Blythe aside to make room on the cobbled lane, and a well-dressed, short, stout fellow marched past, glaring at them while tapping his walking-stick on the ground. "Young people nowadays," he growled.

"I've also yet to meet your brother and sisters—I mean, talk to them and all," Blythe stammered, unable to keep himself from grinning idiotically even as his face burned.

"Unlike Papa, they're a little more difficult to hold down," Edrik replied. He walked on, leading Blythe by the hand. "They tend to wander off to the most unexpected places at the most unexpected time. Let me think—Cranston went west, Edith went east, and God only knows where Corliss and Guendolen are right now. They dressed up like a pair of boys, though, and disappeared with their sketchbooks."

"Ha! You're no better than they are, you know, with your habit of showing up when and where I least expect you to."

Edrik just laughed, coloring, and said nothing to that. They'd reached the town square at that point, and what used to be a quiet, idle, romantic walk—half-ruined by grumpy adults who couldn't comprehend or had lost their understanding of young love—was now a saunter through a loud and active wilderness of color, smell, and sounds.

"Wait a moment. You mean to tell me that your sisters run around unescorted?" Blythe asked, amazed. "That's a bit dangerous, don't you think?"

"It depends on the time of the day. Oh, what's this? Would you care for something sweet?"

Edrik had half-dragged Blythe to the window of a tiny sweets shop a block away from the bustling square. Blythe's eyes boggled at the sight of so many colorful confections on display. The shop was a far cry from Mrs. Brainswell's odious bakery in its simple nondescript appearance. Peering through the glass, Blythe could see an interior that didn't boast understated elegance, opting instead for an obviously plain design of painted walls and tables in stark white. Blythe was quick to notice, though, that the brightness of the interior worked very well in showcasing so many brightly colored sweets of all shapes and sizes. There were simple little balls or squares, and those were easily balanced by dozens and dozens of fanciful shapes: ladies' hats, animals, trees, flowers, cameos, and houses.

Blythe grinned at the offerings, feeling like a child all over again. He eventually pulled back from the window and regarded Edrik with a grateful smile. "I'd love some, though not now. I need to go back home."

"All right, fine. You're not upset at being spoiled, are you?"

"Well—no, not really, but I do feel a little badly for not giving you something. I mean—you've already bought me a small cake from that awful woman."

Edrik pursed his lips a bit as he thought. "I really don't mind doing it, but if you want to take turns, I'm not one to complain." He grinned, coloring for the third or fourth time since he surprised Blythe with a visit toward the end of the boy's bread route. "You'll have to excuse me. You're my first. I can't help but be excessive."

Blythe chuckled and gently led him away. "You shouldn't spoil me too much," he said, "or I'll be expecting a lot from you. But fair's fair, and I think it's my turn to buy you something sweet. I want to."

He tried not to think of how he could afford it but failed in the end, leaving him restless and utterly dissatisfied with himself.

Edrik demurred, but Blythe insisted, and soon the two were lost in a sea of exchanges that Jack Wicket would describe as "tooth-rotting" and "bile-churning", which made Blythe all the more grateful that his friend wasn't there to see him helplessly caught in the sugary web of romance.

He took Edrik around to the Wicket cottage, though, in order to satisfy the other boy's curiosity as to the nature of the giant beanstalk. There were only a handful of gawkers there, who were being kept at a distance by Mrs. Wicket through a cleverly worded sign, Blythe discovered.

"She's only worried about your safety," Blythe said as he read the sign that had been propped against the beanstalk's base.

Do not come near this thing and encurridge the devel. You don't want your sole eaten by Hell's fowl gardyan. Go home and prey instead. If you insist on climbing this thing, we demand money fur your bowldness.

"Safety? What safety? She's now demanding money from anyone who wants to climb that thing," a particularly tall, lanky fellow groused.

"From what I heard yesterday, it might as well be a safety issue," an old man piped up in between puffs of his cigar. "That thing's bewitched. Jack Wicket managed to climb it yesterday, I heard, but he says there's nothing up there but clouds, dangerous winds, and birds that shit all over you. I say it's best to give up any fool plan of climbing."

"I heard about strange things in that beanstalk," a boy about Blythe's age said, his eyes bigger than saucers as he spoke in awed tones. "Ghosts in the shadows of the vines and leaves, some said. Faces staring out from the shadows, my uncle told us last night, warning you of death and hellfire if you carry on."

The silly men scratched their heads and exchanged fearful looks. "Good to know Mrs. Wicket's looking out for us."

Edrik, for his part, appeared to be barely paying them much attention. Still grasping Blythe's hand, he stared at the beanstalk, wide-eyed and drop-jawed. "Lord," he breathed, "there's one for art!"

"Is the madness inspiring you yet?"

"Yes—I think it is."

Blythe sighed as he looked around him and took in the sight of dispersing onlookers. "At least one person in this silly town is moved to do something good."

"Oh, come now, darling," Edrik said, startling Blythe with his endearment. "Anything unusual and magical should be opening people's minds to endless possibilities."

"What if it's black magic?"

Edrik shrugged. "It's still magic, isn't it?"

"You really are a radical. Now let's go. I'm expected home, and if I'm late, Molly will deprive me of my blanket-wall privileges." Blythe gave Edrik's hand a tug.

"Blanket-wall privileges? Dare I ask what those are?"

"Um—no. I think it's best to just pretend that I never mentioned it because I really regret saying a word now."

The two had walked a few paces around the Wicket cottage, about to lose themselves in another "tooth-rotting" and "bile-churning" moment, when the weather-beaten shutters of one of the ground windows flew open. Almost literally.

Not only did those shutters fly open with such force as to hit the walls with loud bangs, they were also so old and badly kept that after hitting the outside walls of the cottage, they both tumbled down and rested on the grass.

"Oh, blast!" Mrs. Wicket poked her head out, and she stared, aghast, at the ruined shutters. "Damned things finally tore off their hinges."

"Hello, Mrs. Wicket," Blythe said. He glanced at Edrik, who stood frowning as he contemplated the shutters. "We were on our way home."

"Oh—Blythe Midwinter," she said, red-faced and blinking. "Pardon me. This is what happens when your one and only child refuses to help around the house. I'm amazed that cottage remains standing, given all the work that needs to be done to it."

"Is Jack home, ma'am?"

"No, he's gone—" Mrs. Wicket broke off when she looked at Edrik as though noticing him for the first time. Her eyes widened, turned a little glassy, and a tight smile froze her face. "Jack's gone off on an errand," she stammered, and it took everything Blythe everything he had not to roll his eyes. Jack had gone off on another beanstalk-climbing adventure without him.

The miserable scum-dog-worm-bastard! I hope he finds man-eating ogres up there with an appetite for peasant boys' piss snakes!

It took nearly fifty deep breaths for Blythe to calm down. "Mrs. Wicket, I'd like you to meet my new friend, Edrik Vicary."

"Edrik Vicary? You mean from that mad old artist's family?" she echoed incredulously while giving Edrik a once-over, her scowl deepening.

Edrik marched forward, extending a hand. "The one and only mad old artist, ma'am," he said, laughing, and he shook her hand heartily. "My papa's got odd habits, I'm afraid."

Mrs. Wicket continued to regard him warily. Then she shrugged. "Well, you're good natured enough to be normal, it looks like." She paused and stared hard at him first before looking past Edrik's shoulder toward Blythe. "New friend, indeed. New sweetheart, more like."

"I'm glad you approve, Mrs. Wicket," Edrik said. The bastard practically crowed, Blythe noted, feeling pleasantly mortified.

"Yes, yes, well—Blythe, Jack wants you to come by later if your sister will spare you."

Blythe's heart leapt. "Of course. I'm sure Molly will let me go for an hour or something."

Mrs. Wicket nodded. She waved a hand as she withdrew from the window. "I'll have some tea waiting for you, dear."

They finally walked on, Edrik practically bubbling over with delight. "One person outside my family approves," he said, beaming in that way that made him indescribably handsome to Blythe. "Now I want to buy you something sweet to celebrate."

Blythe laughed. "You're disgustingly sappy." Of course, he himself found Mrs. Wicket's approval just as exhilarating, but he wasn't used to shouting his joy for the rest of the world to hear. Was this something normal in situations such as his? Yes, it had to be. Giddy idiocy had to have a place somewhere.

He was so giddily idiotic, in fact, that he didn't even care when they finally reached his cottage, and Edrik saw its old, weathered state for the first time. Not that Blythe was in any trouble for mockery or rejection, seeing as how Edrik was equally giddily idiotic as he was, and he kept Blythe at the little wooden gate for several more minutes, kissing him and whispering broken tooth-rotting declarations of first time love before walking home.

When Blythe finally entered the cottage, he was in such an obnoxiously happy state that Molly had to throw him back out and order him not to come back until he got over his delirium.

• • • •

"WE HID OUR GOLD IN the basement," Jack said, eyes wide, pupils darting side to side as though he were looking out for spies in the vicinity.

Not that it would've mattered, really, since all windows and doors had been shut—except for that window with the broken shutters, of course. But Mrs. Wicket had taken care to set a couple of potted plants on the window sill to partially screen out the world. Inside the cottage it was dark, with only candles breaking up the oppressive gloom.

Unfortunately, Blythe had learned, resorting to such measures was necessary given the Wickets' turn of fortune lately.

In brief, Jack found his gold in the clouds earlier that day after spending much of the previous day simply exploring the landscape at the end of the beanstalk. He'd managed to steal a sack of gold coins, which he'd offered to share with Blythe but that Blythe had refused because he couldn't take anything he didn't earn—or had smuggled out himself. Besides, he was still sore for being left behind, and he alternately sulked and gaped in wonder at Jack's wild adventures in what appeared to be a fantastical land filled with giant things. With the freshly stolen sack of gold—yes, it was stolen—precautions needed to be made to avoid suspicions and possible burglaries, hence the shut-out world and the furtive whispers in the dark.

It was also proving a tad inconvenient for poor Mrs. Wicket, who was trying to go about her chores in the near darkness. Here and there, Blythe would hear her stumble, drop something, or bump into a piece of furniture or even a wall, so that Jack's hushed talk was offset by occasional curses in the dark from his mother.

"What's going to happen now?" Blythe asked. "You've only talked about a strange place with giant plants and a giant castle filled with gold—that you stole some of. Is that all there is to it?" That didn't sound hard at all. The giant plants and castle would take some getting used to, but if nothing was going to stand in his way, Blythe would be more than happy to risk his neck following his friend. As for the thieving, well, if no one owned the gold, it wouldn't be called stealing, would it?

Jack hesitated. "Well—I might've skipped talking about the risks."

"Risks? You mean like falling off and breaking my neck and worse?"

"Yes and no."

Blythe fell silent, waiting. "What?"

"There are man-eating ogres up there, and they've hoarded so many things—all of them gold!" Jack replied, excitement spiraling. "I'd love to take all of those, but it's impossible, and I'm sure by the time I empty out their coffers, I'd be eighty years old." Then he nodded emphatically. "Come on, you'll enjoy the adventure! And you don't even need to steal everything—just take what you need, and you'll be set for life!"

A moment's pause followed, with nothing else said between the two, though Mrs. Wicket bumped hard against something somewhere in the darkest part of the cottage and let out a muffled, "Oh, sod it! Jack, I'm going to work! This is ridiculous! And while I'm away, you'd better not be climbing that damned beanstalk, and you'd better not be corrupting your little friend!"

"Oh, lord, Mama!" Jack hollered back.

"Don't you 'oh, lord' me, young man! And before you chop that thing down, harvest as many beans as you can! We might as well put that hellish thing to good use!"

Blythe stared at his friend. "Man-eating ogres?"

"They're fond of the taste of Englishmen, but don't worry about them. They've got treasures—lots of them! You can't even begin to imagine the—"

"Man-eating ogres?"

Chapter 19

"You don't have a fever."

"Then why do I feel like I'm at death's door?"

Molly snorted. "Because you're making things up." She pressed her hand against Blythe's forehead again. "You're not hot, Blythe. You don't have a fever."

Blythe groaned, pulling the covers around him more tightly as he curled up into the smallest ball he could manage. Given his miniscule size to begin with, he hoped he looked as pathetic as he possibly could. And who on earth could be so hard-hearted against the small and the helpless? Like kittens? Puppies? Chicks? Baby brothers?

Blythe had taken care to add two more layers of blankets when Molly wasn't looking the previous night, and that seemed to work in heating him up so much that he tossed around in utter misery, soaked in sweat. The discomfort also disrupted his sleep a number of times throughout the night, for which Blythe was partially grateful. It meant that he looked quite dreadful—pale and sunken-eyed and just a hair's breadth away from being Death's next traveling companion—without even trying.

"My stomach hurts," he said, his voice cracking. "And so is my head."

"What do you mean it hurts? Both at the same time?"

Blythe's eyes and the top of his head were the only visible parts of him, and he made good use of them. He blinked several times, making sure to slow those movements to less than half of his normal blinking speed. On top of that, he didn't open his eyes fully, wondering if half-opened and deeply shadowed eyes made for an effective picture of a terminal disease that none of Mrs. Pugsley's famed potions could ease.

"Everything's so foggy," he said. "I can hardly see you. I think my eyesight's going."

Foggy eyesight was true, at least, because of his voluntarily heavy-liddedness. With the time being the usual godforsaken one and the only light coming from the hearth across the living area, Blythe could barely make out his sister's silhouette hovering above his bed. She'd taken her hand off his forehead now and was likely readying herself for a violent struggle to get her suddenly ill brother out of bed.

"Oh, for God's sake, Blythe. I knew letting you play with Jack Wicket when he and his mother moved here was a bad idea," Molly said in a dull monotone.

"This has nothing to do with Jack," Blythe protested, carefully adding a few more cracks to his voice. He sounded as bad as when his voice had just begun to catapult itself up and down the register, making him seem as though he were suffering from a severe and permanent case of the sore throat. "I've been working without rest for two months now. It shouldn't come as a surprise to you that my poor, sickly body couldn't stand all the harsh demands of such a life."

He shifted under the covers again, blinking sluggishly and throwing out a weak cough or two in the bargain. "I hope you're happy. You should've known well before I was dragged into the thankless life of a bread-seller that working seven days straight would take its toll on a body like mine."

He curled up into a tight ball again, mortified. In the course of being theatrical, he'd somehow straightened himself out again, and he hoped that Molly didn't notice it.

"Just look at me. I'm wasting away. Considering how many times I'd fallen sick in the past, that's saying something." He paused, swallowing audibly. "This time around, things could be lethal." He coughed again. "If I were to die from this, would you be convinced of the direness of my situation? I can't wait to show myself to Mama and Papa—and even Grandmama and Grandpapa from both sides. They'll see just how badly I've been used, and they'll haunt you till you go mad. Unless your dark, dark conscience has already taken care of that, of course."

Molly waited a moment. "Are you finished yet?"

"I have to be done talking," Blythe retorted. "Every word I speak brings me one step closer to the Other Side. Unless you want to be rid of me now, in which case, I'll go on and talk your ears off till I talk myself to death."

"At this rate, Blythe Midwinter, you're well on your way to talking me to death."

"You're cruel, Molly, and I won't forget it when I'm nothing more than a ghost doomed to haunt this cottage."

"All right, all right, you win. Stay home today and don't bother with the bread sales. I'll take care of those, myself. Just rest and get your strength up for tomorrow."

Blythe perked up. "Really? Thank you!"

He would, if he could, have added something like, "You won't regret this, Molly. I'm doing this for us, and I'm sure you'll be shocked speechless when I come home, carrying a bag of gold for us enjoy for the rest of our lives. And you can show our wealth to that poxy Mrs. Brainswell and tell her where to shove her stupid bakery." He couldn't, though, because he wanted it to be a surprise, and besides, Molly would kill him first before allowing him to climb that beanstalk.

Molly snorted again and walked off. "Humph. Boys," she muttered. From the other side of the blanket wall, Bertie farted—a loud, full-bodied horn blast that added just the right kind of punctuation to Molly's words.

▪ ▪ ▪ ▪

BLYTHE'S NECK SCREAMED, startling him out of his terror-induced trance. He bowed his head, grimacing as the aching muscles of his neck were forced forward. "Oh, God, that hurts," he said, now rubbing his strained muscles. "Damn that beanstalk and its stupid height."

"Are you ready?" Jack asked as he stood next to him, grinning.

"I think so. I've never climbed anything this high before."

Jack waved a hand dismissively. "Don't think too much about that, and don't look down. Just keep your eyes on the clouds and move closer to them."

"Easier said than done, it looks like." Blythe meant every word, too. "Are you sure your mama's out?"

"Yes, yes, don't worry about her. She's working. Looks like a genteel life doesn't sit well with her, and she's better off keeping herself busy than sitting around the cottage, ordering a servant around or something."

"Is there a place for me here where I can vomit before I go?"

"And don't be so negative! Think of all the gold you can take back with you. You'll never have to sell bread or cakes again. You'll have a nice, comfortable cottage to live in—one that's bigger than your balls."

Blythe nodded, the queasiness abating. "I'll try. You'll have to help me, though—at least talk me through the climb. I should be all right on the way down. Unless I faint and fall off, in which case, I'll be haunting you forever for convincing me to go ahead with this stupid thing."

"I promise." Jack stepped forward and felt around the thick tangle of vines. "Do this first before pulling yourself up one step. Find a strong part to hold on to, and when you climb, don't pull yourself with your hands and arms. Use your legs to push your body up. Your hands hold on to things only to keep you from falling, and you save a lot more energy that way."

Blythe nodded as he took his place opposite his friend, the beanstalk's thickness hiding Jack from his sight. He felt the vines at shoulder height and grabbed on to them. Glancing down, he placed one foot on a particularly solid tangle of twisting vines which didn't move under his weight, encouraging him. Alternating hand and foot movements to propel himself up, Blythe was soon climbing the giant beanstalk with Jack.

• • • •

"COME ALONG! WE'RE NOT even halfway there yet!"

"Oh, shut up, Wicket!"

"What's wrong? Are you stuck?"

Blythe panted, his grip on the beanstalk tightening even more, something he thought was an impossibility at this point. His brain had gone blank and had filled the vacuum with terror—extreme, debilitating terror from a newly discovered fear of heights. His hands seemed to fuse themselves around whatever it was they held, and Blythe swore that he could feel his fingers burrowing into the giant vines and turning themselves into permanent parts of that confounded beanstalk.

His legs seemed to have received frantic warning signals from his upper half and had also stopped functioning. Getting any of his limbs moving again had been excruciating at best, and with every foot climbed, his movements slowed more and more till Blythe found himself quite stuck and practically sobbing as he pinched his eyes shut from the surrounding countryside and its vicious reminders of how high he'd gone so far.

"I can't climb anymore!" he cried out, pressing his sweat-and-tear-drenched face against the beanstalk.

"You're tired already?" Jack actually sounded incredulous, which only made Blythe hope for a particularly murderous vulture to come around and start pecking away at his friend till nothing was left of Jack Wicket except his hands, which would still be holding on to the infernal beanstalk.

"I'm not tired! I can't move! I'm scared of heights!"

The beanstalk shook a little, making Blythe's heart stop for the millionth time since he started this fool errand. It was Jack's movements that did that, and the higher they were, the less stable the beanstalk seemed. And that didn't even count the horrifyingly strong winds that blew well above ground.

"I told you not to look down!"

"I don't have to look down to know how high I am!" Blythe was practically hysterical now. "Lord, why did I agree to this?"

He heard Jack grumble something. "Then what're you going to do? There are a lot of things waiting for you up there!"

"Nothing's worth a broken neck." Blythe tried to uncurl his stiff, bloodless, and aching fingers and saw that they still refused to move. "I can't do this, Jack. I can't."

"No! You've come this far to give up!"

"What do you mean? You said we're not even halfway there." The beanstalk shook again, this time more violently than usual. "For God's sake, stop moving!"

"All right, then—rest a bit. I'll rest with you. Take your time."

If he weren't so terrified, Blythe would've felt a good deal of gratitude toward Jack. There'd also be quite a bit of humility there. But he *was* terrified beyond hope, very much on the verge of losing his mind unless he felt good, solid earth under his feet, and even Jack's generosity couldn't melt the solid block of ice that had become what was left of Blythe's humor.

"I'm not resting, and I'm not moving another inch upward!" he roared, his face still pressed against the vines. "Leave me alone!"

Did he just wet himself? Oh, dear God, no! He didn't even know if another crowd of idle gawkers had gathered below. What a miserable thought. He and Jack had taken care and made sure that no one was anywhere near the cottage when they started; in fact, they waited about half an hour before people's curiosity was satisfied, and those idle gawkers shuffled off, muttering among themselves. From what he'd heard from Jack, less and less people had been coming around to stare, the novelty of a giant magic beanstalk already losing its charm. Upchurch, bless that absurd town, had moved on to the next gossip involving randy squires.

"I'll guide you up," Jack called back. He remained utterly unfazed by Blythe's panic and sounded just as light and careless as ever. "Wait. Let me go down to your level."

"No, no, don't. No, Jack, let me go back. I can't do this. Go ahead and collect your treasure."

You're giving up too soon!"

Blythe sighed, feeling some relief at the calm that was slowly taking hold of him. "I'm not. I know what my limits are. Please go on. This is your adventure to enjoy, not mine." How he hated saying that, but at that moment, there were far more important things than endless gold for the taking: his sanity, his skull, and his under garments.

Jack was silent for a moment, and Blythe didn't know if his friend had heard him.

"Are you sure about this?" Jack finally asked.

"I've never been surer of anything in my life. Good luck up there."

"Bah. I'll bring you something, then. A small token if you're so damned noble about earning gold and all that nonsense."

"I don't care what you do. Just go. I need to move on before I die permanently."

The beanstalk shook. Jack was most likely climbing again. He said something back, but a sudden gust of wind drowned his voice, and Blythe could only cling onto the beanstalk and wait for the wind to die down. He could hear nothing but its ghostly howl, his thundering heartbeats, and his ragged breathing.

He waited—he didn't know how long it took him—before he found a smidge of bravery that got his limbs moving again. Inch by inch, it seemed, he worked his way down the beanstalk, urging himself under his breath.

"There you go," he whispered with each successful step down. "Good work. Now another one."

The closer he got to the ground, the more tension left his body till at length, his movements had grown less jerky and more fluid. His self-talk also shifted from quiet encouragement to a firm scolding.

"What on earth were you thinking, climbing up this thing just because your friend could do it?"

His breathing had also evened out as the words slowly built up steam and flowed out of him. He paused and braved a quick glance down. A surge of delirious delight coursed through him when he saw that he was about one belfry height away from safety. When he moved again, the scolding picked up, and he filled his own ears with his anger. Before long he was so, so close to the ground, and he descended more quickly.

"Did you hear me, Blythe Midwinter? What did you hope to accomplish by going up there? Were you trying to prove something? To whom? And what if you lost your hold and fell? What then? Would that be worth some grand adventure at the end of the beanstalk? If your friend told you to jump off a cliff, would you do it? Of course you would! You can't seem to function without him around!"

Blythe didn't know if it was exhaustion, unspeakable relief, or simple extreme emotionalism, but somehow the closer he got to the ground, the more his voice sounded like a girl's—a grown woman, at that. And not just *any* grown woman, but Molly.

"Oh, thank God!" he cried as he scrambled down the final ten feet and hopped to the ground, his knees giving way under his weight so that he crumpled in a pretty ugly sort of way, but he didn't care. He landed on his face and remained there, breathing in the lovely scent of grass and soil. If he could, he'd embrace the ground, and it was all he could do to lie prone with his arms and legs stretched out and touching as much earth as they could. Oh, bliss.

"And this is your idea of rest?"

Blythe rolled to his back and looked up, startled. Above him towered a livid, red-faced Molly. Her baskets sat on the grass nearby, and her hands were firmly planted on her hips. Blythe stared at her for a moment before looking up at the beanstalk.

"Was that you talking the whole time I was climbing down?" he asked.

"What do you think?"

Blythe blinked. "I thought it was me. No wonder I sounded like a girl."

Molly marched forward, bent down, and grabbed Blythe by the collar. "You're coming home with me, Blythe Midwinter, and when we get there, I'm going to—"

A litany of threats that ranged from torture on the rack to being burned alive poured out of Molly as she dragged him up to his feet by the collar, surprisingly strong for a woman her size, which was not much taller than Blythe, but it could also be feminine rage that powered her. Blythe and Bertie had caught glimpses of such power once a month, in fact, and heaven only knew how things would be should it be unleashed completely.

Still gripping his collar, she brought her brother home—after ordering him to carry the baskets.

I'm about to die a horrible death, Blythe thought as he stumbled alongside his sister, squawking and panting, *but at least I didn't wet myself like I thought I did.*

If he were to die that day, at least his final moment on a grand adventure wasn't an embarrassing one.

Chapter 20

Blythe wasn't slaughtered, but he had to sit through almost twelve hours—or what felt like twelve hours—of hysterical scolding from Molly. He couldn't really remember the details of what she'd said—no, shrieked—like the unholy child of a harpy and a banshee. His ears rang long after, of that he was certain, and the best his scorched brain could manage when it came to remembering Molly's point was that he was Satan's child who was sent to earth to lay waste to it after driving his siblings mad and then wearing their flesh for his traveling cloak.

After being soundly harangued into meek obedience, Blythe was sentenced to a week of vegetable-peeling and laundry duty. He was also expressly forbidden from visiting Jack Wicket through the duration of his punishment.

"Can I at least talk to friends at the gate?" he asked sullenly. "You don't really expect me to live like a monk, do you?"

"I admit to regretting not sending you off to a monastery when I had the chance," Molly replied evenly. She'd stopped her agitated pacing by now and stood before her drooping brother, arms crossed on her chest.

Blythe looked up, ignoring his ragged shoes, which he'd been contemplating the entire time he was being lectured. "When you had the chance?" he echoed. "When was that?"

"When you were born. A group of monks traveling on a holy pilgrimage passed through Upchurch, and I thought that to be a bad omen about you. Little did I know how right I was."

Blythe scowled. "You're cruel."

Molly smirked as he grumped. "And you're good at manipulating me by looking as tiny and helpless as you possibly can."

It was actually a great deal harder than she thought, but Blythe said nothing about it. He did feel the strain of his efforts, though. On their arrival home, Molly had ordered him to sit his "saucy arse" down, indicating his bed, but he pulled out his old stool and plopped himself down on it. He'd chosen it, of course, because sitting on it made him look smaller and younger to whoever towered over him in a rage. He'd also taken care to shrink into himself some more while bowing his head and staring dolefully at his shoes.

After an eternity of holding that position, Blythe was beginning to panic at the thought that his body had locked itself up in that little crouching goblin position, as he now called it.

"I'm younger and sicklier than you," he retorted. "Of course I'm going to be smaller."

"Blythe, there are clothes that need washing. They're waiting for you outside."

Blythe sighed as he stood up. "All right, fine," he said. When he was outside, standing in utter helplessness before the tub of clothes soaking in water, he shook his head. "All this trouble, and I never even got as far as halfway up that damned beanstalk."

* * * *

HE DIDN'T KNOW HOW to check for thorough cleanliness, but Blythe figured if the clothes had been soaked in water, dunked in the same a few more times, and then wrung out before hanging, he should be safe. Then again, he also didn't want to spend any more time on such a tedious chore considering how drenched he was. As he struggled with clothes that weighed five times more with that water in them, he cursed under his breath. Wet fabric kept slapping his face and head as he draped the damned things on the clothesline. He was only about a third through when he decided to rest for a moment. His arms and shoulders ached from handling the laundry, and his mood had long grown even more sour than before.

The sun was quite pleasant, at least, so he could try to dry himself a little before finishing up. He was convinced that he was in danger of coming down with the most dreadful cold if he kept this up.

"Psst! Blythe!"

He whirled around and was shocked at seeing Jack standing by the low stone fence that partly bordered the cottage. A tree stood just beyond the fence as well, offering Jack a shadowy retreat. Blythe spared the cottage a quick and cautious glance. Seeing Molly nowhere, he jogged over to where Jack stood.

"You're back already?" he asked, wide-eyed.

Jack nodded, looking rather shocked, himself. "What an adventure!" he whispered hoarsely. "You should've been there!"

"You know I couldn't." Blythe's spirits sank at the reminder of his failure, but at the same time, he could still vividly remember how nightmarish it was, being up so high, with nothing to save him should he lose his hold or his footing. He shuddered at *that* reminder. "Tell me what happened," he added. "This one didn't last you all day."

"It was the same as yesterday, but this time, I knew my way around, so it wasn't hard taking the chicken."

Blythe stared at him. "Chicken," he said. "You risked your life for a chicken."

"No, no!" Jack frantically waved his hands, his eyes practically bulging out of their sockets. "It's the kind that lays golden eggs!"

"No! Really?" When Jack answered with a vigorous nodding of his head, Blythe sniggered. "What I'd give to have golden eggs for breakfast. Can you even eat something that's cooked but made of gold?"

"Or if it hatches, it's a gold chick!" Jack hissed before dissolving in a fit of mad giggling and snorting. After another moment of shared silliness, their laughter died down, and he said, "Seriously, though—remember all those things we talked about? You know, how there's much more to the world—"

"Or sky," Blythe interrupted.

"—or sky than what meets the eye? You really should be up there, Blythe, seeing what I've been seeing. It's incredible. Just amazing."

Blythe clucked as he regarded Jack narrowly, his ambivalence stirring again. "You're stealing treasure, though. How does that justify the danger?"

"Am I?" Jack replied, looking incredulous. "Lord, I call it justice! I told you a couple of man-eating ogres live up there, didn't I? They've been eating Englishmen—or more like English *boys*—so I'm not particularly sympathetic."

Blythe shook his head and chuckled. "How many more times do you expect to go up there, anyway?"

"However many times it takes for me to make off with their treasure before I'm caught."

Blythe listened, horrified. "You're mad! If they catch you, you'll be that night's supper!"

"Ha! Not if I can help it. I'm going back tomorrow morning. I wish you could come. You know, give it one more go if you can. At least you can say that you tried."

"I already have."

"One more time, then. Just one more time."

Blythe sighed, pinching his mouth into a tight line. "No, Jack, I'm sorry. I'm being punished for attempting it today. After my morning route tomorrow, I'm expected back immediately, or Molly will double my sentence."

Jack whistled low. "Lord, she's cruel!"

"I told her so, but you know how adults are—always think they're justified in being ghoulish to their younger brothers."

"Well—try to come by on your way home, anyway, if only to see me off. And I want you to see my new chicken. It's quite large and but squeezably soft."

Blythe grimaced. "I can't help but think that what you just said sounded a bit—wrong—somehow."

"Now that you mentioned it, I think so, too. And I feel a bit dirty for saying it." Jack sighed and moved away from the stone wall, raising a hand. "Try to come tomorrow!"

Blythe nodded and moved back. "I will!"

• • • •

THERE WAS SOMETHING about a boy's first love that compelled him to do, or attempt, one fool thing after another, utterly unmindful of warnings from overly emotional adults.

Blythe had plenty of time the previous night to mull over the error of his ways because Molly told him to. And he understood what it was, having done it and faced death along the way. At the same time, the lure of possibilities tugged at his mind, insistent and even rude, in a manner of speaking.

Blythe had to admit that he couldn't ignore the temptation of independence that came with wealth. He once again pictured himself and his siblings living comfortably in a larger and warmer cottage that didn't leak in five hundred different places or groan dangerously during a storm. Molly didn't have to sell anything, and Bertie would have enough to buy himself a cottage and support a wife and children. Blythe could pick up where he left off on his education, and he could finally enjoy good books and have something clever to say in everyday conversation.

There was, above all, the matter regarding Edrik Vicary and all the time he could spend in the other boy's company. He pictured all the things they could do or all the places they could travel to. He'd yet to meet Edrik's father and other sisters, let alone spend time in their company, learning about their art. Edrik, at the moment, didn't seem to show much interest in, or inclination toward, novel-writing, choosing instead to spend his time in learning and in being with Blythe.

Normal adolescent things, in brief.

And it was also a normal adolescent desire to want to have the resources necessary in order for Blythe to shower Edrik with endless attention and occasional gifts. He sighed as he burrowed under the covers in the cold darkness, his mind still whirling wildly as it went back and forth, back and forth.

By the time sleep claimed him, he'd decided to give the giant beanstalk one more chance. Perhaps this time around, he'd be able to muster enough courage to go all the way to the clouds. Surely it had to be nothing more than a matter of getting used climbing great heights.

• • • •

AS LUCK WOULD HAVE it, it took him longer than usual to sell all the bread loaves that morning, so he was too late to see his friend off. When he arrived at the Wicket cottage, a few gawkers—a much, much smaller number than the last time, thank God—were being driven away by Mrs. Wicket, who chased them out with a broom and strings of curses so vile they made Blythe's blood curdle.

"I couldn't keep that little bastard away from this horrible thing," she said once they were alone. She leaned tiredly against the broom, jabbing a finger in the beanstalk's direction.

"You let him go, Mrs. Wicket?" That was a surprise.

She nodded, shrugging weakly. "I didn't want to let him go, but he came home with a chicken that can lay golden eggs yesterday, and he was so convincing about all kinds of treasures that could be had still."

"But he steals them!"

"Steals them? From whom? He never told me someone lives in that giant castle he visits."

Blythe regarded her for a moment and found, to his dismay, her looking sincerely puzzled. If Jack were there, Blythe would've taken the broom and shoved the whole thing up his villainous arse for lying to his mother. Then again, Jack Wicket had been lying since he started breathing, which would render that imagined punishment impotent.

"Um—how long ago did he leave, ma'am?"

"Two hours at least," Mrs. Wicket replied, casting a few nervous glances up the beanstalk. "I specifically told him to be back by noon, or else. He was in a bit of a hurry, it seemed—said he couldn't wait for you and that he needed to leave earlier than usual."

"Did he say why?"

"No. He was very keen, though, to go up there again. You know, I'm not sure if I heard him right, but I think he mentioned something about a magic harp he had his eye on." She paused, shrugging and still looking confused.

Blythe looked at her, surprised. "What can he do with a magic harp?"

"I don't know. Work magic, maybe? God knows what goes through that boy's head. That's what I get for not having him baptized like any regular Christian. Now look at him—that hollow body of his filled up with black essences from the fiery pit."

Blythe couldn't help but nod in agreement. "The more I think about it, the more I'm convinced that he's fueled by Satan's farts like you said."

"Your parents are lucky they had you even with all the ridiculous things you do every now and then. At least you're not as hopeless as Jack. Now, dearie, would you like to have something to eat?" Mrs. Wicket paused, glancing around them cautiously. Then she dropped her voice to a near whisper. "We can afford to buy good food now, but we still have to be careful not to let on about the gold in the sack and the chicken with the gold eggs. Living our days always looking over our shoulders like fugitives is a small price to pay for unexpected wealth, I'm afraid."

Blythe smiled at her and shook his head. "No, thank you, ma'am. I have to go back home and report back to my sister."

"Such discipline," Mrs. Wicket said, sighing. "You're a remarkable boy, Blythe Midwinter, and I suspect you'll get very far someday."

"I seem to be stuck in a rut at the moment, but thank you. I hope so."

Oh, Hell's balls, there it was again—that nagging voice in his head, reminding him about the miracle of wealth, and his resolution grew. He glanced back at the beanstalk and hardened himself.

"Mm-hmm. I know what you did yesterday, young man," Mrs. Wicket said, clucking and shaking a finger at him. "It was an uncharacteristically stupid thing you did. Little silly scrapes every so often I can understand, but trying to go with Jack? I knew nothing about your plans, you know, and that demonic boy of mine hid everything from me. I was ignorant about it until after I got home from a long day's work, and your sister paid me a visit to tell me all. I promised her that I wouldn't let you near that beanstalk if you were to appear today."

Blythe shifted uncomfortably as he wracked his brain. How annoying to have to run into this roadblock now that he'd committed himself to this. If he delayed much longer, his courage would fail him altogether, and he'd have another day of nothing but regrets for his inaction.

"Very well," he said once he'd settled on a plan. "I suppose you're right, ma'am. I'll go on home and stay put because, you know, I'm being punished for doing something stupid yesterday."

Mrs. Wicket sighed heavily, nodding and smiling at him. "You do that, dearie. Trust me, this is for your own good. At least we can all be assured that, unlike Jack, you'll learn something from this, and you'll come back from your punishment a wiser boy than before."

Blythe tried to look meek. "I hope so, too."

"You've got a good deal more sense than my son," Mrs. Wicket said. "I'll be off, too, to buy myself a new gown. Lord, it's been ages since I got myself someone's cast-offs!" She shook her head as she pondered that fact. "I can afford to buy a new dress. Imagine that! I never thought—never expected—"

She abruptly broke off when her voice cracked with emotion. With a final wave goodbye, she entered the cottage with the broom, and Blythe ambled back to the road that led him home.

Instead of going straight to his cottage, though, Blythe turned off the path and went to the river. There he whiled away the time, watching the currents and thinking about the hopeful turn his life was about to take.

Once again, he pictured his family living comfortably, his education, and, of course, his time with Edrik. No longer would he feel so self-conscious and embarrassed at being seen in the company of a boy who was his superior in every way.

Money was the only way for him to bridge that gap, and the little profits his family made from honest efforts weren't going to give him—or them—what was needed the most. And one more thing he needed the most was to reach that goal as soon as he could, with opportunity right there, within his grasp. How often did Fortune come around, after all, to offer simple human beings the chance to change their lives forever? The beanstalk could be gone for whatever reason tomorrow or the day after or the one after that. No one knew for sure, and he couldn't afford to gamble away his chances.

"I need to get up there," he muttered, "and I need to get up there today. I can't wait anymore. I don't have any excuses left." Around him, the chirping birds and gentle breezes seemed to encourage his resolve with their cheerful noise.

He waited a few more moments before walking back, assuring himself that Mrs. Wicket would've left by then.

Chapter 21

Blythe returned to the Wicket cottage and saw that it was empty. He heaved a sigh of relief as he hurried toward the beanstalk after depositing his baskets against the cottage wall. He had no idea how long Mrs. Wicket was going to be away, but he figured it wasn't going to be an issue. By the time she returned, that is, he should be well above ground and beyond her reach—or at least beyond her shouting range.

Grabbing hold of some sturdy vines, Blythe took a few deep, calming breaths and started climbing. This time, he was a great deal more aware of what he doing. He took his time and focused on using his legs to push himself up.

At the same time, he reminded himself about the rosy future that was in store for his family. No more baking! No more hellish morning hours spent shivering in the cold, dragging his still-sleepy self from one doorstep to another! No more irate, lovestruck, or gossiping servants and masters! No more dreadful costumes for market day! And, considering the possibility of a larger cottage with separate bedrooms, no more nightly poisoning from Bertie's bottom!

Feeding his mind with dozens of wonderful scenes of a comfortable existence, Blythe felt his resolve harden even more, his courage enjoying a much-needed spurt, and pressing his mouth into a firm, determined line, Blythe climbed.

Not once did he look anywhere but up. After several moments of inspired climbing, his body seemed to have developed its own movements, which didn't require much conscious thought. It felt as though his hands knew where to grab hold of a strong cluster of intertwining vines, and his feet knew where to plant themselves for perfect leverage.

He noticed his movements at least vaguely through the lovely, colorful haze in his mind. It felt like a smooth, graceful dance even though Blythe had never danced in his life. He started to sing under his breath without breaking his momentum, the sound of familiar old tunes adding to his eagerness for adventure and wealth.

And it was with a fond flutter that he realized the song he was singing was one he and Molly sang together a couple of years ago, when she'd first recruited him to help in her baking and needed a little assistance here and there in the kneading and dividing of dough into loaves. He'd been curious and eager at first, but being his age, he'd also grown tired of it within moments, and Molly read enough into his mind to keep him going with a number of round songs. Yes, he'd thought it silly at first and reluctantly joined her, but he found that it really did help make the hour pass quickly and the repetitive work much less tedious.

He didn't know if it was because of his singing, his surging energy levels, or all the pretty pictures that continued to flicker in his mind, but he was able to steal a glance down to gauge his progress without freezing up into a terrified statue. The fact that he'd managed to advance beyond the estimated panic point from yesterday only made him sing more lustily and move upward with greater zeal.

The beanstalk's contortions, spirals, and extreme curves also provided him with occasional places where he could rest a little and re-energize, the amazingly strong, solid collection of vines and leaves holding his weight well even when he practically lay horizontally. He never even managed to do that on his first attempt, and he had to blame both Jack's relentless progress, whose pressure on his confidence was dreadful, and his resulting panic attacks.

Blythe had lost himself in his daydreams completely that he didn't recognize the sudden violent shaking of the beanstalk for what it was. He paused, blinking, and listened to the familiar wailing of the winds at that height, and he was surprised to hear none. In fact, the air was very calm and pleasant.

Yet, there it was again.

Not only that, but along with the sudden shaking of the beanstalk came sounds—distant ones, but still easily recognizable. They were voices raised in—something. Fury? Terror? Shock? Blythe couldn't tell, given the distance and the odd distortions created by it.

No, he corrected himself as he held his breath and strained to listen more closely. No, it was one voice, not several.

His eyes widened as he glanced up. "Jack?"

There were movements above him, well away, in fact—much closer to the clouds than to him. Blythe still couldn't make out much, but he could see a small shape near the top of the beanstalk, and it appeared to be climbing down quickly.

"Oh, blast," he said. "He's done already? I never even got to reach the clouds for a peek!"

He continued to climb in hopes of meeting the figure at some point, though the distance between them seemed daunting. But he was still riding on that earlier shot of enthusiasm and energy, so he found it somewhat easy to ignore the chasm of a distance that remained between him and Jack.

Jack, who'd fallen quiet for a moment, suddenly started yelling, but though his voice carried well enough in the calm air, his words remained intelligible. From where he was on the beanstalk, Blythe could now make out his friend's figure as well as the fact that Jack was carrying something that glinted in the sun. Something made of gold, to be sure.

"Oh—is that the magic harp? He managed to steal it?"

Blythe sighed at the thought of being left behind. He wished that he'd resolved to rebel against Molly's injunction sooner and had told Jack the previous day of his desire to join his friend again. If he weren't such a damned coward, he thought, his friend would've waited for him, and they'd both be clambering down the beanstalk together at that moment. As for what Blythe could've taken with him, he could barely begin to guess, but with Jack's sack of gold, gold egg-laying chicken, and now the gold harp, he figured that he'd have made off with something like a large atlas with gold paper. Maybe even a gold bread loaf for a laugh.

Jack had paused in his descent and was yelling again. This time he'd freed one hand—that fool was born with nerves of steel—and had begun to wave it wildly at first before gesturing with it. He'd obviously spotted Blythe, who frowned as he slowed his ascent.

"What on earth is he trying to do, kill himself?"

Jack stopped waving and descended some more, this time shouting nonstop. After a few more moments of climbing, Blythe reached a point where he could finally make out a few words.

"Go back! Go back! Hurry!"

Blythe sighed. "Oh, come on, Wicket, I haven't even reached the clouds!" he shouted back.

"You can't go up there! Go back down!"

"Oh, so now you want to pocket all the treasure, is that it? A fine friend you are!"

Jack shouted a string of obscenities that a sudden breeze mercifully swallowed up, and he continued to move down while Blythe carried on with his determined climb. No, indeed, he wasn't going to be bullied by a friend who, only yesterday, wanted him to join him again in a grand adventure.

"You idiot! Do you want to die?"

"Oh, so are you threatening me now?"

"I said go down! He's coming!"

Blythe rolled his eyes. "I see *you* coming, Jack, with more treasure on your back! And it looks like you changed your thick, thieving mind about sharing your spoils with your best friend!"

"Oh, for God's sake—stop being such a steaming pile of cow shit for once, Midwinter, and go back down before you're caught!"

Blythe could see his friend clearly now. Jack had, indeed, made off with the magic harp—which was made of gold, of course—and it was secured against him with the help of his belt.

"Blimey, that's a fine thing!" he said, whistling. He couldn't help himself.

"You'll have time enough to admire it up close later, now stop stalling and climb back down, or we'll both be done for! No—stop! Stop right there, and don't you move another inch!"

"Ha! What're you going to do, kick me off your precious beanstalk?"

"You're tempting me to do just that!"

Blythe stopped. His earlier good mood and even better momentum were now gone, and he was feeling the effects of his efforts. His arms and legs felt sore and tired, and his head spun a little, seeing as how it had been hours since he enjoyed a decent meal. Damn Jack Wicket and his selfish interruptions. He glanced up and found his friend still negotiating his way down a wild spiral toward him.

"Oh, come on, Jack," Blythe said, not at all caring if he sounded like a petulant child. "Look at how high I've come. I've gone well past the halfway point, and I'm still going." He paused, reconsidering what he'd just said. "All right, so I'm feeling tired now, but it's all your fault my concentration's completely broken!"

A distant roar interrupted his complaints.

"I see that you didn't have anything to say to that except to fart in space. Humph. I might have guessed you'd stoop to that."

The roar came again, and this time, the beanstalk shook quite violently, drawing a horrified cry out of Jack. What the devil did Jack eat for breakfast?

"Bugger it, he's caught us!"

Blythe glanced up, irritated. "What are you—crikey!"

He could see the point in the clouds where the beanstalk disappeared, and from that point, a head, shoulders, and arms appeared to hang down for a moment in a way that one of those exotic monkey things did when swinging by their tails. While no one in Upchurch, even more so Blythe, had ever seen a monkey, one of the magicians at the market conjured up a troop of magical performing monkey things about a year ago, entertaining their audience with an intricate demonstration of tree-swinging in a dazzling cloud of color.

This creature thing—for lack of a better word, anyway—was hideous. That Blythe could make out its features at a distance only showed how shockingly large it was. The complexion was a horrid shade of green, with broken shadows here and there that suggested badly mottled skin—perhaps some despicable disease that affected its species. No, ogre! That was the man-eating ogre that Jack had talked about, Blythe thought. Perhaps its vile skin condition was caused by one of the monster's countless victims—preferably a drunk sailor who was also dying from a horrific mix of herpes, gonorrhea, smallpox, and the gout.

The creature had dark, deep-set features that Blythe chose to ignore in favor of its huge, gaping maw that dripped ogre slime as it roared again from its cloudy perch. Its arms—long, thick, and clumsy—flailed away at nothing, offering Blythe some measure of comfort.

If all it could do at the moment was poke its head out of the clouds and flail about in a vain attempt at grabbing Jack, who was well beyond the monster's reach, then it was a pretty stupid ogre that was going to be easy to run from. Or so he hoped, anyway. As though reading his mind and finding offense at the insult, the creature grabbed hold of the beanstalk and shook it for several seconds, nearly throwing Blythe off, and it was all he could do to cling tightly and wait out the shaking. Above him, Jack did the same, cursing soundly at the same time.

The ogre stopped at length and locked gazes with Blythe, letting out another bone-chilling howl when it saw that it had failed in shaking off anyone, and this time, Blythe cried out a terrified answer. No, he screamed—worse than a girl, at that.

"Move it, Wicket!" he yelled, his voice a shrill, ten-octave-higher screech.

"Now you're telling me?" Jack shrieked back, and both boys clambered down the beanstalk as quickly as they could without sacrificing safety.

The beanstalk shuddered violently now, not only from their frantic efforts, but also because of the ogre's. It had somehow realized that the beanstalk was the means with which Jack had trespassed its property and ruined its murderous snacking on unsuspecting Englishmen. Or English boys. It roared again as it followed them down, and this time, Blythe was quite sure he'd just wet himself.

"Oh, God, oh, God, oh, God!"

"Hurry, hurry, hurry!"

Blythe and Jack's furious chanting melded their voices together so that Blythe didn't know who said what. They could have taken turns, but it didn't matter.

All his hopes and dreams for a better life—gone forever. Fortune was always fickle, and heaven knew when another chance were to come his way. In fact, he didn't know if he'd be given another chance anytime till the day he died.

Despite his terror as he half-clambered, half-slid down the beanstalk, Blythe couldn't help but think about his lost opportunity. Just when he'd resolved to go and just when he'd found the courage to overcome his fear for a small share of the treasure—just when everything had begun to fall into place for him, this gluttonous monster had to come around and ruin things for him.

Blythe was doomed to suffer the tedium of early morning bread-selling for the rest of his life. All right, the rest of his fifteenth year and possibly well into his twentieth at the very least. He was also doomed to stand before people at the market, looking ridiculously fashionable just to help sell cakes. He was doomed to be derided by Edrik's cousins and social circle as a ragged, uncouth boy who had overly high aspirations and pretensions in his choice of romantic partners. He could see their smirking faces, hear their tittering and their whispers.

With his hopes dashed, Blythe felt anger well up—exasperation and anger at the unfairness of it all as well as self-directed anger for not taking the chance when it first landed on his lap with that old man's offer of magic beans—dreams gone forever because of that foul thing awkwardly making its way down the beanstalk and howling its fury at being bested by a fifteen-year-old boy who'd sooner steal than work.

The ogre let out another horrific holler, straining Blythe's nerves.

"Oh, shut up!" Blythe yelled as he redoubled his efforts. Age and size worked to his advantage, and frustration gave him wings of a sort.

Without giving a thought as to the speed of his progress, Blythe shut his mind off against any and all distractions and descended faster. He heard Jack calling out, but as to what his friend was saying he didn't know, and neither did he care. All that mattered was the ground below getting closer and closer, and when he felt it was a safe distance for him to jump, he leapt off the beanstalk.

Blythe landed a bit hard on the grass, but he had enough sense in him, despite the shock of firm ground jarring his bones and knocking the breath from his lungs, to roll over and ease the fall. Above him he could hear Jack shouting and the ogre roaring. A quick look up showed that he'd managed to outdistance his friend, who was about one belfry high still. The monster, though, was making good progress despite its clumsiness.

Blythe ran to the side of the cottage where a pile of firewood was stacked and thickly covered in cobwebs. Another typical sign of Jack Wicket's laziness—he'd chop the wood and gather them, but he'd leave them there, not bothering to bring any in unless roundly thrashed by his mother. Then again, as of late, because of good weather, he didn't even obey, period, contenting himself instead with sharpening the ax and calling that a good, productive day.

Blythe grabbed hold of the ax and ran back to the beanstalk. He swung and started chopping away at that infernal plant, letting out his own rage with every stroke.

"It was my turn!" he cried. Whatever energy he had earlier had returned, and this time, it was all bent on justice over his loss. "I could've had a little bit of the treasure! I'd have earned it!"

Earned it, anyway, because he'd have overcome his doubts and his fear, though the treasure still technically belonged to someone else, but it was perhaps splitting hairs at this point. At any rate, Blythe, hopelessly incensed, could only see one thing, and that was everything he'd lost. Possessed with a madman's zeal, he continued to hack away at the beanstalk.

"What are you doing? Let me down first, you idiot!" Jack bellowed.

"Hurry up and jump off, Jack Wicket! I'm not stopping this for your stupid hide!"

And Jack did. Once he was a couple of feet above Blythe's head, he let go and jumped off with a cry. Blythe didn't bother to see how his friend landed, but he kept swinging that ax, feeling the sharp blade slice nicely into the vines and listening to the groans and creaks of the weakened plant. Amid those, he could also hear vines tearing as the beanstalk's combined weight with the ogre's added more stress to the compromised area.

Not only that, but Blythe had also begun mixing in a few hearty kicks in between a few ax strokes. While on normal days he wouldn't have managed to raise a leg waist-high for a violent effort at hitting something with his foot, he was now practically drowning in heated energy that made him do things he never had done before, with a strength that he never knew he had.

"This isn't fair! I deserved a chance!"

Chop, chop, kick, chop.

His kicks were meant to be nothing more than an emphatic punctuation to his furious railing. He didn't realize till it was—happily—too late that his kicks had added to the beanstalk's weakening.

"You're going to die!"

The ogre had barely finished shouting his threat when the beanstalk tore with a loud crack, its upper part falling, taking the monster down with it.

Chapter 22

Justice seemed to have a rather bizarre way of defining itself. On one hand, it was more than obvious that all of England was now free of cloud-residing-ogre threats. That the monster was also fond of English blood and meat only seemed to ground home the reality of an entire country's emancipation.

On the other hand, there was also the more than obvious risk of destroying a countryside with both a fallen giant beanstalk but also a fallen ogre, one that stood about thirty feet tall.

When the beanstalk came down hard, taking with it its horrid burden, it was nothing more than pure blind luck that it crashed in the open, barren heath, which wasn't too far from the borders of Upchurch. A young shepherd, who'd been driving his flock just over a nearby hill, claimed that the crash was so loud and so sudden that he'd shat all over himself, and so did his poor, terrified sheep.

And that one lonely, neglected hill would forever be known as Terror Manure Hill, which would be haunted by petrified piles of sheep droppings.

The ogre, naturally, died on impact, thereby adding to the concerns as to its body's proper disposal. The prospect of allowing it to decompose naturally wasn't an option. Carrion crows would've helped, but it would still take them too long to reduce the ghastly mass of battered flesh to nothing but bones.

"It'll take a great deal of money and resources we don't have to deal with this matter, which, I'm sure, will pose a serious threat to the general health of Upchurch residents," the mayor said, flailing wildly as he paced back and forth next to the mangled ogre carcass.

People of every station gathered around to gape first and then get sick afterward.

Blythe and Jack stood nearby, slouching and sullen, whispering and nudging each other. Both of them were in deep trouble now: Jack for trespassing and luring the ogre out, and Blythe for felling the beanstalk and heaping an unexpected health hazard upon the heads of innocent townspeople.

"Do you think it'll be hard labor for us?" Jack whispered. He stood without his magic harp, of course, having had the good sense to run into the cottage and hide it before the mayor and others charged out into the open to see what had happened.

"I don't know, but I suppose I can learn how to milk cows," Blythe replied. "The skill might come in handy down the road."

"I miss poor Sarah. I hope she's being cared for."

"You have gold," Blythe hissed, now twice as sulky. "I don't. And it's your fault I never got a chance. If you didn't wake that stupid ogre up, I'd be home now with my own treasure, planning my future."

Jack let out an outraged sound. Before them the mayor continued to rail about the decline in family values and the rise of adolescent delinquency. "I told you it wasn't me! The damned harp called out when I took it, and I had to run!"

"And you just *had* to steal a loudmouth harp."

Jack didn't answer right away. "It sings, and it's very shiny."

People continued to come and go, and a tiny group of one man and three women appeared with sketchbooks and pencils. Blythe shrank back when he recognized Cranston Vicary.

"Oh, lord."

"Blythe?" a voice called out. "Are you all right?"

"Oh, *lord*." Blythe gave Jack a quick nudge. "Stay with me, Jack. I need someone here in case I die of embarrassment."

Jack only rolled his eyes, and Blythe turned to find Edrik stumbling over uneven ground toward him, an elderly gentleman only a few steps behind.

"Edrik," Blythe said, grinning ruefully as relief and mortification warred inside him. "I'm all right, and so is my friend. Oh—I've never introduced you two before."

And so he did, with the mayor now launching a tirade against a failed educational system for the poor. No one anywhere paid him any heed; the ogre's gruesome corpse was considered by all present to be a thousand times more interesting and worth their while.

"And this is my father. Papa, this is Blythe Midwinter, whom I've told you about—"

"Several times, yes, with no pause for breath," Mr. Vicary cut in as he awkwardly walked up to them, huffing a little. "Damn this gout!"

Edrik colored, grinning. "And this is Jack Wicket, whom I've just met."

"No doubt you'll be talking endlessly about him as well, my boy."

"Lord, no," Jack spluttered, reddening. "I'm not Blythe!"

Mr. Vicary shook their hands and offered his congratulations for their in-genuity in "freeing England from the ogre scourge even before it began".

"Well, to be fair, we also added the threat of the plague," Blythe said sheep-ishly. He jerked his head in the direction of the mayor, whose passionate solilo-quy remained ignored.

"What, plague? What on earth is *that* about? We've got magicians, don't we? Why aren't we asking for their help? What use are they if all they offer us are silly market theatrical things?" Mr. Vicary retorted, scowling at the ogre's body with his hands on his hips. "Let me talk to him." Off he went, huffing and hollering for the mayor.

"You'll have to tell me everything," Edrik said. He paused, his gaze moving up and down Blythe, inspecting him closely enough to make Blythe redden and Jack mutter something about his teeth falling off from extreme rot. "Oh, sorry. Just trying to see if you were hurt."

"I'm fine, Edrik, really." Blythe let out an embarrassed laugh, which Edrik matched with one of his own. "And I promise to tell you everything you need to know."

Edrik looked puzzled. "Not now?"

"No. I'm about to be slaughtered before being sent off to milk cows as pun-ishment."

When Edrik's confusion deepened, Blythe pointed at the three figures hur-rying up the low, uneven incline toward them: Mrs. Wicket, Molly, and Bertie.

"Well, Blythe Midwinter, it's been nice knowing you," Jack said, drooping. "I'll see you in the afterlife if you believe in one."

"I've a feeling that my afterlife will be more Purgatory than simple nothing-ness."

Jack gave him another nudge and whispered, "I owe you a golden egg. My chicken laid a couple last night, and I want you to have one. You know, for be-ing my best friend and sticking with me through all this. And for not getting your chance."

Blythe regarded him in amazed silence for a moment, feeling himself choke at the sincerity in Jack's voice and expression. "I don't feel right taking it, Jack, but can you keep it safe for me? I might change my mind later."

"I will." Jack smiled and offered his hand, which Blythe shook.

When they pulled apart, Edrik took hold of Blythe's hands in his, and he looked at Blythe steadily. "I want a full account after your punishment." He leaned closer and whispered, "I really doubt if cows are a part of that."

Blythe grinned before being kissed soundly; unfortunately, justice being a capricious little bugger, Edrik was forced to pull away just as Mrs. Wicket's voice cut through the confusion around them.

"Jack Wicket! What the devil's stinking arse are you doing, destroying the countryside with beanstalks and monsters? I'm tearing your balls off and throwing you into a blasted monastery if that's the last thing I'll do, you no-good devil's dung pile!"

It was a hellish chorus with Molly's hysterical screeching, which overlapped Mrs. Wicket's. "Blythe Midwinter, I'm going to hang you up by your entrails!"

Bertie, for his part, appended a breathless, "Blimey!" He stopped, gaping at the dead ogre even as the women continued their charge toward the little group.

"Ah. I suppose now isn't the best time to meet your family."

"I'll have to face this on my own," Blythe said, turning to Edrik, who nodded.

"I'll be here to scrape your body parts off the grass." He kissed Blythe one more time before fully releasing him and rejoining his father, who was now deep in conversation with the mayor.

• • • •

BLYTHE WRACKED HIS brain for a certain story he swore he'd heard Mr. Ruffle tell him once upon a time, while Blythe stood and waited, shivering in the morning chill. What story was that again? He frowned as he scrubbed away at a particularly stubborn spot of ground-in dirt. Actually, it looked more like a bit of food that had turned into a particularly disgusting, lumpy birthmark on the floor of the hearth.

He'd been cleaning and scrubbing the cold fireplace for only God knew how long, but he was ordered not to stop until Molly decided it was clean enough.

Now what piece of insane gossip was that again? It had something to do with a girl who'd been roundly abused by her stepmother and someone else.

Somehow, Blythe thought as he looked as his soot-covered hands and clothes, this girl's story was somehow a good one to mull over at that moment, though for the life of him, Blythe couldn't figure out why he made that connection.

He paused when his arms ached, sitting back and sighing, dragging a soiled arm across his brows. His stomach growled, and thank heaven for Molly's momentary absence. Stumbling to his feet and grimacing at his sore leg muscles and throbbing knees, Blythe made a drunken zigzag to the table, where some bread and cheese sat.

"What a long day this will be," he grumbled, scowling at the half-finished hearth while gnawing away at his bit of food.

He'd just finished sweeping the cottage. After hearth-cleaning duty, he was supposed to scrub the cottage floor as well. It could've been worse, he supposed. At least he didn't need to do the laundry.

The execution-by-disemboweling-and-entrail-hanging was bad—at least for his ears. Molly somehow had mustered enough righteous rage to subject her cringing, grimacing little brother to a tirade that would make her Monthly Molly Monster counterpart green with envy.

"You could've died climbing that thing! I don't care if you didn't! You still put yourself in a situation where you could've!" was one his bubbling brain managed to remember. "And what would you do with stolen gold, eh? No, I don't care how many Englishmen that monster had for pudding! Nobody in this family steals, do you hear me?" was a good one. "We might be poor, but we damn well earn our keep through hard, honest—why, in God's name, am I screaming?" that was another good one, but Blythe wasn't allowed to answer that unless he wished to have one more back-breaking chore added to his punishment.

Blythe wondered about Jack. Was his friend still alive? He'd stolen treasure from a monster, and while Blythe's opinions continued to swing back and forth between support of Jack's views and of Molly's, he still couldn't help but feel the sting of unfairness.

He gazed around him and took in familiar details again, resentment bubbling up inside him. Every piece of battered furniture, every inch of the interior that was shrouded in darkness because of the lack a good number of windows, every frayed and patched up article of clothing—all served as stark reminders of the daily hardship he and his siblings faced.

Is that all you see, dearest?

He blinked, his breath hitching, as a beloved and sorely missed voice cut through his dark, self-pitying thoughts. It was his mother's voice, of course, still preserved and jealously protected in his memory. He hadn't heard it chastise him in a while, and now it sound loudly and clearly. The lively cadence, the irrepressible humor, and the teasing manner with which Mrs. Midwinter used to pose her questions whenever her youngest child needed comfort and reassurance—they made Blythe sit up and take notice just as much now as they did when she was still alive.

He looked around the cottage again, taking his time this time, and at length started to see things. Not ghosts or phantasms, but clear pictures he'd learned to ignore in his foolish attempts at fixing the burden that came with one's accident of birth.

Blythe spotted snatches of happier times—both while his parents were alive and after their deaths. Moments of insane joy that came not in spite of hardship but because of it. Stripped of all the glittering trappings that came with wealth, his family had great fun over simple things: jokes, silly accidents, gossip, bizarre and unexpected things that happened. There was nothing complicated about those scenes, and that was perhaps why Blythe could see them vividly in his mind still despite the cobwebs of time.

Those moments had helped them through long days of cold and want, when Blythe fell ill several times. Those saw the siblings through the loss of both parents. And those were seeing them through hard times that—if Blythe were to be honest with himself—weren't as difficult now as before. He was, after all, contributing to their survival, helping Molly achieve her dream of success as a baker, which would lead to his own dreams as well.

Is that all you see, dearest?

Blythe smiled ruefully. "No, Mama," he said.

An ogre's treasure, however justifiable it might be in taking it, would have cheapened his parents' legacy and his family's dreams of a better future. He thought about the gold egg Jack had earlier offered to keep for him and decided he didn't need it. No matter how he looked at things, he was always reminded that this great adventure up the beanstalk wasn't meant for him. Whether or not he'd enjoy a turn of good luck through the strange, unpredictable workings of Fortune or through simple hard work, the issue was that those magic beans and all that came with them were never his to begin with. Let Jack deal with the consequences of his choices; that wasn't a burden Blythe should carry, but at the very least, he could still learn from his mistakes and, hopefully, gain wisdom from it.

In a way he did, he supposed, sometime ago, while in Mr. Ruffle's company. "Remember as well that a person's worth can never be measured in gold," the old gentleman had said. Blythe nodded, smiling at the memory.

Then go back to work.

He did. After finishing his snack, Blythe went back down on his hands and knees and scraped away at the sooty hearth.

• • • •

"SO IT LOOKS LIKE UPCHURCH now has a new guild of magicians, though beyond ridding the countryside of an ogre's carcass, its purpose is still being determined," Molly said, stirring the contents of the pot.

"Did they make the beanstalk disappear?" Blythe asked meekly. His sister's mood was a great deal improved, but she was still punishing him for the rest of the week. At least she'd relented and shortened his sentence from a fortnight.

"They did, but Mrs. Wicket insisted on leaving the base alone. As a reminder to Jack, she said. And they let us gather as many green beans as we could before they took everything away."

Molly had returned with a sack of green beans she'd picked from the beanstalk, reporting that people practically murdered each other in a frenzy of gathering beans from a magical plant. She didn't believe that the green beans would yield anything special beyond additional nutrition in their meals. Unfortunately it also meant that they needed to eat as many of those things in as short a time as possible in order to avoid losing them to the ravages of time.

Blythe nodded and continued to snap the green beans in half, thrilled at the thought that he'd be seeing something other than carrots and potatoes in his food that evening. He paused for a moment as he regarded the vegetables.

"Molly, may I stop by Mrs. Wicket's cottage on my way home from my bread route tomorrow?"

"Why?"

"The beanstalk's base still has beans growing off it. I'd like to take some more as I'm sure it'll be sprouting more of those things as long as it exists."

Molly snorted. It sounded like one of Bertie's horrific farts, but Blythe dared not comment on it. "I gathered enough beans to last us at least a week unless these things rot before their time. You're free to gather more when we're done with ours, Blythe."

"What if Bertie and I like them so much that we finish them well before then?"

Molly looked repulsed. "How? By eating them raw?"

"It's good for our health," Blythe offered weakly.

"Uh-huh. I expect you to come straight home tomorrow. And the day after. And the day after that until the end of your punishment. Do you understand? If it means escorting you from start to finish, I'll do it."

"No, thanks. I'm sure I can manage following your orders on my own."

"I should hope so."

Blythe sighed and nodded, grabbing another handful of green beans to snap into smaller pieces. What he'd give to see Jack being thrown into a monastery after castration, he thought, and he had to suppress an absurd fit of giggling.

"By the way, that boy you kissed?"

Blythe started and looked in shock at his sister, who was now flinging salt and possibly arsenic into the pot.

"What about him?"

"He looks like a good, decent, intelligent sort, like the kind who'd be an excellent influence on you. I've yet to meet him, but from what I could tell, I approve." Without looking at him, Molly stirred the pot and tasted its contents, wrinkling her nose.

Blythe slowly broke out into a silly, idiotic grin. Thank God, indeed. There was something he did right, at least.

Don't miss out!

Visit the website below and you can sign up to receive emails whenever Hayden Thorne publishes a new book. There's no charge and no obligation.

https://books2read.com/r/B-A-LFQC-JWHV

About the Author

I've lived most of my life in the San Francisco Bay Area though I wasn't born there (or, indeed, the USA). I'm married with no kids and three cats.

I started off as a writer of gay young adult fiction, specializing in contemporary fantasy, historical fantasy, and historical genres. My books ranged from a superhero fantasy series to reworked and original folktales to Victorian ghost fiction.

I've since expanded to gay New Adult fiction, which reflects similar themes as my YA books and varies considerably in terms of romantic and sexual content.

While I've published with a small press in the past, I now self-publish my books. Please visit my site for exclusive sales and publishing updates.

Read more at https://haydenthorne.com.